The Note

*Also by Angela Hunt
in Large Print:*

The Pearl
Gentle Touch

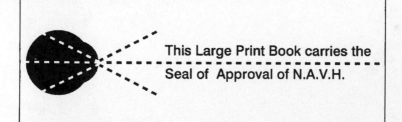

L (Inspirational)

The Note
A Story of Second Chances

Angela Hunt

Thorndike Press • Waterville, Maine

Published in 2006 by arrangement with Thomas Nelson, Inc.

Thorndike Press® Large Print Christian Fiction.

The tree indicium is a trademark of Thorndike Press.

The text of this Large Print edition is unabridged.
Other aspects of the book may vary from the original edition.

Set in 16 pt. Plantin by Christina S. Huff.

Printed in the United States on permanent paper.

Library of Congress Cataloging-in-Publication Data

Hunt, Angela Elwell, 1957–
    The note : a story of second chances / by Angela Hunt.
      p. cm.
    ISBN 0-7862-8756-X (lg. print : hc : alk. paper)
    1. Large type books.   I. Title.
  PS3558.U46747N68 2006
  813´.54—dc22   2006009139

The Note

One

Wednesday, June 13

The sultry breeze carried not a single hint that the summer afternoon would give birth to the worst aviation disaster in American history. At New York's bustling LaGuardia Airport, thousands of passengers clutched belongings, flashed driver's licenses, and gripped boarding passes before departing for far-flung destinations across the globe.

Every one of them had made plans for the evening.

At gate B-13, 237 passengers waited for a jet that would carry them to Tampa International Airport. Their reasons for traveling were as varied as their faces: some hoped for a few days of fun, others looked forward to work, others yearned to see family. A pleasant mood reigned in the lounge area despite the jet's late arrival. Chuck O'Neil, one of the PanWorld gate attendants, told jokes to pass the time. Four standby passengers smiled in relief when they were told seats were available.

PanWorld Flight 848, which had originated at TIA, touched down at LaGuardia at 2:38 p.m., almost an hour late. Two hundred fifty passengers and crew disembarked from the Boeing 767, which had developed problems with a pressure switch in the No. 1 engine. The trouble was nothing unusual, considering the age of the twenty-two-year-old plane, and Tampa mechanics had corrected the problem while others performed routine maintenance.

In the gate area, families kissed their loved ones good-bye while other travelers placed last-minute calls on their cell phones. Five passengers were PanWorld employees utilizing one of their employment perks: free travel on any flight with available seating. Debbie Walsh, a ticket agent with PanWorld, was taking her nine-year-old son to visit his father in Florida.

Forty-nine-year-old Captain Joey Sergeant of Tampa stepped out for a cup of fresh coffee before returning to the cockpit. With him were flight engineer Ira Nipps, sixty-two, of Bradenton, Florida, and first officer Roy Murphy of Clearwater. Together the three men had logged more than forty-six thousand hours of flight experience.

On the tarmac, PanWorld employees

loaded the belly of the plane with golf bags, suitcases, backpacks, and two kennels — one occupied by a basset hound belonging to the Cotter family from Brooklyn, another by a ten-week-old Siberian Husky, a present for passenger Noland Thompson's grandchildren in Clearwater. While baggage handlers sweated in the afternoon sun, mechanics poured twenty-four thousand gallons of fuel into the jet.

The flight attendants boarded the waiting travelers with little fuss. Among the 237 passengers were Mr. and Mrs. Thomas Wilt, who planned to cruise the Caribbean from the port of Tampa; Dr. and Mrs. Merrill Storey, who hoped to buy a condo in St. Petersburg; and the Darrell Nance family — two parents and four children, all bound for Disney World after a day at Busch Gardens. First-class passenger Tom Harold, defensive coach for the Tampa Bay Buccaneers, boarded with his wife, Adrienne. To celebrate their fortieth wedding anniversary, the couple had taken a quick trip to New York to catch her favorite play, *Les Misérables*, on Broadway.

Forty-eight of the PanWorld passengers were students from Largo Christian School — recent graduates whose senior class trip had been postponed until mid-June to avoid conflicting with final exams. The students and their nine chaperones had missed an earlier flight, and many were openly thanking God that the airline could accommodate the entire group on Flight 848.

Shortly before 4:00 p.m., flight attendants sealed the doors, then airline workers pushed the 767 back from the gate. On the flight deck, Captain Sergeant started the four Pratt & Whitney engines. After checking with air traffic controllers in the tower, the plane taxied to its assigned runway.

At 4:05, controllers cleared the jet for takeoff. By 4:15, Flight 848 was airborne, her wheels tucked back into the well, her nose lifted toward the stratosphere. After a short circling climb over New York Harbor, Captain Sergeant began a graceful turn to the south, toward Florida and sunny skies.

The pilots couldn't have asked for better weather. Temperatures in Tampa were in the high eighties, the humidity a sultry 70 percent. No clouds marred the horizon for as far as the pilots could see. The captain took the jet to 35,000 feet, typical cruising altitude for the 767, and held it at 530 miles per hour. Once the plane was safely settled into her flight path, he checked the passenger list and noticed that he flew with two empty seats. Florida flights often sold out at this time of year.

The passengers set about the business of making time pass as quickly as possible. They closed their eyes to nap, clamped on headphones, browsed through magazines, or peered at dusty paperbacks they'd picked up from the airport bookstore. The high school graduates in the back of the plane laughed and shouted across the aisles as they shared stories of their Manhattan adventure.

The flight attendants unfastened their seat belts and whisked out the drink carts, murmuring "Watch your elbows" with every step they took down the aisle.

One of those flight attendants was Natalie Moore. She had joined the flight in New York at the last moment, filling in for a steward who had taken ill. Before leaving New York she told a roommate she was looking forward to her first visit to Tampa. A rookie with the airline, she had graduated from flight school in Atlanta and moved into Kew Gardens, a New York neighborhood primarily populated by young flight attendants who worked out of LaGuardia and Kennedy Airports.

As the hands of her watch moved toward five o'clock, Natalie and her coworkers began to serve dinner. Passengers had a choice of entrées: baked chicken breast or sirloin steak, both accompanied by green beans and salad. As soon as the flight attendants served the last of the dinner trays, they cleared their cart and pushed it aft to begin cleanup. The flight from New York to Tampa did not allow much time for lingering over dinner, and only because Flight 848 flew during the dinner hour was a meal offered at all.

At 6:06, after nearly two hours of uneventful flight, Captain Sergeant began his descent. At 6:18, air traffic controllers at Tampa International cleared the incoming flight to drop from 15,000 to 13,000 feet. As usual, the pilot responded by repeating his instructions: "PW 848, out of one-five for one-three."

On board, passengers on the right side of the plane caught a dazzling view of Florida's Sun Coast — white beaches, pool-studded backyards, and green treetops, all bordered by the wide, blue expanse of the Gulf of Mexico.

In the galleys, flight attendants locked the drink carts into their stowed positions, getting ready to make a final pass down the aisle. Natalie Moore moved through the cabin reminding passengers to be sure their seatbacks and tray tables were in their upright and locked positions. As she waited for a rambunctious teenager to comply, she bent to glance at the horizon. The sun, slipping toward the ocean, had painted the sky in a riot of pinks and yellows.

At 13,389 feet, while Natalie and the other crew members went about their work, the torrent of air rushing past a loose screw on the fuselage outside the fuel tank created a spark. The electrical fuses tripped, and at 6:29 the plane's radio and transponders fell silent. Captain Sergeant sent a distress call, but no one heard it.

The loose screw continued to spark.

A few moments later, a man sitting in row 24, seat C, noticed three of the attendants huddled in the galley, their arms around each other. One wiped away a tear, while another bowed her head as if to pray.

"Isn't that nice." He nudged the woman sitting next to him. "Look — they've had a tiff, and now they're making up."

Their disagreement must not have been serious, for the flight attendants immediately separated. "Ladies and gentlemen," a male voice called over the intercom, "this is the captain. Please give attention to the flight attendant in your section of the plane. We have experienced a loss of power due to an electrical disruption, but we can still land safely. In order to prepare for this event, however, we ask that you remove all eyeglasses, then give your attention to the flight attendants as they demonstrate the crash position."

Leaning forward, the man in 24-C looked out the window and saw that they were descending in a curving path, moving over water toward land. Though the atmosphere in the cabin hummed with tension, he remained hopeful. The jet was coming down in a relatively smooth spiral above the choppy waters between the Howard Frankland and Causeway Campbell Bridges. The airport lay just beyond.

As the people around him fumbled to obey the flight attendants, he pulled a sheet of paper from his coat pocket and scribbled a message. Glancing out the window again, he saw the blue of the water and felt a flash of inspiration. Digging in another pocket, he produced a plastic bag, then tucked the note inside and secured the seal.

Smiling, he looked up at the pale stewardess standing in the aisle, her mouth a small, tight hyphen. "Sorry," he said, noticing that everyone around him had already bent forward to prepare for an emergency landing. "I wanted to take care of something. I'm sure we'll be all right, so tonight I'll laugh and give this to my —"

He never finished his sentence. A spark from the fuselage ignited the fuel vapors, and Flight 848 exploded. At 6:33 p.m., pieces of the plane began to rain down into the waters of Tampa Bay.

Among the shards and debris was a note.

Two

Two hours earlier

Across town, at the *Tampa Times* office, Peyton MacGruder received a note. The summons came in the form of an e-mail, and, as usual, Nora Chilton minced no words:

Need to see you at once.

Peyton sighed at the imperial command from the lifestyles editor, then checked her watch. Four-forty-five, which meant she couldn't slip away and later claim she hadn't seen the message. E-mail at the *Tampa Times* flew through the office at the speed of electricity, and Nora didn't miss a trick.

Peyton made a face at the computer monitor. If Nora kept her more than fifteen minutes, she could kiss her tennis game good-bye. Karen Dolen, a news writer and Peyton's tennis partner, had a husband and three hungry kids to feed by six-thirty, so tennis couldn't be postponed.

After checking her computer's "in" basket to be sure nothing more appealing had arrived, Peyton stood, picked up her backpack, then glanced at the blonde head hovering over a keyboard at the desk across the aisle. "I'll see you tomorrow, Mandi, but probably after lunch. If anyone asks, I've got a morning appointment in St. Pete."

Mandi Sorenson, a college intern who had filled Peyton's morning with insistent and irritating offers to help, looked up and blinked. "What was that, Ms. MacGruder?"

"It's Peyton, and I said I'll see you tomorrow."

"Okay." As Mandi lowered her wide gaze back to the obituary forms some soul from local news had contributed to the cause of Keeping Mandi Quiet, Peyton shouldered her backpack and tried to remember if she had ever been that bug-eyed with wonder. Probably not. One of her college profs claimed she'd been hard-wired for skepticism, and even as a student reporter for the *Independent Florida Alligator* she'd not been easily impressed. What was a newspaper office, after all, but a collection of computers and a motley assortment of writers?

"And the older I get," Peyton mumbled, moving through the maze of desks, chairs, and rolling file cabinets, "the more motley the writers."

Nora Chilton's office was situated in a

row of offices at the back of the building. As Peyton moved toward the expanse of wide-windowed rooms, she nodded to two men in navy suits — out of towners, from the look of them. No Floridian wore dark colors in June. She watched the strangers disappear through the senior news editor's doorway, then leaned against the doorframe of Nora's office and rapped on the open door with her knuckles.

From behind her desk, Nora glanced up over the rim of her tortoiseshell reading glasses. The petite editor was sitting erect in her chair, her head capped by a curled mass in a uniform shade of brown, the surest sign of home hair coloring.

"Come on in, Pat," she said, lowering her gaze to the papers in her hand.

Stepping into the office, Peyton resisted the urge to correct the woman. Her name was *Peyton,* not Pat, Pate, Patty, or Mac, but Nora Chilton insisted on giving everyone in her department a nickname. Peyton wasn't sure why, but she suspected Nora wanted to cultivate friendlier relations between writers and editors.

Fat chance.

"Pat," Nora said, dropping the papers as Peyton slid into the guest chair, "thanks for coming in. This will only take a moment."

Peyton waited, one brow lifted, as Nora glanced out at the newsroom beyond her door. After a moment of silence, she spoke again, her voice lower. "Did you happen to see the bean counters out there?"

The corner of Peyton's mouth lifted in a wry smile. "The two guys in suits?"

Nora leaned forward, the grim line of her mouth thinning. "Accountants from New York. They're after us to tighten up."

Folding her hands, Peyton waited while Nora shuffled the pages on her desk. "We've been asked to give special attention to the figures from our latest readers' survey."

Readers' survey? Like malevolent genies released from a bottle, the words loomed up and shadowed the office, killing Peyton's hope of a pleasant meeting. Her column, "The Heart Healer," had never scored high in the *Times*' reader polls. Peyton liked to think she had lots of readers, people who were too busily productive to bother with questionnaires.

"Here are the figures." Nora slid one of the pages across the desk. "According to the latest focus group, your column ranked lowest of our five regular features. I'm sorry, Pat, but the numbers don't lie. And if a column isn't pulling its weight, something's got to change."

Peyton's lips parted as she stared at the paper. "The Drive-Through Gourmet" occupied the top position, followed by "The Pet Vet," "The Quick Cook," and "The Car Caretaker." Like a lead weight, "The Heart Healer" sat heavily at the bottom of the list.

For a moment her head buzzed with rationalizations. Plucking the most obvious defense from the top of the swarm, she said, "It's not entirely my fault, you know. I inherited this column. If it were up to me —"

"It's not up to you, and, if it's any comfort, the column does rank high with one particular audience." Nora's thin mouth curved in a barely discernible smile. " 'The Heart Healer' came out on top with women over eighty-five. I suppose that's because nursing-home residents don't drive, cook, have pets, or eat often at McDonald's."

Peyton narrowed her gaze. Nora's sense of humor — if that's what it was — left something to be desired. "I don't know if I'd put much stock in those polls, Nora. They're only collections of random opinion."

"But opinion is important in the lifestyles section. We're not producing hard news — we're what people read for pleasure." She leaned forward, the set of her chin telegraphing her infamous stubborn streak. "Emma Duncan had *great* numbers when she was writing 'The Heart Healer.' At one point, this department was receiving over a thousand letters a week, all for Emma —"

"Yeah?" Peyton's voice went hoarse with frustration. "Well, Nora, let's not lose sight of one important fact — Emma Duncan is deceased. And because you didn't want to lose her readers, you gave her column to me. I'm doing my best to keep the thing going, but did you ever think that maybe the entire *concept* is dead?" She leaned back, scrubbing her hand through her short hair. "I mean — 'The Heart Healer.' How sentimental is that? No professional writer would volunteer to write that sappy stuff today. It may have been timely twenty years ago when Emma began to write, but now —"

"The concept will still reach readers." Nora's voice held a note of irritation. "But perhaps it's time we had another writer take a crack at it. We can always move you to something else."

Peyton's inner alarm bell began to clang. Move her? To what? She'd left the frenzy of the sports department to write "The Heart Healer." While the homespun column wasn't much of a creative challenge, the regular schedule had been good for her peace of mind. Sports writing required too many late nights, too many encounters with testosterone-fueled men, and too many squabbles with Kingston Bernard, the senior sports editor.

She couldn't deny that "The Heart Healer" had done better in years past, but she'd made considerable progress in the ten months since Duncan's death. The readers had rebelled at first, probably resenting Peyton's professional approach, and for a few weeks reader mail virtually disappeared. But over the last six months Peyton had received an average of twenty-five letters or e-mails per week. Not huge by Dear Abby standards, but respectable. Peyton liked to think that while her version of the column may not have appealed to Emma Duncan's readers, she was appealing to *someone*.

"Nora," she firmed her voice, "the problem is a difference in approach. I came out of journalism school; I learned to write from a properly detached perspective. Emma got plucked from the neighborhood; she wrote about her kids and dogs. My work may not resonate with Emma's crowd, but the column is accurate and useful. A lot of local people are looking for practical, simple information —"

"I can't afford to reserve front-page space for a useful column appealing to only a limited number of people." Nora's brown eyes snapped behind her glasses. "I hate to be the one to tell you, but few of our readers are interested in step-by-step procedures for conducting a title search. Nor do busy families want the recipe for modeling clay. And what was that piece you wrote last month? How to seal seasonal clothing in plastic by reversing the hose on a vacuum cleaner? Honestly, Pat, no one's interested in those things." Her brows rose, twin wings of disdain. "I have a hunch those topics don't even interest you."

The words stung, but Peyton knew she held the upper hand. As an over-forty female, if they let her go she could sue them for both age and gender discrimination . . . and they knew she wouldn't hesitate to call a lawyer.

Peyton pulled her shoulders back. "I'm a good writer. You can't say I haven't met my responsibilities and deadlines."

"No one's saying you don't write well." Nora leaned back in her chair, some of the frostiness bleeding out of her expression. "Your speed amazes me, and you have a great eye for detail. But there's more to doing a column than putting all the words in the proper place. A good columnist writes with passion, and I just don't feel that in your work. Emma Duncan, God rest her

23

soul, had it. If she wrote a piece about tomatoes, by the time you finished reading you not only knew how to plant them, you wanted to run out and plant an *acre*."

"You want me to get excited about tomatoes?" Peyton threw up her hands. "I'm sorry, Nora, but I'm not what you'd call *passionate* about gardening. But I can write a competent column about anything you'd want to name. I've come up through the ranks; I've paid my dues. I can't help it if 'The Heart Healer' attracts readers who want to know about title searches and clothing storage. They write letters, I answer them. It's that simple."

Nora leaned back in her chair, then pulled off her glasses and set them on the desk in a deliberate gesture. "Honestly, Pat" — she inclined her head in what seemed a condescending posture — "I don't think you're a bad writer. You're good, and you've got the awards to prove it. But 'The Heart Healer' isn't pulling its weight. Let me put one of the other girls on it, someone who's married and has a kid or two. And we'll move you back into the sports pool or maybe give you a shot at local news."

Not trusting herself to speak, Peyton shook her head. No matter how Nora presented Peyton's transfer, her move from columnist to reporter would be seen as a demotion, especially if she got tossed back into the reporters' pool. The thought of once again covering dull city council meetings made her head ache. After fifteen years of newspaper writing, she should have been promoted to editor. She might have been, if she wasn't continually butting heads with anal-retentive types who clung to outmoded rules and regulations like children who refused to be weaned from the breast.

"My column is fine," she insisted, lifting her gaze. "It's working."

"The numbers don't lie." Nora tapped the report with her glasses. "Only little old ladies are reading your stuff, Pat, and I think those numbers came from nursing homes where the residents read everything out of sheer boredom." She lowered her gaze, stubby lashes shuttering her eyes. "I think it's time you let me give 'The Heart Healer' to someone who cares less about writing to her peers than to her readers."

Again, the words stung. What was wrong with writing to a certain standard of excellence? Did the *Tampa Times* want writers to dumb down their work and appeal to the lowest common emotion? Emma Duncan, not exactly the most brilliant bulb in the chandelier, had written maudlin stories about her poodle and Chihuahua, for heaven's sake. The lady had never won an award, while Peyton's résumé was liberally peppered with honors. Yet Nora seemed to be saying that "The Heart Healer" needed someone who had kids and pets in order to make the column work.

Odd that, in a day when women were empowered, emancipated, and responsible for their own fulfillment, the old prejudice against unmarried females could rear its head and nip at an exposed ankle. In the office Peyton made no secret of how much she enjoyed her freewheeling singleness. Few people knew that she had once reveled in a husband's love and the scent of a man on a freshly slept-in bed. Yet a rain-slick road brought that life to an end, erasing a wonderful man and the family that might have been . . .

Abruptly, Peyton closed the door on memories she'd locked away a thousand times before. Raking a hand through her hair, she struggled to find a weapon against the editor's relentless logic. "Nora, I'm receiving twenty-five letters a week. And you know what they say — for every letter we get, at least a hundred people intend to write but never do."

"Even twenty-five hundred readers are

not enough to convince the bean counters."
Nora's voice scraped like sandpaper against
Peyton's ears. "We live in a major metropol-
itan area with a substantial population of retirees. 'The Heart Healer' is intended to
appeal to the upper-age demographic, so it
should be reaching at least seventy-five
thousand people. You should be receiving
over seven hundred letters a week." She
paused, then added: "Emma Duncan did."

Peyton swallowed hard, realizing how
little her twenty-five letters meant to the
number-crunchers in the executive offices.
The newspaper's daily circulation was
250,000, so her reader mail represented
only 1 percent of the total daily subscribers.

"The Heart Healer" *wasn't* working.

But how could she surrender it? She'd
worked so hard to make certain her column
differed from Dear Abby and Ann Landers
and all the other advice columnists. In each
"Heart Healer" column she answered only
one letter from a reader, going far beyond
the usual pithy answers to give specific, de-
tailed guidance. Along with the admittedly
dry topics of title searches and insurance,
she had given advice to mothers who
needed to comfort daughters who'd suffered miscarriages, fathers who feared
losing angry teenage sons, and mothers who

worried about teenage daughters. Quoting whatever psychology expert's book she happened to have within reach, she'd given practical, expert, useful advice.

Her readers didn't need passion — they needed understandable answers.

"Please" — she scarcely recognized her voice — "don't take me off 'The Heart Healer.' Give me some time to adjust it; let me rethink my focus."

Nora's eyes glinted behind her glasses. "I was hoping to give Janet Boyles a shot at that column. I think she's ready for it."

Peyton forced a smile even as Nora's words spread ripples of pain and betrayal. Peyton had thought she and Janet were friends, but if the television writer had been jockeying for her spot . . .

"I'm ready for anything." Peyton forced herself to hold the other woman's flinty gaze. "Give me three months. If the numbers haven't improved by then, let's retire 'The Heart Healer' and institute a new column with a different concept."

"I'll give you three weeks," the editor said, crossing her arms. "That's when we'll take our next readers' poll. If 'The Heart Healer' hasn't shown marked improvement, I'm giving Boyles a shot." She glanced toward the sea of desks beyond the door. "In the meantime, you might want to think about where you'd like to go next — back to sports or regional news."

Peyton clenched her fist, well aware that she was occupying sacred ground. Emma Duncan's untimely death from a heart attack, at her desk, no less, had elevated the woman to virtual newsroom sainthood. "The Heart Healer" could tank with *ten* different writers, yet Nora and the top brass would still want to keep Emma Duncan's column on life support.

So Peyton had to do something . . . and her approach had to work. She needed something incredible and novel — and she'd need breathing space to pull it together.

"I have vacation time coming," she said, exhaling slowly. "Why don't I take next week off and give this some serious thought? That will give me two weeks to try out a new approach."

Nora's gaze rested on her, as remote as the ocean floor, then the editor nodded. "Sounds like a good plan. Sure. File your Friday column by deadline tomorrow, and we'll run the 'on vacation' notice beginning Monday."

"My Friday column's done. I'll file it now."

Nora lifted a brow. "Topic?"

"How to select a good laptop computer. One of my readers has to buy one for her grandson." Rising from the chair, Peyton slung her backpack over her shoulder. "Thanks," she called as she left the office, though she felt anything but grateful.

And as she wandered through the newsroom, she pressed her hand to the back of her neck and wondered how in the world she was supposed to produce passion in a how-to column that had outlived its usefulness. Clearly, Nora Chilton didn't think she could do it.

Peyton would have to prove her wrong.

Comment by Nora Chilton, 52
Senior Editor/Features

I've been working at the *Tampa Times* for thirty years. I like being an editor — most of the time. When the process works, there's nothing like the electric feeling of pulling a team of writers together and beating the clock. When we're on, nothing — not balky computers, recalcitrant interviews, or penny-pinching accountants — can stop our momentum. Rocky Balboa's sweat-drenched "Yo, Adrian! I did it!" can't compare to the thrill of dogging a breaking story until the last minute, then turning out great copy just under the wire.

But people like Peyton MacGruder, talented though they may be, can make me want to tear out my hair.

She didn't take my direction very well when I spoke to her a few moments ago. She's probably ticked at me for giving her an ultimatum, but what else could I do? I've tried subtle hints over the last few months, but Peyton's always turned a deaf ear to my guidance. I was blunt with her today, but someone had to be. Someone needs to be blunt with all of us.

Back in the days of paper and typewriters, when I was coming up, our editors thought nothing of throwing a story back on our desks and barking an order to write it again. Those pitiful pages would *bleed* with red ink, and we had to make changes in a heartbeat, often starting from scratch — no word processors, you know. We learned the hard way, in a real pressure cooker, and if I have any ability at all, it's been developed in the school of hard knocks and inflexible deadlines. But writers like Peyton came up in a softer, easier atmosphere. Everything's electronic, so telling a writer to go back and fix something in his or her story is far simpler, and the reporter who changes a phrase or two doesn't have the advantage of starting from a blank page and rethinking every word. We lost something important when we lost the effect of red ink on a stark white page.

That's why I take my job as features editor seriously. While the older writers cling to their venerable traditions and the executives fret over market surveys, profit and loss statements, and circulation figures, I'm always trying to reach the men and women who have enough free time to pick up my section and look for something special. That's why I push my writers to produce exceptional copy.

I feel like I'm venting, but I can't talk about these things with my superiors, and I certainly can't lay these responsibilities directly on the younger writers. They're struggling to make ends meet, take care of their kids, and produce clean copy on a deadline. Most of them don't have time to worry about the Big Picture.

But I do — that's my job. And that's why I told Peyton MacGruder to either rethink her approach or prepare to move on. She's a good writer and a mature one, but her work has all the warmth of a glacier. Not once in her tenure as the Heart Healer has she revealed a glimpse of the woman beneath the permafrost. Emma Duncan, may she rest in peace, was nothing but heart, and the readers miss her.

It's not Peyton's fault, exactly — these days journalists are encouraged to keep any sense of themselves out of their work. A good journalist, according to conventional wisdom, writes tight prose that covers the bases without revealing the writer at work. That kind of writing wins awards and warms the cockles of other writers' hearts.

It does not, however, touch readers'.

This is a tough business. I was hard on Peyton, but I know there's more to her than meets the eye. She's bright, extremely methodical, and she works hard — once she decides to apply herself. Time and again I've told her to loosen up and let herself relax in her work, but she only shakes her head and goes back to her step-by-step writing. Just once, I'd love to see the woman, not the writer, shine in that column.

I think today I was trying to light a fire under our resident heart healer . . . but who knows how she'll take my coaching? I'm hoping she'll understand and use her talents to make a good column more appealing.

Truth is, we need strong-willed people like MacGruder in the newspaper business, no matter how hard they are to corral. The American daily paper is going to have to change, and we've got to winnow out those who are stuck in inflexible patterns.

Peyton MacGruder will either move into the future with me or she'll move into another department. It's her decision.

Driven by an intense desire to vent, Peyton headed for the east side of the building, home of the *Tampa Times* sports department. As she moved past the copy desk, she saw Carter Cummings, the outdoors writer, huddled with Bill Elliott, who covered the Bucs beat.

"Hey, Peyton," Carter called as she walked by. "How's life with our own little Martha Stewart?"

"Can it, Carter." Peyton jerked her thumb toward the far wall, where another row of glassed-in offices had commandeered the available windows. "Is King in his castle?"

"Yeah." Carter's mouth curved in a smart-aleck grin. "But you'd better watch your head. I don't think he's in the mood for questions about the proper way to hang curtains."

She flashed him a look of disdain. "He's

34

not the only one in a mood, so don't toy with me, Carter."

The outdoors writer elbowed Elliott, then in a stage whisper announced, "She wants the boss. Can't stay away. Mark my words, there's something going on between them."

As Elliott waggled a brow, she permitted herself a single, withering stare in their direction, then swallowed her irritation and moved down the aisle. Boys will be boys, she reminded herself, and she'd had her fill of them during her stint in the sports department. Though women had made tremendous gains in all areas of reporting, some males, stuck in adolescence no matter *what* their chronological age, apparently expected all women to behave like cheerleaders with raging hormones. When she had to conduct interviews in locker rooms, more than a few male athletes stood before her in various states of undress, obviously trying to either embarrass or rattle her. But she would look at their eyes only, and she'd learned how to navigate through the locker room by watching the ceiling. Her writing tended to suffer, though, when the only telling details she could add to a story were the color of an athlete's eyes and a mention of the water stains on the ceiling tiles . . .

She paused outside the office labeled

Kingston Bernard, Senior Editor/Sports.
The door stood ajar, so she pushed it open.
King sat behind his desk, the phone to his
ear. His rugged face was scrunched in a
scowl, his gaze fixed on his flickering computer monitor. "Whaddya mean, he's not
signing?" he growled, but his face lightened
considerably when Peyton rapped on his
door and stepped into the room. He pointed
toward the chair, then pounded the desk.
"Listen — that rookie's dumber than he
looks if he can't recognize a golden deal
when it's presented to him. You need to get
someone in there to talk sense to the boy."

Sinking into a vacant chair, Peyton
crossed her legs and exhaled slowly in an
effort to lower her rising blood pressure.
King might be on the phone another ten
minutes. He enjoyed talking about sports
even more than he enjoyed reading and
writing on the topic, and he had cultivated
friends throughout the sports world. He
could have an agent, a coach, or some athlete's mother on the phone, but Peyton really didn't care. She had never been able to
understand why perfectly rational men
came unglued while watching others run
down a field or court with an inflated bit of
leather in their hands. She enjoyed competition, she understood the emotional rush in-

volved in a contest of brains and brute strength, but she never could understand why rational adult men could come to murderous blows over a game.

She'd been a competent sports reporter when she worked for King, but still they'd had their run-ins. He was always pushing her for more — more details, more background, more of this and that — and she resisted all the way. She'd done a personality piece on Tiger Woods in '98, driving two hours to interview Woods at the Pine Barrens golf course in Brooksville. After spending another two hours with the young golf pro, she'd come back and typed up a profile covering every who, what, when, where, how, and why any reader would want to know. She'd done a good job and she knew it, but she found herself stuttering in exasperation when King sent the story back for reworking. "It's a collection of facts," he'd said. "Nothing you couldn't have pulled from the Web. Tell me something I don't know about the boy."

They'd argued for three hours. Peyton insisted that a writer couldn't delve deep into a media-savvy subject in one afternoon, while King maintained that if she'd gone in with all the facts, she could have pulled something new out of the golfer. "The story's good," he'd said, "but to lead on my front page it has to be *great*."

In the end, they'd compromised. He ran the story pretty much as she'd written it, but hardly anyone noticed it below the front-page fold.

King Bernard's tendency to drive Peyton crazy had been reason enough for her to jump at the chance to take over Emma Duncan's orphaned column.

With a brusque farewell to his caller, King dropped the phone into its cradle, then grinned across the desk. "Well, well, Peyton MacGruder. Feeling a little aggressive, are you? You never come to see me unless you're looking for a fight."

She glared at him, irritated at the current that moved through her whenever he spoke her name. The senior sports editor was handsome in a just-rolled-out-of-bed sort of way, with strong features, tons of thick, dark hair, and the trim body of a man who spends regular time in the gym. Enough, she supposed, to make a woman look twice even when she didn't want to.

"I'm not looking for a fight; I just had one. Two, if you count the drop-dead glare I gave Cummings and Elliott."

"Really." His dark brows shot up, framing brown eyes that sparked with mischief.

"Sorry I missed that. Who'd you tussle with before you ran into the boys? The publisher or the executive editor?"

She shot him a *don't-toy-with-me* glance. "Nora Chilton. She raked me over the coals because my column's numbers are down. Apparently most subscribers would rather read an IRS audit notice than 'The Heart Healer.' "

His mouth quirked with humor, but wisely he cleared his throat rather than release a laugh.

"Things, um, sometimes go through cycles." He swiveled in his chair to face her more directly. "Maybe this is a down cycle, and things will pick up."

"She gave me three weeks. If my numbers don't improve, I'm going back to the pool, and she's going to give my column to Janet Boyles." A swift shadow of anger swept through her, followed by a possessiveness she didn't realize she felt. *Her column?* All this time, even though her name appeared on the byline, she'd felt as if she were ghosting for Emma Duncan.

King's chair creaked as he leaned back, a finger pressed to his lips. "You know," he said after a moment, "maybe Nora's bluffing. Maybe she thinks you need a swift kick in the pants to inspire you to greater achievement." He laughed softly. "It happens to the best writers, you know. We develop a decent product, and then we sit back and coast on our reputations."

She rubbed her nose, suddenly aware that the office smelled of his cologne. "I've only had the column ten months, so I doubt I'm coasting."

King leaned forward, then parked his chin in his palm, his dark eyes searching her face. "So what are you going to do to bring the numbers up?"

How like him to assume she could do something about it! She was writing a good column, she was being as complete and thorough as she could be, yet here he was, demanding that she do something else —

Her voice coagulated with sarcasm. "What in the Sam Hill do you *expect* me to do? Wear a sandwich board and recruit readers out on Kennedy Boulevard?"

"I think you need to write a better column." His voice was light, but his eyes were serious, with challenge and sympathy mingled in his gaze. "I think you need to pull your material from deeper within instead of giving them step-by-step instructions about things like repotting Easter lilies."

Peyton straightened in her chair. "I'll tell

you what I'm going to do. Tomorrow I'm going through my reader mail to find the wildest, most outrageous letter of the bunch. That's the question I'll answer next. My regular readers might think I've lost it, but if they write in, at least Nora will know someone's reading."

She tilted her head, amazed by a sudden thought. "Wait a minute . . . you read my stuff?"

His gaze shifted. "I read everybody."

"You didn't when I worked in this department. You said the lifestyles columns were nothing but fluff and sentiment, and you couldn't be bothered to waste your time."

"I changed my mind, okay?" A muscle clenched along his jaw, then he closed the laptop on his desk. "It's late and I'm hungry." Pressing his hands to the desk, he pushed himself up, then looked at her. "You got plans for dinner?"

Abruptly distracted from her train of thought, Peyton glanced at her watch. "I was supposed to play tennis, but it's too late."

Rolling down his sleeves, King shot her a grin. "So — you want food?"

Caught off guard, Peyton shook her head. "I don't know. If you want to know the truth, I don't really feel much like eating."

His grin faded. "No problem."

Peyton continued to stare up at him. Had he just asked her out? Or was the dinner invitation one of those casual, grab-a-bite-with-a-coworker things? He had never asked her to eat with him when she worked in his department.

"By the way, that reminds me" — his broad hand reached across the desk and flipped the pages of his calendar — "are you free Sunday afternoon? Tom Kaufman is speaking at a dinner for the Bucs season ticket holders and I've got two tickets."

Peyton felt a smile twitch at the corners of her mouth. He *was* asking her out. A Bucs dinner would be a working occasion for him, but not for her, and he knew it. So the only reason he'd invite her along would be because he enjoyed her company.

"I'm not sure about Sunday." She gave him an uncertain look. "I'll have to check my calendar."

"Well, if you're free, you can have the two tickets." He winked. "Maybe you can invite that new guy who's covering Polk County courts for the news department. I hear he's single."

Flinching under an odd twinge of disappointment, she looked away. "I'm surprised you'd give away Bucs tickets. I know you're a fan."

"I wouldn't miss it ordinarily, but it's Father's Day. I need to be home for my kid."

Peyton cocked her head, not sure she'd heard correctly. King's nineteen-year-old son, Darren, was a sophomore at USF, and quite independent. She didn't know Darren, but from her association with King she knew that father and son were not close. King had divorced Darren's mother when the boy was sixteen, and her death two years ago had done little to bring father and son closer together.

"I didn't know" — she kept her tone light — "that Darren was living with you. For some reason I thought he had an apartment near campus."

"He does."

"So why don't you take him to the Bucs dinner? Sounds like it'd be a great thing for you to enjoy together."

An expression crossed King's face then, a look Peyton had never seen him wear. Bewilderment and pain flickered across his strong features, mixed with a strong stamp of embarrassment. "Because Darren hasn't called to say what he wants to do," he said simply, his gaze shifting to the phone on his desk. "And I want to keep the day open."

Peyton lowered her gaze, overcome by a sudden feeling that she'd managed to stumble into forbidden territory. In all the time she'd known King Bernard, she'd never ventured near the wall around his personal life. Something told her this wasn't a good time to press forward; better to cut a hasty retreat.

"Thanks for reminding me," she said, standing. "I ought to get my dad a card."

King smiled, but with a distracted look, as though he were thinking about something else. "Your father still living?"

"Yeah." She turned toward the door, then paused and looked back over her shoulder. "We don't have much to do with each other these days. He's in Jacksonville." And then, because her words seemed to hang in the air, she added, "I haven't seen him in ages, but if I send a card, at least he'll know I'm alive."

King nodded. "Call me if you want the Bucs tickets."

She tried to give him a confident smile, but the corners of her mouth wobbled uncertainly as she looked up at him. "You keep them. Maybe Darren will surprise you and show up."

Comment by Kingston "King" Bernard, 45
Senior Editor/Sports

The thing I like best about the newspaper

44

biz is that you never know who's going to walk through the door. You could've knocked me over with a breath a minute ago when Peyton MacGruder came into my office — the princess of practical doesn't often come slumming in the sports department. I was kind of glad to see her — as long as she didn't have a gripe with me. I've tussled with thirty-pound grouper that are easier to handle than Peyton Mac-Gruder in a huff.

Don't get me wrong, I like the lady. She's got a brain like a steel trap — not that her brain is the first thing a man notices — and the rest of her's not bad, if you get my drift. But the old adage about red hair being a sign of temper is true in her case, and I've felt the sting of her sharp tongue on more than one occasion.

Since I'm being honest here, I might as well confess. When Emma Duncan kicked the bucket and the higher-ups wanted to keep her column, I told Nora Chilton she could do a lot worse than Peyton Mac-Gruder. It had come to the point where the red-haired wench and I either needed to part as friends or kill each other, and I definitely preferred the former.

Now it looks like Nora's having the same kind of problem with Peyton I did — you can learn a lot from your coworkers if you read between the lines. Peyton's good, and fast as blazes, but she's all surface.

I'll never forget the Friday morning she drove out to Brooksville to interview Tiger Woods. I was thrilled when she came back with four cassette tapes — she'd talked to the guy for two hours! With visions of sports journalism awards dancing in my head, I congratulated her, sent her off to write, and reserved a lead spot on the front page of our Sunday sports edition. That could have been a lead story — and in the hands of almost anyone else, it would have been. Trouble is, it would have taken any of my other writers six hours to pull their notes together.

An hour later, Peyton sends me the file and I print it out. My temper starts to boil as I read a thousand words of elementary stuff — where Tiger was born, where he went to school, how his dad coached him, how he got his start in golf. My *son,* who's no writer, could have written that piece without even going to Brooksville. *I* could have written it without doing any more research than popping up a few Web pages.

So I send it back to Peyton and ask for more depth. By now it's three o'clock, I've got no story, and we're nearly at deadline.

THINGS GOD CANNOT DO

Are there really 3 things that God cannot do? Can't God do everything? Let's take a look at God's own Word to see what He Himself tells us.

1. God Cannot Lie

"Ahh," you say, "yes, I believe that God cannot lie." This may seem rather obvious or even a trick answer, but nevertheless absolutely true. According to God's own Word in Titus 1:2 we see "God, that cannot lie." God, and God alone, can make that claim.

2. God Cannot Change

"Oh, sure," you say, "I believe that God cannot change." This is also a rather obvious truth. God tells us in His Word, in Malachi 3:6, "I am the LORD, I change not." This is another characteristic which is unique to God alone.

3. God Cannot Allow Sinners into Heaven

"Hmmm," you say, "I'm not so sure about that one. I don't know that I believe that." But, do you know how we know that this is true—absolutely true? Because God Himself tells us, and *God cannot lie* and *God cannot change*. So, if God said it, it is true and it is true for all time. Jesus spoke in John 3:3,5 "Verily, verily [truly, truly], I say unto thee, Except a man be born again, he *cannot* see the kingdom of God…. Verily, verily [truly, truly], I say unto thee, Except a man be born of water and of the Spirit, he *cannot* enter into the kingdom of God."

You may reasonably question the truthfulness of whatever you hear from men including myself. But what we find in God's Word (the Bible) is absolutely true and true for ever (Psalm 119:89).

Now, if God cannot allow sinners into heaven, this is very bad news for all of us because God also tells us: "For *all* have sinned, and come short of the glory of God" (Romans 3:23). That may be a difficult truth to accept about yourself, but accept it you must. You may have *believed* that you were pretty good, but you now *know* that you are a sinner. The Bible says in 1 John 1:10: "If we say that we have not sinned, we make Him [God] a liar." Is there more to the story? Is there a way to get to heaven? Let's examine more of God's true words to us.

In John 14:6 Jesus said, "I am *the* way, *the* truth, and *the* life: no man cometh unto the Father, but by Me." Jesus explains that there are not many ways to get to heaven. There is *one* way, and that way is Jesus Himself, because He alone died for our sins: "While we were yet sinners, Christ died for us" (Romans 5:8). Again, we know this is true, because God said it and He doesn't lie and He doesn't change. "Neither is there salvation in any other: for there is none other name under heaven given among men, whereby we must be saved" (Acts 4:12). *Salvation is only through Jesus.*

There is an incident recorded in the Bible where a man asked: "What must I do to be saved?" The answer was: "Believe on the Lord Jesus Christ, and thou shalt be saved" (Acts 16:30,31). You may say, "But, don't

I have to do something else?" God gives the answer: "For by grace are ye saved through faith; and that not of yourselves: it is the gift of God: Not of works, lest any man should boast" (Ephesians 2:8,9). God made salvation so plain and so simple.

Simply take God at His word. His Word is eternally true (Psalm 119:160). You now *know* that you are a sinner; you *know* that there is no salvation in works; and you *know* that you must believe on the Lord Jesus Christ to be saved.

"Repent ye, and believe the gospel" (Mark 1:15). "If thou shalt confess with thy mouth the Lord Jesus, and shalt believe in thine heart that God hath raised Him from the dead, thou shalt be saved" (Romans 10:9).

If you have repented and believed on the Lord Jesus Christ as your Saviour, then you may know that you have eternal life. God says in 1 John 5:13: "These things have I written unto you that believe on the name of the Son of God; that ye may *know* that ye have eternal life." In the past, you may have *hoped* that you were going to heaven. Now you may *know* it!

Crusade Baptist Church
2982 Copley Rd, Copley, OH
crusadebaptist.org
330-665-1076

If you have questions or want to talk to someone about what it means to follow Jesus Christ, visit SeekLife.net

Gospel Series #232 (KJV)

MOMENTS WITH THE BOOK
MWtB PO Box 322, Bedford PA 15522
814-623-8737 • www.mwtb.org

9 781614 163336

The next thing I know, she's in my office going on about how she's covered all the bases, and I keep telling her she hasn't even scratched the surface. She tells me I'm acting like an editor for the *Enquirer*, that all I want is dirt and scandal, and I tell her she's way off base. I don't want scandal, but I do want a *story*, not facts and trivia. I want to know the *person* of Tiger Woods, I want to *see* this whiz kid, but all I've got from her is boring biography.

We probably would have carried on all night, but the deadline stopped us both. Peyton made a halfhearted effort to rewrite, but all she did was rearrange her facts. I ended up running her story, but I placed it below the fold and moved Bill Elliott's Bucs Report into the lead spot.

Peyton MacGruder is . . . exhausting. You know, now that I think about it, I wouldn't be surprised if those Tiger Woods interview tapes contained nothing but dead air. Tiger probably answered a few of her questions, recognized trouble when he saw it, and played on by, leaving her in the clubhouse.

I was hoping she'd do well with that features column — through "The Heart Healer" she could boss people around to her heart's content and bring Emma

Duncan's readers into the twenty-first century at the same time. Guess it's not working out the way I'd hoped.

You know . . . for a moment, when I mentioned the tickets for the Bucs shindig, she had sort of a deer-in-the-headlights thing going on in her eyes. I almost laughed. She probably thinks I wanted to take her to the dinner myself.

Not that I'd mind — ordinarily. She's a great gal, lots of spunk, always has an opinion. She knows I'm no saint, but she still speaks to me, so that's something in her favor. I once ran into her in the parking lot of the Hyde Park United Methodist Church near downtown. She was covering a 10K race, and actually thought I was checking up on her until I explained that I had come to the church for my AA meeting. She let it slide and didn't say anything else, but she was one of the few people who didn't give me grief when I chose to drink fruit punch at the office Christmas party — or is it Holiday Party? I can't keep up with all the PC lingo we're supposed to employ.

Peyton's also been pretty sensitive about Darren — nice of her to say that maybe he'd surprise me so I'd get to use the Bucs tickets anyway. I doubt it — I sometimes think Darren would rather undergo oral surgery than spend time with me — but if he's needing money, he might call and play the dutiful son on Father's Day. I can always hope.

So while I wouldn't mind having a sandwich and coffee with Peyton MacGruder, I don't think I'd want to take the relationship beyond that. I could, of course, now that she no longer works in my department . . .

Nah. Like I said, she's exhausting. And I have enough trying people in my life.

The last thing I need is the heart healer.

Ninety minutes later Peyton was standing in an Eckerd's drugstore on Hillsborough Boulevard, poring over a colorful array of Father's Day cards. She dismissed all those with sappy messages, and cringed at most of the funny ones. Her relationship with her father wasn't the kind of thing that could be summed up or acknowledged in a card, unless Hallmark decided to publish a line of greetings for those who wish to bestow only a perfunctory nod to the occasion. But still . . . Father's Day came only once a year, and if it had not been for Dr. Mick Middleton's biological contribution, she wouldn't exist.

She picked up a card with a picture of a

woman gazing through a photograph album. *When I think of love,* the caption read, *I think of you.*

The sentiment made Peyton's throat tighten. When she thought of her father, she thought of a squalling mob — at least, that's what had filled his house the last time she visited. Her father and his wife, Kathy, had six children, all of them spaced two years apart. The youngest had been a toddler when Peyton left Gainesville, but by now the youngest was probably — she paused to count on her fingers — eighteen years old.

She winced. Had so much time passed? How could the baby have progressed from infancy to adulthood while Peyton remained in the same season of life?

Sheesh. She glanced toward another section on the display rack, a sparse selection of graduation cards. If the baby of her father's new family had graduated from high school, then the oldest kid must be finished with college by now. She closed her eyes in order to riffle through her memories. She'd received all kinds of graduation announcements over the years, from her half-siblings as well as from Kathy's relatives, people whose names were as unfamiliar as the faces in the stiff photographs. How could they expect her to keep up with them all?

50

It wasn't like she and her dad had ever been close. Mick Middleton, a proud native of Jacksonville, Florida ("the biggest city in the world!"), had married Elaine Huff at eighteen and buried her at twenty-two. During the three-year marriage, he fathered a child — Peyton.

Because Peyton's mother had died of a severe asthma attack — an event Peyton mercifully had not witnessed — Mick Middleton turned his young mind toward medical science. Peyton stayed with her grandmother while her father put himself through medical school. When her grandmother died from complications of diabetes, the new Dr. Middleton enrolled his daughter in the Bolles School in Jacksonville, a private coeducational boarding facility with an emphasis on arts.

He married Kathy, ten years his junior, when Peyton was in the ninth grade, and by the time she left Bolles the new family consisted of two kids and another on the way. By the time she met Garrett, the love of her life, her father's new brood included three children, two dogs, and a station wagon.

Fearing a complete circus, she decided not to invite her father or his kiddie clan to her wedding. In '78 she and Garrett were married in a small church in Gainesville — the same year Kathy conceived the fourth child of Peyton's father's second family. In late '81, Peyton received a card announcing the birth of her fifth half-sibling . . . only a few weeks before a minister held Garrett's funeral at that same small Gainesville church.

No. When she thought of her father, she did not think of love. She thought of separation.

Sighing, she placed the sentimental Father's Day card back in the rack. The only person who came to mind when she considered the word *love* was Garrett, who'd been an assistant professor at the university when they met and her world turned upside down.

They dated, they kissed, they sparred — and for the first time Peyton felt she had found a person in whom she could anchor her soul. They married quickly, starved through lean months, and wrote profound poetry for one another alone. They had just moved into a rental house that seemed to have more good points than cockroaches when she answered the door and discovered two polite highway patrolmen in pressed uniforms who came to explain that she was a widow.

Darkness followed . . . a depression so deep she couldn't fathom it even now, then the light began to shine again, slowly and steadily. After her time of mourning and adjustment, her father begged her to come back to Jacksonville, but Peyton accepted a job with the *Orlando Sentinel* and professed a sudden liking for all things Disney. Jacksonville seemed distant and stifling, and the thought of visiting her father amid the happy bedlam she often heard in the background of his phone calls did not appeal.

She'd only been in Orlando a few months when her new friends accused her of despising the male species. Peyton was quick to point out that she did not hate men — after all, her father was a man, and she tolerated him. But the two men with whom she later developed semi-serious relationships never seemed interested in marriage. The first bolted when he met a blonde cocktail waitress who dipped her cleavage toward him, the second seemed content to merely talk about commitment. When Peyton asked him if he ever intended to live up to his lofty conversation, the talking ceased. As did the relationship.

In the passing years she grew accustomed to living alone and, to her surprise, found she enjoyed her freedom. She had two cats for company, a dozen hobbies for pleasure, and a host of friends at the office. After moving from Orlando to Tampa — after a while, too much Disney could blur the line between reality and fantasy to even the most discerning eye — she found herself delighting in a career that utilized her talents and satisfied her curiosity. Her column even had the potential to provide practical help for people's lives —

If she still had a column.

She made a face as the memory of Nora's conversation came flooding back. In three weeks, she might find herself in the business of padding obituaries for influential Floridians, so she might as well go home and sketch out some ideas to improve the column. She had a week to laze around and think, so maybe she'd paint the guestroom and hope that inspiration would strike as she slapped paint on the walls.

She plucked a plain, unvarnished card (Happy Father's Day from Your Daughter) from the top of the rack and moved toward the cash register. A small boy of three or four crouched in the candy aisle, his greedy eyes fastened to a basket of bubblegum balls.

"Mom, where are you?" Peyton murmured, moving down the aisle. "He's going to end up with a pocketful of candy if you don't watch him."

Peyton took her place in line, then rocked back on her heels and turned to search for the wayward mother. A pair of teenage boys in jeans and T-shirts had draped themselves over a video game by the door; a sunburned tourist with a Walkman on his waistband checked out the bottles of Solarcaine in the first aid supplies.

Out on the street, the wail of a siren rose and fell.

"Miss?"

Peyton turned to the freckled woman behind the register, then handed her the card. "That's it for me."

The siren grew louder.

"Musta been a wreck out there," the cashier said as she turned the card over in search of the UPC. "Traffic's terrible this time of day."

Peyton smiled. "I know."

The clerk swiped the card beneath a scanner, then punched a couple of keys on the register. "Six-thirty-five," she said, cracking her gum as she shifted her gaze toward the glass doors.

Peyton gasped. Six dollars for a *card?*

"It's been a long time." She pulled her

wallet from her purse. "I had no idea cards were so expensive."

"It's a ripoff," the clerk agreed amiably, sliding the card into a bag.

Outside, a different siren howled, then another, from closer by, joined in the caterwauling. As Peyton glanced toward the doors, she saw that the two teenagers had stepped outside. One was pointing to the street and jumping in consternation.

"What in the —," she began.

The tourist, red-faced and sweating, came toward them. Earphones dangled from his neck. "I heard it on the radio!" Beads of perspiration shone on his upper lip and the Adam's apple in his throat bobbed as he swallowed. "A jet just went down in Tampa Bay."

Struggling to mask her disbelief, Peyton painted on a smile. "Surely you're mistaken. We've never had a crash in this area."

"Look for yourself, lady." The man jerked his thumb toward the front of the store. "Every emergency vehicle in the area is en route to the scene. It's all over the radio."

Peyton felt the wings of tragedy brush past her, stirring the air and lifting the hair at the back of her neck. Could the unthinkable have happened? The airport lay right next to Tampa Bay, so if a jet had gone down in those waters, there might be survivors. There would definitely be a story . . .

Gulping for breath, she left the cashier and ran for her car.

Only later would she realize that she never did send a Father's Day card.

Three

Wednesday, June 20
Sitting at a booth in a dark corner of a sea-food restaurant, Peyton held a sweating glass of iced tea to her forehead and struggled to keep her eyes open. Every time she closed them, visions of the previous week played on the backs of her eyelids, and she didn't think she could stand to witness such tragedy again. She'd seen enough sorrow in one week to last a dozen lifetimes.

Immediately after the crash, spurred by a reporter's instinct, she had driven down Memorial Highway until she reached a roadblock north of West Cypress Street. Abandoning her car by the side of the road, she tossed her keys into her pocket and ran toward the water, joining a crowd of others — kids on bicycles, men and women, white- and blue-collar workers from the sur-rounding commercial buildings, all drawn by the spectacle of disaster.

At the end of West Cypress, she stood with the others and stared past the emergency vehicles at . . . nothing. A dark remnant of cloud hovered over the water, stretching gauzy fingers toward the north, but nothing marked the gray-blue sheen of the bay.

"It'll take time," the man next to her said, his gaze sweeping over the water. "For things to . . . surface." Taking mental notes, Peyton studied him. He wore a white dress shirt, rolled up at the sleeves, with a navy tie loosely knotted at his neck.

"Do you work around here?" She gestured over her shoulder toward the tall buildings lining the bay.

"There." Without looking, he pointed toward the Bob Hawkins headquarters at the end of Cypress. Peyton thought Bob Hawkins, Inc., made manufactured homes; she made a mental note to check.

The air shimmered with heat haze and vibrated with the wail of sirens as other emergency vehicles rushed toward the water and stopped. A pair of Tampa cops were attempting to cordon off a stretch of sand close to the water, but Peyton couldn't see anything on the beach to protect . . . only a few stands of grass, a handful of scrub oaks, and an occasional sea gull.

For things to surface. Heaviness centered in her chest as the words hit home — the police would soon need this beach for recovery. The remains of human life would eventually rise from the deep.

Gulping back a sudden rise of despair, Peyton turned from the water. Behind her, a teenage boy in oversized tennis shoes balanced a boom box on the handlebars of his bike while he stood slack-jawed. From the radio, a deejay announced that traffic had come to a standstill on both cross-bay bridges, effectively shutting down two counties. "This is truly terrible," he said, his voice breaking. "We have never known anything like this. If you believe in a higher power, now is the time to pray."

Peyton lengthened her stride, setting her jaw as she moved away. What good would prayer do now? The plane had apparently dropped out of the sky, and God had done nothing to stop it.

Once she reached her car, traffic had so backed up that it took her three hours to travel less than a mile. At the entrance to Tampa International Airport, she parked on the shoulder and jogged toward the terminal, then threaded her way through the mob gathered in the airside serving PanWorld Airlines.

Behind the desk at the gate reserved for Flight 848, a pale PW spokesman was assuring anyone who approached that help was on its way. When pressed for further information, the man admitted that "help" was a trauma team from the airline's New York office. "For now," he told Peyton and a horde of other insistent reporters, "we can confirm that Flight 848 has experienced an in-flight incident. The plane dropped off our radar at 6:31 p.m., and we are doing everything possible to search for survivors. An Accident Operations Center has been established at PanWorld headquarters in New York, and trauma experts are en route to Tampa."

Over the next few hours, time stopped for Peyton — and for much of the city. Like a tall oak draws lightning, the tragedy drew hundreds of people to the Tampa airport — counselors, rescue workers, clergy of every stripe, and, of course, members of the media. Airside C, serving PanWorld Airlines, was temporarily closed off to serve the families of victims, while other PanWorld flights were shifted to different gates. A public relations team from PanWorld's New York office arrived to handle the news media.

Peyton wasn't surprised to learn that reporters had been barred from Airside C. Tampa policemen guarded the entrances, protecting the mourners' privacy, and even local reporters who had friends in airport administration found themselves having to rely upon press conferences for updates and information. Within twenty-four hours of the crash, however, local writers from the *Tampa Times* and *St. Pete Post* were displaced by television newscasters from all the major networks. As reporters jockeyed for position inside the airport hotel, news trucks from the local stations jostled in the airport pickup lanes with vans from CNN, ABC, CBS, NBC, FOX, and the new World News Network. After each press conference, the print reporters retreated to quiet corners to type up their impressions on laptops or mumble into digital recorders while the TV newscasters scrawled out quick scripts, adjusted their makeup, then taped interviews with stricken family members and somber airport officials.

In all the media madness, one reporter stood out, both on the air and off. Wherever Julie St. Claire of the World News Network went, an appreciative crowd followed. Though she'd never heard of the woman before, Peyton thought it wasn't hard to understand St. Claire's appeal — the twenty-something brunette was not only beautiful, but poised. While Peyton noticed other reporters pacing, yelling, and snapping during the few moments before a live interview, Julie St. Claire remained as calm and cool as an ice princess. But she delivered news of the tragedy with compassion and warmth, and in the newsroom, when Peyton lifted her gaze to the TV sets hanging from the ceiling, she usually found herself watching WNN's coverage.

On Thursday afternoon, as she waited in the Marriott ballroom for a press conference called by the Tampa Bay Bucs' head coach, Peyton watched Julie St. Claire do a live interview for WNN. A team of personnel surrounded the reporter, one man fluffing her hair while a woman applied pancake makeup with a sponge, but St. Claire could have been a mannequin, so concentrated was she on her task. She stood with her eyes open and mouth closed, her gaze focused on the waiting camera, a steno pad in her grasp. When the director lifted his hand and began the countdown with his fingers, the makeup artists stepped back, and St. Claire sparked to life.

"Good evening," she said, her voice level as her blue eyes stared into the wide camera lens. "Grief still roams the halls of the Tampa Marriott Airport hotel, where weeping relatives remain on scene for news of their loved ones aboard Flight 848. But no longer are they hoping for a miracle. As PanWorld released the complete passenger list this afternoon, recovery teams brought the first of the bodies up from the wreckage. Later tonight, in the area behind me, the coach of the Tampa Bay Buccaneers will formally announce the death of Tom Harold, beloved defensive coach of the Bucs, who helped move the team from last place to the Super Bowl in the space of one season . . ."

Peyton listened with admiration as the reporter moved from news to sports. She'd heard other television and radio reporters stumble and fumble their live reports, but Julie St. Claire performed as if she had been born for the job. She certainly looked the part. Dressed in a tasteful blue suit, with nary a stain or wrinkle . . .

Peyton glanced down at her own outfit — jeans and a cotton shirt, topped by a sweater she'd tied around her neck to ward off the air-conditioning chill. Her short hair was probably standing on end, considering how many times she'd raked her hands through it, and as for makeup, who had time for such foolishness in a situation like this?

Newspapers, Peyton decided, had been invented for communicators who had more brains than beauty. It wasn't fair that television reporters made more money and reached more people than print reporters, but being high-maintenance had to have a downside.

Though she was technically on vacation, an irresistible power drew Peyton to the airport and the newsroom. Reporting was too much a part of her, the experience too close to ignore, so day after day she hung out at the airport, then drove to the newsroom and sat at her desk, helping out where she could, providing snatches of overheard conversations and facts for writers who needed dashes of local color. The newsroom throbbed with life — phones ringing, fingers flying over clattering keyboards, and tempers flaring — but Peyton wouldn't have missed it for the world.

Questions flew back and forth at the speed of thought.

"Who do you know at the FAA?"

"I need a warm body to run over and get me a quote from the president of the airline!"

"Anybody know anyone at the New York mayor's office?"

"I need a contact at Boeing, and I need it *now!*"

The calls for help came thick and fast,

frightening Mandi and the young copy kids into scared-rabbit silence, but Peyton found herself energized by the electricity that zipped through the newsroom. Though "The Heart Healer" wouldn't appear at all in the coming week, she stayed at the office, jotting down questions for her fellow reporters, answering phones, and logging on to the Web to help with research. When things grew quiet in the newsroom, she headed off to the airport to gather whatever information she could.

Except for the daily ritual features — the comics, syndicated columns, and the classifieds — all stories seemed to revolve around some aspect of the crash. The news reporters worked round the clock to concentrate on airline problems and the recovery efforts, the economic writers focused on the financial prospects of TIA and PanWorld Airline, King and his sportswriters investigated the blow dealt the Tampa Bay Buccaneers. Other writers took their cues from the crash as well — the health/medical writer did a piece on how the human body reacts to a time of severe grief, the guy covering retail and tourism wrote an article on how Tampa Bay's image might suffer, and the woman who covered social services featured the charitable organizations who were offering relief and counseling during the aftermath of the tragedy.

Milton Higgs, manager of the archive and research center, moved a cot into the library and sprouted a beard, choosing to sleep in his office rather than miss an opportunity to provide photos and background on prominent citizens who had perished in the crash.

Nora Chilton had her features writers considering every angle of the tragedy not already covered by the news department. She sent people out to interview local victims' families, arranged for photography shoots, and reserved front feature page coverage for the most heart-wrenching stories. The events coordinator spent so much time on the phone in his effort to compile a list of times and dates of local victims' memorial services that he ordered a telephone headset, and the children and families writer did a three-part piece on how to gently teach children about death. Peyton thought Nora was treading dangerously close to overkill when she assigned the home/gardening/pets writer, Diane Winters, a major feature on memorial statuary for the residential garden.

Compelled to help her coworkers, Peyton attended every press conference she could squeeze into, conducted spot interviews with willing PanWorld employees, and made a list of the various approaches employed by other reporters. She took notes as the mayor of New York, who had lost personal friends on the flight, lashed out at the airline for not notifying family members in a timely manner. She listened as Red Cross workers, priests, and rabbis led stricken family members in prayer at the airport chapel. And she studied other members of the media — some of whom handled interviews with tact and grace, others who ran over trampled emotions like freight trains on a fast track to nowhere.

The reporters weren't the only strangers in town. The promised airline trauma experts, Peyton learned, came in three varieties: white-shirted officials from PanWorld, who grew thinner and paler with each passing day; burly mechanic-types who wore biohazard suits and carried boxes of notepads and disposable cameras out to the crash site; and cardigan-clad counselors. The counselors spoke in urgent whispers and crept through the airport in soft-soled shoes, tissues and Bibles their weapons against grief. While the white-shirts argued at the airport and the biohazard guys snapped pictures on the beach, the counselors sat with weeping family members.

The most common question, one that Peyton asked herself, was "why?" Within days, the airlines had presented not an answer, but a reaction.

Julie St. Claire broadcast the official blurb as she stood outside the PW Baggage Claim Office. "Investigators," she said, steadily eyeing the camera, "have reported that the flight data recorder recovered two days ago revealed nothing unusual. Yesterday the U.S. Federal Agency of Civil Aviation ordered inspections of all Boeing 767 passenger planes belonging to U.S. airlines. An inspection of another 767 had revealed the destruction of three of the four safety bolts holding the engine to the wing. Two-hundred-thirty Boeing 767 airplanes are currently in service worldwide, and one hundred twenty of them belong to eight U.S. airlines. Despite these inspections, the 767 is considered safe. John Hollstrom, an aviation consultant, describes the jet as 'right behind the 747 as the backbone of the world's aviation fleet.' "

St. Claire paused a beat, then continued in a softer tone. "While such news might assure apprehensive travelers who will be flying 767s in days to come, it is small comfort to the grieving families who mourn the loss of loved ones aboard Flight 848."

Peyton felt suffocated by secondhand grief. After two days, the counselors moved the grief-stricken families from Airside C to the ballroom of the Tampa Marriott, which reporters referred to as "heartbreak hotel." PanWorld had devised a formula for arranging food and shelter for the victims' families — for every passenger, they figured, two to six mourners would show up in Tampa. They grossly underestimated the number. Peyton met one family who brought forty people to claim the body of a woman who had been daughter, mother, niece, aunt, cousin, and beloved friend.

With a vast host of anxious companions, Peyton felt her heart go numb as evidence of 261 lives began to appear on the shores of Tampa Bay. Photographs, waterlogged paperbacks, charred seats, ceiling panels, battered suitcases, knapsacks, and an empty pet kennel either washed up or were brought to the surface by the recovery teams. All recovered detritus was logged in, then either placed in cartons for the airline or carried to the Marriott ballroom. Long rows of tables displayed these personal items, and after every delivery a host of anxious relatives swarmed forward in hopes of identifying a bit of a lost loved one.

Though reporters were still forbidden in

restricted family areas, Peyton saw grieving people everywhere — on the shuttles, walking through airsides, standing at the windows with their hands pressed to the glass. And though she didn't want to intrude, she often stood within eavesdropping distance to listen. What she heard amazed her. Though many families had been completely shattered, still people spoke of faith, comfort, and love. The trauma counselors, brought in to comfort families, often withdrew from the restricted areas to counsel each other.

Peyton quietly sat alongside families as they filled out forms for the Hillsborough County medical examiner: Did the deceased have any identifying scars? Do you have access to dental records? Had the deceased, if female, given birth to a child?

Some of the mourners wore lapel photos of their loved ones. After two days they grew restless, having had their fill of counseling and commiseration. They wanted their loved ones' bodies, wanted to take them home. Peyton knew of at least two families who flew home to New York in tears, only to return a day later. They could not find peace until they laid their loved ones to rest.

One woman haunted the halls, refusing to sit and wait in the families-only areas. She wore a voluminous black dress imprinted with some sort of stenciled design, and topped the outfit with a straw hat.

Peyton first saw her on the shuttle. When their eyes met, the woman's hand flew to her mouth, then her knees buckled. As everyone around rushed to help, the woman lowered her hand to point at Peyton: "Karen?" she asked, her voice quavering.

Peyton shook her head. "Sorry."

"You look just like her." The woman leaned heavily on two other shuttle riders, who were now glaring at Peyton as if she'd done something terrible by not being Karen. "My daughter. They haven't found her yet, you know, but they did bring up her suitcase."

Peyton couldn't get off the shuttle fast enough, and for the rest of the week she kept glancing over her shoulder for any sight of the straw hat, ready to sprint around the nearest corner should it appear.

On Thursday divers recovered twenty bodies. By Saturday, they had recovered two hundred twenty, with one hundred positively identified, thirty tentatively. The positive IDs were turned over to family members.

The funeral services began on Sunday. At the Largo Community Church, the forty-eight high school graduates were eulogized in song and poetry. After the service, somber mourners released 213 white and 48 silver balloons into the clear sky while a choir sang about friends being friends forever if they knew the Lord.

Two hours later, the city of Tampa held another service on the beach south of the airport. Peyton stood with the mourners on the sand and listened as a priest recited ecumenical snippets of Scripture: "When this corruptible has put on incorruption, and this mortal has put on immortality, then shall be brought to pass the saying: 'Death is swallowed up in victory.' Oh death, where is your sting? Oh grave, where is your victory? Thanks be to God, who gives us the victory . . . God has not given us a spirit of fear, but of power and of love and of a sound mind . . . Yea, though I walk through the valley of the shadow of death, I will fear no evil; for You are with me; Your rod and Your staff, they comfort me."

The minister then switched to a more practical tone. Well aware of the resentment many families felt toward PanWorld, he said, "People on both sides of this tragedy are mourning today. Twenty-four of the two hundred sixty-one who died were airline employees. Common sorrow could do much to reunite those who are bearing this grief. A shared anguish can be a bridge of reconciliation."

Peyton watched as family members dropped roses into the waves, then waded into the water, ankle-high, some knee-high, oblivious to the creeping wetness rising up pants and dresses. Through the water, she supposed, the mourners felt a connection to their loved ones . . . and to each other.

She didn't think she would ever be able to look at the beach without seeing roses in the wavewash.

Now, a full week after the catastrophe, Peyton pulled her iced tea glass from her forehead and stared at King, who sat across the booth. She'd run into him at the office, and this time when he wearily suggested dinner, she had accepted, too tired to engage in a mental debate about his intentions.

He leaned his elbow on the table, his hand supporting his head. His dark hair gleamed in the weak light from the overhead lamp while an aura of melancholy radiated from his strong features like some dark nimbus.

She couldn't recall ever seeing him look so defeated.

"Is it over?" she asked, her voice heavy in the silence.

He nodded slowly, staring at the menu on

the table. "As far as the world is concerned" — he lifted his gaze — "it's over and done. The families have mourned, the bodies are buried, and the president's talking about peace in the Middle East. The world is ready to move on."

"Are we?"

A corner of his mouth quirked in an almost-smile. "We'll move on, too. Tampa doesn't want to be known as Disaster City. In a couple of days, I'll be writing about the Bucs' new defensive coach, and you'll be telling readers how to get grape juice stains out of white carpeting. Nora might even urge you to stick to safe, practical topics. We've filled our quota of raw emotion. Our readers will want something . . . *gentler* . . . for a while."

Peyton pulled the paper wrapper from her straw, then dropped the straw into her glass. She had written an as-yet unpublished column on Flight 848, departing from her usual format to write a letter to her readers, but Nora wouldn't run it until after Peyton's supposed week of vacation. Though only a few days before the editor had been urging her to write with more passion, Peyton suspected Nora might not trust the resident Heart Healer to address a true crisis in the column.

King frowned at the menu. "What are you going to have?"

Peyton sipped her tea, then gave him a smile. "Truth is, I'm not really hungry. I think I'm too tired to eat."

"Me, too." He closed the menu with a weary sigh. "How about a snack, then? Feel like having popcorn on my sofa? I've got to write about a tight end the Bucs have their eye on, but I haven't even begun to look at his tapes."

Ordinarily, the prospect of an evening alone with King Bernard would have repelled Peyton faster than skunk scent, but the thought of curling up on a sofa and watching mindless football seemed a lot more comforting than going home to her dark house.

"I'm there," she said, closing her menu.

Four

Amazing, Peyton thought, how the newspaper kept prodding life forward. Though the crash of Flight 848 had left an indelible mark on the Tampa Bay community, within ten days the news writers at the *Times* had moved on to entirely different topics. By the last day of her official "vacation," the headlines had shifted. Stories about the president's statements on the national budget dominated the front page, while NASA's announcement of a manned mission to Mars occupied the space below the fold. Israel and the Palestinians were bickering again on page 2A, and officials from North and South Korea made the right column of the front page when they officially opened the newly rebuilt, 309-mile train track running from Seoul in South Korea to Pyongyang, the capital of the North.

On the front page of the local section, Florida's governor awarded medals of valor to the rescue workers who spent hours salvaging the remains of Flight 848, and the ten surviving children of Mr. and Mrs. Thomas Wilt offered their inheritance to establish a scholarship fund for needy students who wished to attend Largo Christian School.

And though no one would ever find the story printed in the pages of the *Times*, Peyton knew she and King had made news with their renewed friendship. Two nights ago she'd been calmly eating popcorn and vegging out on King's couch when Carter Cummings stopped by to drop off a pair of press passes to a Lightning function. Though the night had been about as exciting as a worn pair of bedroom slippers, Carter's eyes had widened and his mouth quirked in a mischievous smile. For a moment Peyton thought about telling him to keep his mouth shut, but that would imply that he had something to keep his mouth shut *about,* and there was nothing, absolutely nothing, going on between her and the sports editor.

So now she pretended boredom and indifference when she caught winks and twitters from her coworkers. *Let 'em talk.* They were talking about zilch, zero, zippo. She and King were friends and coworkers, nothing more.

Besides, she had other things to worry about. As of Sunday, Peyton would return as the Heart Healer . . . for two probationary weeks. She'd had neither the time nor the energy to consider revamping the format, but, remembering King's comment about a readership weary of despair, she tossed the column she'd written about the air tragedy and pulled a question about finding a lost love from her file of reader mail. Ignoring the feeling of emptiness at the bottom of her weary heart, she explained how the Web could be used to search for lost classmates and childhood friends, mentioned the extensive computerized database maintained by the Latter-day Saints, then ended with a sentimental paragraph about how childhood memories grew sweeter as they grew fainter.

Sometimes, she finished, *we do ourselves a disservice to yearn for what we've lost. For if we try to find it again, we might discover faults and blemishes memory has been kind enough to erase.*

Satisfied with the result, she reread the column a second time, then a third, making small edits as she scanned it. When she was certain it could not be improved — at least not by her tired eyes — she marked the column with Sunday's date, then sent it to the copy desk with a click of the mouse.

She still had to write a column for Monday, but she could work on that over the weekend and zap it into the copy desk via modem. As a "soft" feature, her filing deadline was usually 11:30 a.m. the day before a column was scheduled to appear. Late afternoon deadlines were reserved for news writers, who presumably needed more time to root around for hard news. Sunday feature columns were due by noon on Friday, because nobody in features — not even diehards like Nora — wanted to work on Saturday.

After pulling a couple of interesting letters from her reader mail so she'd have something to consider for Monday's feature, Peyton spent twenty minutes answering e-mails. Two of them were annoying urban legends demanding *"Pass this on to everyone you know!"* She was in the middle of explaining that Neiman Marcus had never charged anyone for a recipe (though the attached instructions would result in an excruciatingly delicious cookie), when her phone rang. Anita, the receptionist in the main lobby downstairs, was calling to announce a visitor.

Frowning, Peyton glanced at her calendar. No appointments. And since she'd technically been on vacation all week, it wasn't likely that an irate reader had rushed to the newspaper office in a fit of temper. Still, one never knew what sort of person might walk in.

Lifting her gaze, Peyton peered around the vast newsroom, hoping to catch a glimpse of a giggling prankster, but no one moved among the mostly empty desks. Most of her exhausted coworkers had filed their weekend stories and gone home to crash, and those who hadn't gone home had gone to lunch. The only sounds were the quiet chatter of Mandi's keyboard, a distant telephone, and the muffled buzz of an over-hanging television. The lull after a storm.

"Did she give a name?" Peyton asked the receptionist.

Muffled sounds followed, then Anita said, "Gabriella Cohen. She says it's very important that she speak to you."

Peyton glanced at her watch. Only twelve-fifteen, but she was done with her work, and as soon as she emptied her in-box she was planning to head for home. Moreover, she was bone tired — not quite up to appearing fresh and friendly to an eager reader.

Peyton strengthened her voice. "Tell her I'm sorry, but I can't see her today — I'm on my way out. She can leave a message, though, and I'll try to call her next week."

An odd premonition strummed a shiver from her as Peyton dropped the phone back into its cradle. Though most of her mail ranged from sweet to fawning, occasionally she received the odd letter from a nut case. Last year a woman had taken her to task for giving the fictitious name "Birdie" to another reader. *I understand why you want to protect the privacy of individuals who write you,* she had written. *But of all the beautiful names in the world, why did you choose the name Birdie? You might as well have called her Rat, Roach, or Weasel.*

Peyton sighed as she closed her notebook, then slid it in a desk drawer. No one could please everyone all the time, but some people were impossible to satisfy. And if the visitor in the reception area wanted to gripe about a name Peyton had used or a topic she had chosen, well, she'd have to wait. Maybe forever.

Peyton logged off the computer network, slid the keyboard tray under her desk, and stuffed the last of her notes on the genealogy column into a file, then tucked it into a drawer. After a quick look around her desk to be sure she hadn't forgotten anything, she picked up her backpack, called good-bye to Mandi, and headed toward the elevator.

Nora approached as the elevator doors

slid open. "Just the woman I wanted to see," she said, giving Peyton a stiff smile. "I read your column for Sunday. It's nice. And it's about time someone pointed out that dwelling on old memories isn't always good for a person's mental health."

Peyton gave her a frosty smile and stepped into the elevator, then pressed the button for the lobby. "Thanks."

Peyton bit the inside of her mouth as Nora followed, and for a moment they waited, the empty air between them heavy and uncomfortable. When the doors closed, Nora broke the silence.

"I think it's what people need to hear right now." Nora didn't turn, but met Peyton's gaze in the mirror images on the brass doors. "I think people are still numb from . . . well, you know. You're encouraging them to look forward, and that's good."

Not knowing what else to say, Peyton murmured another thank you. She didn't know how these compliments fit into Nora's plan to take her column away, but appreciation was always nice — even if it was intended to soften a coming disappointment.

"Have something special planned for next week?"

The question hung in the air between them, shimmering like the reflection from the brass. Peyton gritted her teeth, resenting the editor's fishing expedition. She probably wanted to hear that Peyton had something new and improved and exciting in mind, but she'd been so benumbed by the events of the past week she'd scarcely given any thought to her personal crisis. She'd wanted breathing space, but she'd been handed a nightmare.

"I'm not sure yet," she said, forcing the words off her unwilling tongue. "I'm taking some reader mail home with me. Maybe something will strike me." She shrugged.

"Something always seems to," Nora said, but the phrase didn't sound at all like a compliment.

Peyton lifted her head, grateful that Nora didn't work weekends. Whatever she scraped up and pasted together for Monday's column would probably go straight from the copy desk to the pressroom, with nary a Nora to poke and prod at it. Not that it mattered. Monday editions were traditionally light.

When the doors slid open, Peyton stepped out of the elevator with long strides, leaving Nora in the shadows. The marble lobby gleamed with the rosy glow of afternoon. The floors, walls, and even the circular stone reception desk seemed alive with light.

A group of men huddled near the desk — Carter Cummings, Bill Elliott, Tom Guthrie — all sportswriters, Peyton noticed, and King's friends. Bill was holding his month-old baby, a foolishly proud grin on his face, and something in the cozy tableau set Peyton's heart to pounding within her rib cage. Lowering her head, she walked swiftly toward the revolving doors.

"Miss MacGruder!"

She had expected to hear Carter or Bill call her name, so the sound of a female voice made Peyton start. She looked up, hearing the echo of her name above the clacking sound of wood-soled shoes.

Then she remembered the phone call. A woman had wanted to see her . . . Gabriella somebody-or-other. Drat! Why had she told Anita she was on her way out? The receptionist must have relayed the information, because the woman had obviously decided to stick around for an ambush.

Peyton kept walking in time with her pounding heart, but knew she wouldn't be able to outrun the woman she saw from the corner of her eye. Why did the paper have to include a photo with the byline of every columnist? There'd be no getting out of this one.

"Miss MacGruder, wait, please!"

Peyton came to a dead stop and cast a longing glance toward the door. Monday she'd make it a top priority to find a back way out — through the pressroom, perhaps. Or maybe she could park by the loading docks —

No, the others would think she was being pretentious. Better to stand and face the downside that accompanied even a dribble of fame.

Pasting on a small smile, Peyton took a deep breath, then turned. The approaching woman was young, probably in her early to mid-thirties, with clipped blonde hair and a slight frame. Blue eyes dominated her face, and a heavy shoulder bag swung with every step, seeming to tilt the petite woman to one side.

"I'm sorry," Peyton began, lifting her hand. "I'm in a bit of a hurry. Can we chat next week?"

"This won't take long." Breathless, the woman stopped by Peyton's side, one hand clutching the leather strap of her shoulder bag as if she feared purse snatchers haunted the *Times* lobby. "Please, Miss MacGruder, I've fretted all night about what to do, and I think you're the one. I mean, I think you'd know how to handle this."

Caution and curiosity warred for a moment in Peyton's brain. Curiosity won. "Know how to handle what?"

The woman pressed her lips together as her eyes filled with tears. "I scarcely know where to begin. But I know this is a big story — huge — and I believe you can do it justice. I wouldn't want to give this to anyone but the Heart Healer."

Peyton inhaled deeply, her heart warmed by the praise even as her brain warned her against swallowing wholesale flattery. "Walk me to my car, then," she said, giving the woman a final head-to-toe glance. She didn't seem deranged or dangerous, but it wouldn't hurt to keep the conversation in a public place. As long as the security guard stood in the shack at the entrance to the employee parking lot, this ought to be okay.

"Thank you." Smiling in what looked like sincere relief, the woman pushed her way through the revolving door, and for an instant Peyton was tempted to beat a hasty retreat back to the elevator, leaving this woman blinking in the sun outside.

But she moved through the door and met the woman on the sidewalk. "So what's this about?" Peyton asked, not breaking her forward stride.

The woman hurried to keep up. "It's about Flight 848."

Peyton threw up her hand. "It's been covered, I'm afraid. Extensively. We'll run follow-up stories once the FAA publishes their findings on the exact cause of the crash, but for now that story is finished."

"This isn't about the crash." The woman's voice held a note of disappointment, as though Peyton had failed her somehow. "It's about the *people* on board that plane. It's about a broken heart . . . and that's why I thought of you."

Still walking, the woman opened her bulging purse. Some primal instinct urged Peyton to run — the woman could be pulling a *gun* from that bag — but another impulse forced her to slow her steps, then stop. The woman stopped, too. After withdrawing a square of white cloth — a linen napkin, Peyton thought — she dropped the purse and let it tilt her shoulders again. Silently, with the reverence of one participating in a religious ritual, the woman placed the folded cloth on her open palm.

"We live on Mariner Drive, on the southern side of the Howard Frankland Bridge," the woman said, her voice trembling as her fingers gingerly lifted the fabric. "Yesterday morning I was sitting in my backyard, watching the water and thinking about all those poor people, and I saw this.

It was stuck to the barnacles on one of the posts of our dock."

She nodded at the object within the linen cloth. Peyton looked and saw a clear plastic bag — a sandwich bag, apparently, one with a zip-lock top.

Her mouth twisted as she looked up. "You found a *baggie?*"

The woman bit her lip and nodded, then gently turned the bag over. Peyton hadn't noticed when the plastic lay on the white cloth, but now she could see a sheet of white paper and words scrawled upon the page.

"It's a note. And I believe it came from someone on that plane."

Fascinated, Peyton lifted the bag by a corner. The paper inside appeared perfectly dry — *Zippup bags lock freshness in and odors out* — and the blue ink unblurred.

And the message, though scrawled, was legible:

T—
I love you. All is forgiven.
                    Dad

Peyton threw the woman a sidelong glance. "You really think this is from one of the victims?"

The woman spread her hands. "I don't

know what it is. But of all the writers working for this paper, I knew you'd know how to discover the truth. If this really is from a father on that plane, then somewhere there's a son or daughter who needs to hear this message."

Her voice dropped to a softer tone as she pressed the linen cloth into Peyton's free hand. "You're the Heart Healer, aren't you?"

Peyton couldn't answer. She stared wordlessly at the woman, her heart pounding, the plastic bag hanging between her fingers like a dead thing. What if this note *had* survived the fiery crash? So far the woman's story seemed credible — Mariner Drive *did* lie south of the Howard Frankland, and a row of houses with boat docks did line that street; Peyton gazed over into those lush backyards every time she took the bridge to Pinellas County. So if this woman really did find this note in the water, it could be genuine . . . or it could be a malicious ruse. Was there any way to completely rule out either scenario?

"What do you want me to do with this?" she finally asked. She suspected the answer, but still needed to hear it from this stranger. If this woman had forged the note and invented the story, she could be one of those people who got a kick out of seeing her name in print. If so, Peyton wasn't inclined to grant her even two seconds of celebrity.

The woman took a hasty half-step back. "I don't know what you should do with it. I'm only a housewife, I don't know anything about newspapers or airplanes or the FAA. But I read your column all the time, so I feel like I know you. I was sure you'd know what to do."

Peyton gingerly wrapped the bag in its linen covering, then tucked it into a pocket of her backpack. "I'll need your name," she said, fumbling within her bag in search of her notebook. "And a phone number, in case I need to contact you. And I'll need your exact address, and the time of day you found this — I have to have all the details."

The woman took another half-step back, her expression tight. "I really don't want to become involved, not publicly. But I do want to help."

Peyton pulled a pencil from her bag, then flipped her notebook open. If the woman had written the note and *didn't* want publicity, then she might be the worst kind of sicko — the kind who savored maliciousness in private.

Pausing with her pencil above the page, Peyton lifted a brow and looked at the woman. "I'm ready — name, address, phone number?"

The woman opened her mouth, closed it, then opened it again. "Okay. I'm Gabriella Cohen, I live at 10899 Mariner Drive, and the number's in the book — my husband is Dr. Eli Cohen, but we're listed under my name." She lifted one shoulder in a shrug. "We try not to have patients calling the house."

Peyton jotted down the details. "What kind of doctor?"

"Family practice," Gabriella answered. "His office is in east Tampa."

"Thanks." Looking at the information, Peyton racked her brain for other questions, but Gabriella Cohen had already begun to back toward the parking lot. "Can I call you if I think of something else?" Peyton asked, raising her voice.

Gabriella lifted her hands. "I've already told you all I know. But I'll be praying you find the one . . . who should receive the note."

Walking slowly to her car, Peyton absently pulled the Jetta keys from her pocket and unlocked the door. She sat in the driver's seat with the door open, letting the dry heat dissipate in a stifling wave. Moving robotically, she put the keys in the ignition and cranked the engine, then slid the AC level to maximum blast.

As the cold air gathered strength to chase out the heat, she pulled the linen square from her backpack, then unwrapped the plastic bag and stared at it, overcome by an unanchored but strong sense that she had come to a major crossroad in her life. She had been given a gift — perhaps worthless, perhaps priceless — and the future might well depend upon what she did with it. Or if she did anything at all.

The scrap of paper inside that baggie could either launch her to stardom or send her crashing into oblivion.

Both prospects terrified her.

Five

Saturday, June 23

Peyton spent the better part of Friday night pacing and arguing with herself — the note was real; it was a sure fake; maybe only the FAA, the FBI, the CIA, or some other alphabet soup group could ever tell for sure. She should pursue the story wholeheartedly; she should toss the note in file thirteen and forget she'd ever seen it. She'd be a hero if the story played out; she'd be a laughingstock if it proved to be a hoax. If even *one* adversarial reporter coaxed an FAA official to say a note in plastic could never have survived the fire, the impact, and the water, she — and all her hopes — would be crushed.

By 2:00 a.m., she'd decided to test the waters. In her initial column, she'd *hint* at what she'd discovered, and she would couch the premise in ambivalent terms. She'd say she'd found something that *might* have come from the flight, but on the chance that it had, she was following every lead, making every call, doing everything in her power to follow through. Like a dedicated and conscientious reporter, she would investigate and write, then let her readers make the final decision. They would read her columns, weigh the evidence for and against the note's authenticity, and make up their own minds.

Of course, as an objective reporter, she would remain impartial and uncommitted.

As her cats, Samson and Elijah, reclined on the bed and listened with rapt attention, she moved on to the debate about Whom to Trust with the news. Nora Chilton was out. Nora would want to assign the story to a feature writer, or maybe hand it over to one of the investigative reporters in the news department. She'd take it to the publisher, Curtis DiSalvo, who'd congratulate her on finding a unique tidbit, then they'd call in experts and spend more time testing and prodding and proving than they would *searching*.

But Gabriella Cohen had been excruciatingly right about one thing: if the note were genuine, then in those terrible moments when the plane spiraled down from the sky, one father had thought only of his estranged child. That child needed to know the truth.

She briefly considered talking to Janet Boyles about the note, then cast the idea off.

If Janet had been hinting that she'd like a shot at "The Heart Healer," she'd probably jump at the chance to run with the story of the note. Karen Dolen was a good writer, and a friend, but Karen was from the news department, and she'd probably advise Peyton to feature the story in only a column or two. But you couldn't find a needle in a haystack in only a couple of days, and this story might require much longer. It might, in fact, take up the majority of Peyton's remaining two-week probation.

She could talk to Mandi about the project — but the intern was about as savvy as a girl on her first date. Oh, she'd be thrilled — for her, filing expense reports was as exciting as a Chinese fire drill — but she had no real understanding. No . . . Peyton needed someone who could remind her of the risks. She needed the voice of experience, the most knowledgeable and objective newspaperman she knew . . .

Kingston Bernard.

She called him at 3:00 a.m. King grumbled when he answered the phone, and he grumbled more at the prospect of a 9:00 a.m. breakfast, but he showed up at Peyton's door with her Saturday morning paper in hand — a copy of the *St. Petersburg Post*, the competition from across the bay.

She accepted the paper with a smile and led him into the kitchen where the mingled scents of fresh-baked muffins, scrambled eggs, and bacon provided a warm welcome. Samson and Elijah sat under the table, staring at the approaching sneakers with undisguised curiosity.

"Um." King sniffed appreciatively. "Maybe this was worth getting up for." He stood in the kitchen doorway for a moment with his hands in his jeans pockets. "What's the occasion? You didn't say much earlier this morning."

"If I had, neither of us would remember it." Pouring a cup of coffee, Peyton noticed with some surprise that her hand trembled. Had to be from lack of sleep.

She glanced at her guest, then gestured toward the kitchen table. "Just move that pile of magazines off the chair and have a seat. Sorry about that. I know the place looks cluttered, but I really do know where everything is."

King lifted a brow. "A woman of many interests — I like that."

She frowned. "Just sit, will you? You make me nervous standing there."

Laughing softly, King lifted the stack of mingled *Newsweek*, *Journalism Review*, and *People* magazines, then dropped them into a third chair. He sat, then leaned back and grinned. "Okay, I'm sitting. Now are you going to tell me what this is all about?"

"In a minute." She wiped her hands on her shorts, then glanced around the kitchen, overwhelmed by a feeling that she'd forgotten something. The eggs were steaming in a Pyrex bowl, scrambled and ready to go, the muffins filled a basket, and the bacon waited in the microwave . . .

Why was she nervous? Good grief, she was behaving like Mandi, and a dizzy girl was the *last* thing in the world she wanted to be.

"The thing is" — she turned to pick up the coffee mugs — "as I was leaving the office Friday, a woman came up and gave me something. She's convinced — and I'm not, not completely — that she found something from Flight 848."

"Another piece of debris?" King's anticipatory smile drooped as she set one of the mugs before him. "All kinds of things have washed up, MacGruder, and most people are taking debris to the PanWorld office at TIA. That's what she should have done. You never know what bit of evidence will be useful to the FAA guys —"

"This wasn't part of the plane." She sat down, then leaned forward over the corner of the table. "It's a note. From a passenger."

Amazement blossomed on his face. "But how could it —"

"It was encased in a plastic bag — one of those with the little zipper tab. If you ever watch TV, you've seen the Zippup commercials. They're the ones who feature a little dog singing about locking freshness in and odors out."

She leaned back, eager to watch the play of emotions on his features. Though they'd disagreed in the past, she trusted his instincts. If Kingston Bernard — veteran newsman, seasoned reporter, and exemplary editor — didn't think the note constituted a story, it didn't.

He pressed his hand to his face, then lowered his elbow to the tabletop, ignoring Samson, who decided to jump into his lap. "You think," he said, apparently thinking aloud, "someone had time to write a note? While the plane was crashing?"

"Why not? We know the plane went down in a curving path because the pilot was trying to reach the runway. We know at least three minutes passed between the disruptive event and the explosion." She leaned forward again, and tapped the table. "Why couldn't someone have reached for paper and pen and written a note?"

His eyes narrowed in the devil's advocate

2290443

expression she knew well. "But if a plane is going down, the flight attendants are busy showing people how to assume the crash position. It's unlikely anyone would be writing a note in the face of blind panic."

"What if you didn't care about your own safety?" Peyton persisted. "What if reaching out to your kid meant more than being seated properly? If you were motivated by something bigger than concern for your own safety? Why wouldn't you try to reach out to someone who needed to hear what you had to say?"

His eyes warmed slightly as he stroked the cat. "What did the note say?"

Peyton pulled away and picked up her coffee mug. "That's for me to know," she said primly, "and for the recipient to find out."

He scowled, his brows knitting together. "That's not fair, MacGruder."

"Yes, it is." She stood and moved back to the counter to fetch the eggs and muffins. "I'm not going to divulge the contents of the note until I find the person for whom it was written."

"And that person would be?"

"I'm not sure." Peyton carried the bowl of eggs to the table, then leaned on her chair. "But I have clues. The note was signed

'Dad,' so I know it was written by a man who intended it for his child. The child's first initial is *T*."

King's brows lifted as his gaze shifted toward the window and thoughts unknown. "Anything else useful in the content?"

Peyton shook her head. "Not really. An *I love you*, of course. And an offer of forgiveness." She leaned back against the counter, crossed her arms, and frowned at him. "Now you've done it. I've told you everything, and I didn't intend to. Be sure to keep your mouth closed about the details, okay?"

"That's it?" A half-smile crossed his face. "I love you, I forgive you, signed Dad?"

"That's pretty close to the exact wording. Now you have to promise to keep quiet about it, or I'll have to kill you."

"I won't say anything." Taking a deep breath, King adjusted his smile. "Well, kiddo, if you want to know what I think —"

"I do. I don't cook breakfast for just anybody."

"Then I'll say this — I think you've saved your pretty little neck from Nora's cleaver."

Peyton couldn't stop a grin from spreading across her face. "You really think so? I knew the note would make a great story, even a series, but —" Good grief, she was as giddy as a two-year-old with a new toy.

King sipped his coffee, then nodded slightly. "This thing has major tearjerker written all over it. I'm almost jealous. This puppy will run for a week, maybe even two." He glanced down at Samson, still in his lap. "Sorry, kitty. Didn't mean to offend."

"I was up all night thinking about it." Peyton picked up her coffee mug and grinned at him over the rim. "In the first column I can explain how I got the note — and I'll be honest about not being certain of its authenticity. It *could* be genuine, but I can't think of any way short of an FAA investigation to prove it."

"People will believe it," King said. "They will want to believe a bit of good could rise out of the tragedy."

"And I'll ask Mandi to help me with the research — it'll be good experience for her. We have the passenger list, so that's where we'll start. We'll go through the list, name by name, and look up every single obituary. We'll search for men who had children whose first names begin with T. Those children, the survivors of the victims, will make up our pool of prospects."

King nodded, his eyes flashing as he followed her thoughts. "If you have time and space, you could write about each of them.

Profiles of the children, with an emphasis on how the tragedy has affected their lives."

Peyton's mouth opened as another thought struck. "I could *visit* them — that's so much more personal than a telephone interview. And during the visit, I could learn about their relationship with their fathers. At some point, if all is going well, I will share the message of the note —"

"And see how they respond." King reared back in his chair, then pounded the table for emphasis, scaring the cat into flight. "This is solid gold, MacGruder."

Peyton bit her lip as her spirit soared. In her ten months of writing "The Heart Healer," she had never encountered such a unique opportunity. Not only would this column interest every reader in Florida, but the story suited the stated purpose of her column: mending wounded hearts. One in particular.

"This project will require a lot," she said, pointing out the first obvious pitfall. "Nora may not be wild about me jetting off to visit these people. There's no guarantee they live in the Tampa area, or even in the state."

"Of course she'll balk." King shrugged. "Part of an editor's job is guarding the paper's assets. But it depends on how many prospects you find and how much interest you generate. If you find several *T* names, perhaps you could invite them to Tampa. I have a feeling these folks would be eager to come if you could promise them another glimpse of their father . . . especially if they've been estranged."

Peyton closed her eyes, mentally envisioning a dozen men and women with *T* names, all clamoring for a piece of the note. "I foresee problems," she whispered, opening her eyes. "What if I have fifty potential prospects? There's only one note."

King rubbed a hand over the morning stubble on his chin. "Wonder if they could pull fingerprints from the paper or the plastic bag?"

Peyton considered the idea. "Even if they could, what good would it do? The people on that plane weren't criminals or government employees. Most of them were ordinary folk, probably including the man who wrote the note. The chances of him being registered in a fingerprint database are slim to none."

"Makes you yearn for the days when Big Brother will have all of us registered in a DNA database." King sipped his coffee for a moment, then looked up at her. "I'm not sure you should go for infallible proof. Think about it — say you have two people whose situation fits the note. What's the harm in letting them both think the letter was intended for them?"

Frowning, Peyton shook her head. "I want to give the note to somebody. The note is the prize, isn't it? I mean, consider that *Survivor* TV show. All of those people won the opportunity to experience the island, but only one person walked away with the million bucks. If this is going to work, I've got to be able to give the note to one person."

A smile broke through King's mask of uncertainty. "How about a lottery? You could have the prospects write letters explaining why they think the note came from their father. You could print the letters over a period of weeks, and let your readers vote on which applicant's letter they liked best."

Peyton shook her head. "Too subjective, and too long. I doubt Nora would let me spend more than two weeks on this. She's already sick of covering the crash. Yes, the story may save my job, but she won't let 'The Heart Healer' turn into an airplane disaster column."

"Maybe you'll get lucky and discover there was only one guy who had a child whose name began with *T*."

Peyton snorted softly. "Are you kidding?

Have you noticed all the Tylers, Taylors, Toms, Tims, Tonys, Todds, Terrys, Teds, Taffys, Tabithas, Teresas, Tinas, Tesses, Tracys, Trixies, and Tallulahs out there? I'll be lucky if our search doesn't turn up four hundred prospects."

"So — when are you going to begin?"

"Soon. With Monday's column, I think. If I can get my thoughts together." She laughed. "Nora wanted me to do something to attract readers. Well, this ought to do it. Best of all, she won't have a chance to stop me. She doesn't work weekends, so this first column will slip right by her."

King's eyes flashed admiration. "Sneaky girl."

She grinned. "I've learned how the game is played."

"So you have." He clapped his hand on his cheek and nodded toward the bowl of scrambled eggs on the table. "Are we ever going to eat or are we going to let the food petrify first?"

"We'll eat. But wait — I've got bacon, too."

Peyton turned to the microwave and pulled out the platter where six strips of bacon lay like burnt offerings above grease-filled ridges. After using a spatula to flip the bacon onto two plates, she set both plates on the table, then dashed back to a drawer for silverware.

Poor King. If he'd ever thought of her as Dorothy Domestic, those visions had been shattered this morning.

Sighing, she dropped a fork and knife next to his plate, then placed her own silverware on the table. After a quick glance to be sure she hadn't forgotten anything else, she slid into her chair and gave him a stiff smile. "That's it — eggs, bacon, muffins, and coffee. If you were expecting anything else, I'm sorry."

"Just one more thing." He pointed to the crowded napkin holder on the table. "I was hoping to find something to wipe my hands, but I can't quite tell if that is supposed to hold letters, bills, or napkins —"

"Hold on, I'll get it." Reaching across the table, Peyton tugged on a white corner, dislodging a clump of napkins as well as a stack of envelopes. After peeling the napkins apart — how long had it been since she used one? — she gave one to King, then demurely placed the others in her lap.

King picked up the scattered letters. "Don't you open your mail, MacGruder?" he said, studying the handwritten address on one envelope. "This was postmarked last month, and you haven't even opened it. And here's another, two months old. Aren't you reading your fan mail?"

Cheeks flaming, Peyton took the half-dozen envelopes from his hand, then tossed them onto the counter. "Not that it's any of your business, but those aren't from fans. They're letters from my dad."

She saw a tiny flicker of shock widen his eyes, then a wry smile twitched at the corners of his mouth. "So you ignore his advice, too?"

"My father and I" — she straightened her spine as she reached for the eggs — "scarcely know one another. I've read his letters, and they're all the same: newsy notes about his wife, his kids, his patients." She dropped a spoonful of eggs — hard, now, she noticed with dismay — onto King's plate, then dumped the rest on her own. "Truth is" — she lowered the bowl to the table — "I think he writes me out of guilt. I think Kathy nags at him, and so he writes. Like clockwork."

King reached for a muffin. "Do you write back?"

She snorted. "I send a card at Christmas."

King didn't answer, but peeled the paper wrapping from his muffin.

"It's cranberry walnut," she said, grateful for a chance to change the subject. "Margie

Stock gave me the recipe. Since she's the food writer, I figured it ought to be good."

King dropped the wrapper onto his plate, then held up the muffin. "MacGruder," he said, examining the bread as if it were an object of great value, "you're hard on all the men in your life, aren't you?"

The question snapped like a stinging whip, but Peyton kept her head down, her eyes upon her plate.

King Bernard didn't know her life story. He didn't know about her father's distance, her husband's death, the missing part of her life. He was just running off at the mouth, a victim of verbal diarrhea if ever there was one.

She picked up her fork and stabbed a stolid lump of egg. "You're on my turf now," she said. "Be quiet and eat."

Six

Monday, June 25

Treasures from the Deep
By Peyton MacGruder
"The Heart Healer" is a regular feature
of the *Tampa Times*

Dear Readers:
I met a woman last week — a woman a few
years younger than I, with blue eyes as
overwhelming as her compassion for
others. This lady, who has asked to remain
anonymous, pressed a priceless treasure
into my hand and begged me to find its
rightful owner.

If you've been reading my column for a
while, you know I'm not easily given to
flights of fantasy. I did a quick investigation
of my visitor — she's a longstanding resident of this community, active in her syna-
gogue, respected by her neighbors. She's
raising two children and supporting a professional husband in her role as home-

maker. As far as I can tell, she's as dependable as the sunrise, so I can find no reason to doubt her story about finding this treasure in the water behind her bayside home.

The treasure, which came to me wrapped in a square of fine linen, is not jewelry or currency, but a simple note. From inside its protective plastic sleeve, its words speak of a love as wide as the sea and as unfathomable as the ocean. The note was, I suspect, another scrap from Flight 848, but no single piece of luggage or debris carries the emotional weight of this fragile slip of paper. It is addressed to a particular person, and it is signed simply *Dad*.

Some of you are already shaking your heads. Flight 848 exploded, you're thinking, and the surviving pieces of debris have already been claimed and cataloged by rescue and relief workers.

But couldn't one small message, scrawled on a scrap approximately the size of a note card, survive the flames and the subsequent impact? The paper is small and the message simple, but perhaps the key to its continued existence lies in those very attributes.

Some of you might suspect this note is a

forgery, a cruel joke. Perhaps it is. But if someone planted this within the waters of Tampa Bay in some cruel machination, I fail to see the purpose. Aside from the possible glow of publicity — which the woman who found the note has refused — no one could benefit from such a scheme.

If, however, if the note is genuine — if there is even a *chance* the message was written in those final few moments of Flight 848, then it is the last communication from that plane to those of us still living.

A popular Paul Simon song from my younger days talks about not giving false hope on a strange and mournful day . . .

Like you, the events of the last several days have moved me beyond words and my limited powers of understanding. In the days since Flight 848 took its fatal plunge into our sun-splashed waters, I have observed both stunning grief and amazing endurance. I have sat with families at the airport and handed out coffee to weeping rescue workers who came streaming out of the bay, their arms burdened with vestiges of sorrow.

Like you, I have lifted my eyes to heaven and demanded to understand why.

I haven't found any answers . . . yet.

But I've been given a treasure, and I'm going to do all in my power to unite the father on Flight 848 with his child, whomever and wherever he or she may be. I have a clue — a strong lead — and in the coming days I will do all I can to convey the last message from Flight 848 to a sorrowing soul.

I would not give you false hope, friends, but I do believe at least one man aboard that PanWorld flight cared enough to send a message in the moment before his death.

There's a father and child reunion coming, and it's only a motion away.

(Peyton MacGruder can be reached at the *Tampa Times* in the following ways: e-mail   pmacgruder@tampatimes.com, phone 813-555-8573, or fax 813-555-8574.)

As usual for any morning when her column appeared, Peyton slept until seven-thirty, took a leisurely shower, and then drove to work. As always, she stopped into the Dunkin' Donuts shop next to the *Times* office and ordered a cup of coffee, then sat at the counter and sipped it while pretending to be disinterested in her fellow patrons. Nearly every regular customer at the bar read the paper as they breakfasted, and this morning she was delighted to see three people — *count 'em, three!* — reading her column.

Smiling, she turned her attention back to her French cruller. The light and sugary doughnut had never tasted quite this good.

She was about to take another bite when her cellular phone chirped. Peyton dropped the cruller to her napkin, then wiped the sugar off her fingertips.

"Looks like they caught you playing hooky." The wasp-waisted, blonde waitress who poured coffee for Peyton on Mondays, Wednesdays, and Fridays paused before the counter, a wet towel in her hand. Her plastic nameplate identified her as Erma.

"Looks like." Peyton pulled the phone from her backpack, the question of who might be calling mingling with musings about whether or not Erma wore some kind of gut-cinching girdle to achieve that tiny waist.

She snapped the phone open. "Hello?"

"MacGruder, where are you?" The voice was Nora Chilton's; the tone was not pleasant.

Peyton rolled her eyes at the bemused waitress. "I'm next door at Dunkin'. I'll be up in five minutes."

114

"Come directly to my office. We have to talk."

Peyton lowered her gaze, her stomach contracting like a fist. She could sit here and say nothing, or she could stand up to Nora —

Time to stand. She had a great idea, solid gold, according to King, so Nora had no reason to complain.

She lifted her chin. "What seems to be the problem, Nora?"

"It's — it's this note business. Where did this come from? When we spoke in the elevator Friday, you said nothing about it. This thing would have made a better feature story, yet you kept it to yourself. If this note did come from the plane, it probably should be handed over to the authorities even now."

"I didn't receive the note until late Friday afternoon," Peyton answered, taking pains to keep her voice low and level. "I didn't give it to you because I didn't think you were interested in any more air disaster stories. And it's not hard news, so I'm not handing it over to anyone. It's a possibility, that's all. An opportunity I intend to fully explore."

For a moment the phone hummed in Peyton's ear, then Nora said, "So why didn't you tell me about it before filing the column?"

"Because you don't work weekends." Peyton caught the waitress's eye again, then pointed to her half-empty coffee cup. "And because I didn't think it necessary. You told me to broaden my readership, Nora, and this seemed like a perfect way to do that." She glanced around the coffee shop, pleased to see a pair of women huddled over the lifestyles section at a nearby booth. One of them was pointing to her column.

"Come to my office as soon as you can." The phone went dead.

Sighing, Peyton disconnected the call, then dropped the phone into her backpack. Erma smiled and came closer, one hand resting on her hip. Laugh lines crinkled the corners of her eyes. "Rough day ahead?"

"Rough week, I'm afraid." Peyton pulled two dollar bills from her wallet, spread the bills on the counter, then gave the waitress a lopsided smile. "I may have made the biggest mistake of my career, but at least I'll go out with a bang."

Peyton did not proceed directly to Nora's office (*do not pass go, do not collect two hundred dollars or a pink slip*), but went first to her own desk and powered up her computer. Sipping on her coffee, compli-

116

ments of a sympathetic Erma, she took a few minutes to fortify her courage for the upcoming encounter with the Dragon Lady. After the computer blinked to life, she logged on to the intranet and clicked on the icon for e-mail.

She blinked.

Her mailbox held forty-five messages, a record for any Monday, and it wasn't yet ten o'clock.

She clicked on the in-box and gaped as a list of messages filled the screen. A soft chime dinged as two additional messages appeared at the bottom of the listing.

Scrolling down, she recognized only one of the return addresses — King Bernard's. She clicked on the envelope icon and smiled as she read his note:

Way to hit one out of the park, slugger! Loved the piece this morning! You not only rounded all the bases, you played the game with real heart.

I would say I did not know you had it in you, but I have always suspected you could write like this.

Keep up the good work, MacGruder. And thanks for the breakfast.

She lifted a brow. King Bernard didn't

117

proffer praise easily, so this was one for the archives.

She clicked on another message, from an address she didn't recognize.

Ms. MacGruder, I cannot express what your column this morning meant to me. I kept thinking — what would I have written to my children if I had been on that flight? Would I have thought of them at all, or only of myself? I hope you find the person you're searching for. A father that selfless deserves no less than your best effort.

— A new fan

Peyton clicked on several other messages, most of which were from readers. Several people wanted to know what the note said; everyone urged her to begin the search.

A final note seemed to sum up her morning mail:

Peyton M —
You're my favorite righter, and I read you in the paper every time I can. I was sorry to hear about the plain crash. And I know that if it had been my dad on that plain, I'd give anything to get the note he wrote to me.

118

Thank you for trying to help. I hope you find the rite person.
                              Tasha Cole, age 10

Laughing softly, Peyton highlighted Tasha's letter, clicked the print icon, then stood and made her way through the sea of desks to the print room. She couldn't postpone her meeting with Nora any longer, but she could at least be well-armed for the firefight.

The Dragon Lady scarcely glanced at the letter Peyton slid across her desk. "At last count, I had nearly fifty e-mails this morning," Peyton said, lowering herself into the guest chair. "And we don't even know what the regular mail will bring."

Nora eyed her with a taut, derisive expression. "You should have told me what you were planning."

Peyton shrugged, feeling momentarily secure in the confidence of reader support. "You've never asked to preview my Monday columns. How was I to know you'd want to see this one?"

Nora's stare drilled into her. "We were done with Flight 848. We've done all the crash features our readers can stand —"

"But what's your favorite maxim?" Peyton rose halfway out of her seat, leaning forward and placing one hand on the desk. "There's always room for breaking news, even in features. This was something different, and it came to *me.* I'd have been the worst kind of fool not to accept it." She sank back in her chair. "Besides, I really do want to follow this thing through. It could be genuine, and if it is, just think — while everyone else on that plane was panicking or praying, one man had the presence of mind to write a farewell note. The least I can do is try to deliver it."

"You don't know what happened on that plane. You never will. You weren't there."

"Some things, Nora," Peyton spoke with a confidence springing from an indefinable feeling of *rightness,* "you have to accept by faith. After all, I've never seen Pluto, but I trust the people who have evidence of its existence." She leaned forward again, her hand gripping the edge of the desk. "This note is evidence of one father who cared enough to say good-bye to his child."

Nora's straight glance still seemed coldly accusing, but she didn't reply for a long moment. Then her gaze dropped to the desktop as she picked up her pen and began to twirl it between her fingers. "Anyway, your column was good. I like this new approach — you're asking questions now, not just giving answers." She paused to clear her throat. "Um . . . any leads so far?"

Relaxing, Peyton shook her head. "Nothing except the note itself. I spent yesterday afternoon in the archives, printing out obituaries from the Tampa passengers of Flight 848. I haven't gone through them yet, nor have I found obits for all the others. So, if it's all right with you, I thought I'd ask Mandi to help me contact the other papers. We'll gather biographical information on all the victims and go from there."

Nora gave her a forced smile and a terse nod of consent. "Now that you've got the ball rolling, you might as well stick with it."

Peyton tented her hands and stared at her boss, wondering at the root causes of Nora's anger and her abrupt change of heart. Was she upset because the note hadn't been given to one of the other writers? Or was she aggravated that Peyton, whose days as the Heart Healer were numbered, had been handed such a sure thing?

Sighing heavily, Nora shifted in her chair. "Let me know if you need any other resources from the office." Her gaze fell to a folder on her desk. "A few moments ago I got a call from Mr. DiSalvo. He's very interested in the outcome of your little search."

Peyton sat still as a thrill raced up her

spine. Curtis DiSalvo, the *Times* publisher and president, had read her column? She pressed her lips together in an unsuccessful effort to stifle a spontaneous smile. No wonder Nora was irritated. Mr. DiSalvo came from a hard news background and made no secret of his disdain for what he called "feature fluff." The man seldom singled out the lifestyles department for special attention, so the fact that he'd mentioned "The Heart Healer" must have put the taste of bile in Nora's mouth . . .

"I'll let you know what I need," Peyton said, standing. "And don't worry, I'm going to try to wrap this thing up in two weeks. That's all the time I have left, right? Two more weeks to broaden my readership?"

It was all she could do to keep from laughing at the exasperated look on Nora's face.

A few moments later Peyton stood on the sports department side of the newsroom, her hand poised to knock, her mind reeling with doubts. The same process of elimination that had driven her to ask King for advice over the weekend had brought her to his door again, and a part of her brain warned against making a habit of the practice.

She never had a chance to knock. The door swung open as she deliberated, and Carter Cummings stood before her. His eyes widened when he saw her, then he looked back at King and grinned. "I *knew* something was going on between you two!"

Peyton didn't have to look toward the desk to know King was growling. "Nothing's going on, Cummings," she said, stepping back so he'd take the hint and leave.

"Sure." Carter sent her a wink, then turned back to King. "I told you she was too classy for you, so why are you leading this woman on?"

Peyton sputtered. "He's not —"

"I'm not doing any such thing." King cut her off, glowering at his coworker. "Get out of here, will ya? Get busy on that grouper fishing piece or I'll have you covering shuffleboard tournaments in St. Pete."

Apparently not even King's glare could dampen Carter's spirit. He winked again as he passed Peyton, and for a moment she stood in the hall and seriously considered fleeing. A half-dozen desks lined this aisle, and at least that many sports reporters had to be listening behind her back with smart-aleck smiles on their faces . . . Steeling herself to her task, she walked into King's office and slammed the door.

Behind the desk, King winced in phony remorse. "Sorry. Was it my crack about the cold eggs?"

Peyton blew out her cheeks. "Forget the other day, will you? I've more important things on my mind."

Grinning, King motioned toward the empty chair. "Take a load off and tell me about it. Good piece this morning, by the way."

Peyton sat. "I got your e-mail. Thanks."

"Was Chilton happy?"

"No, she was breathing fire. She called me at Dunkin' Donuts, if you can believe it, and told me to see her ASAP. But by the time I got to her office, she'd spoken to DiSalvo, who likes the concept of a search. He's all hyped about the note, so like it or not, Nora has to support me."

King leaned forward, all traces of mischief gone from his face. "That sounds good, Peyton, honestly. This could be your ticket to something really big."

"If I can handle it." She bit her lip, a little amazed that the admission had slipped past her lips. She'd made a living out of pretending to have all the answers, and her presence here proved she didn't.

King's brow furrowed. "You feeling insecure?"

"I don't know." She raked her hand through her hair. "If this search were only a matter of looking things up, I'd be home free. But this project will entail interviewing people."

"So what? You've done scads of sports profiles."

"But these people won't exactly be professionals. They may not even want to be interviewed." She pressed her hands together and noticed that her palms were slick with dampness. "And — this is the part that really gets me — they'll be *grieving* people. The accident happened less than two weeks ago, so I may be touching on some sensitive issues." She dropped her hands and met his eye. "I'm not a therapist, King. I don't have the faintest idea how to deal with people who've come through this kind of situation. The idea makes me uncomfortable."

King said nothing for a moment. When he spoke again, his voice was gentle. "What about the grief counselors at the airport — did you happen to meet someone you can call for a few pointers?"

Peyton shook her head. "I stayed out of their way. Any time I saw tears, I backed off."

"MacGruder" — her name was faintly underlined with reproach — "when are you

125

going to learn? You can't run from honest emotion if you want to succeed as a writer. No matter what you're writing, the root of the story always lies in the heart." He snorted softly. "People don't care if somebody hit a home run in a Devil Rays game. They want to know how he *feels* about hitting that homer."

Peyton lowered her eyes, not certain she wanted to answer the challenge in his words, but what choice did she have? She'd taken the first step, stood up to Nora, and announced her plan to her readers. She couldn't turn back now, no matter how badly she wanted to.

With an effort, she raised her chin and met his steady gaze head-on. "I'm willing to do whatever it takes. That's why I'm asking for help."

King lifted a brow. When his lips parted Peyton braced herself for a quick retort — *Why weren't you this committed when I was continually on your case?* — but he only drew a breath and reached for a notepad.

"This is a woman I've known for years," he said, his pencil driving across the page. "She's retired now and lives in Clearwater. She'll be able to give you some pointers, I think."

"Was she a reporter?"

King ripped the page off the notepad and handed it across the desk, his eyes twinkling. "For a while. She wrote features for the *Post*."

Peyton crinkled her nose. Sending her to a veteran member of the competition was bad enough, but feature writers covered everything under the sun. "I don't get it." She took the page. "How is this woman going to help me?"

"Because now she's a preacher."

Peyton looked up. For a moment she thought she detected laughter in King's eyes, but his mouth remained firm as he leaned toward her.

"Not officially, of course, I don't think her church goes in for the woman minister thing. But that's what she is. Spends most of her free time down at the Pinellas County Jail, listening to people and talking to them about whatever preachers talk about."

Peyton felt the corner of her mouth droop. "I don't know, King. My story has nothing to do with religion; it's more about people."

"That's why you need Mary Grace. The woman knows people like nobody I've ever met. She'll be able to help you."

"She wrote features, King. Which means

she covered everything from lawn ornaments to Little League —"

"And she did her job well because she focused on the *people* behind the lawn ornaments and baseball games." He rapped on the desktop. "Get yourself over the bridge, MacGruder. If I'm wrong, I'll buy you dinner when you get back."

Still frowning, Peyton stuffed the paper in her pocket and stood. "And if I end up wasting my afternoon?"

King leaned back, propping one sneaker on the edge of an open desk drawer. "I'll still buy you dinner."

Shaking her head, Peyton moved toward the doorway, but before she left she waved and called, "Done."

Mary Grace Van Owen was home when Peyton called to set up the appointment, but in a hoarse voice — the woman either had a cold or had puffed on a few too many Winstons in her time — she said she had to be at the jail by two-thirty. So if Peyton wanted to talk, she'd best get herself to Clearwater in a hurry.

The sun had disappeared behind a thick cloud by the time Peyton made it to the parking lot, and within minutes of reaching her car the sky opened. Thick bullets of water, blown by the wind from the bay, cracked against her windshield as the wipers thrummed in a steady rhythm. Peyton moaned as the thunder rattled overhead, and for a moment she considered abandoning the trip altogether. She hated driving in rain, hated the long bridge to Clearwater, and hated the thought of spending the afternoon with some old biddy who had a thing for God and criminals.

But she'd made a deal with King, and the biddy was expecting her.

Gritting her teeth, she pulled out of the parking lot and headed toward Interstate 275, which would take her to the Howard Frankland, one of three long bridges leading to the Pinellas County peninsula.

She reached the three-mile bridge with no problem, but as she began the long drive toward the "hump" she couldn't help glancing toward the bay. The restless waves to the north of the bridge were steel gray and capped with white. With a shiver of vivid recollection she remembered that only a few days ago they had been calm, content to swallow the remains of Flight 848.

She looked away, choosing to concentrate on the four-lane, westbound highway. The heavy sky, swollen with rain, sagged toward the high point of the bridge, enveloping the summit with gray mist. Peyton considered pulling over to the narrow emergency lane until the storm had passed, but she'd read about too many hapless drivers being smacked when they stopped to change a tire. Besides, her watch said one-thirty, which left only a little time for her meeting with Ms. Van Owen.

For no reason she could name, the thought of a face-to-face interview raised the hair on the back of her neck. How long had it been since she'd sat down with an ordinary subject? She hadn't had a face-to-face since she'd begun writing "The Heart Healer," and before that most of her interviews had been little more than screaming matches with professional athletes who viewed her as just another PR mouthpiece. Even Tiger Woods — in the interview King had been so impressed with — had given her his standard spiel, then concentrated on his golf game.

"It's okay." Peyton pounded the steering wheel with the heels of both hands, then squinted through the streaked windshield. At her left, the rain made long, wavering runnels down the window, while a slash of lightning stabbed at the roiling water to her right.

Peyton turned the radio to Q105, the local country station, and wailed along with the Dixie Chicks, deciding to sing rather than curse the idiots who rode the left lanes and blew past the careful drivers. Every so often a semi would roar past, tires spitting water onto the driver's side of the Jetta, but Peyton only clung to the steering wheel and sang louder.

She'd always been a careful driver, but ever since Garrett's accident she'd been a paranoid one as well. His life had ended on a rain-slicked road much like this, and the two nice cops who came to her door had been quick to assure her there had been no alcoholic beverages in the car. The accident was one of those things — a wet road combined with wet brakes, the force of momentum combined with velocity. Garrett had been embracing a live oak before he even realized what had happened. (The cops didn't come out and say that, of course, but she could read between the lines.)

And then I turned around and you were gone —

She sang with the Chicks, drowning out the memories with her not-so-subtle voice.

Never had you 'round too long,

And yet you left an empty beat in my heart song —

At the top of the bridge she leaned forward to peer through the ineffective arc made by the wipers. Sunlight lit the road ahead, beginning at the end of the bridge. Blowing out her cheeks, she relaxed her grip on the steering wheel. Thunderheads like this one, apparently confined to one space, were common enough in Florida. She might find the streets in Clearwater as dry as a desert.

Cheered by the sight of streaming sunshine ahead, Peyton eased forward on the gas and sang on.

Mary Grace Van Owen, Peyton soon discovered, lived in a tornado magnet: the Lakeview Trailer Park, off Belcher Road. This park, like most in Pinellas County, consisted of rectangular white trailers parked in diagonal lines around a horseshoe-shaped road. Each trailer featured a tidy carport, usually of painted concrete, decorated with petunias or begonias hanging from a striped aluminum awning.

Cedar signs adorned each trailer in the Lakeview Park, where burnt-in carving identified the lot number and the resident's last name. Peyton found *Lot 137, Van Owen,* in the first curve of the road.

She parked the Jetta in a stretch of grass beside the street, then got out and walked toward the door. Mary Grace's carport was like the others, but a set of four molded plastic chairs sat in the shade, gathered around a small table like wagons around a campfire. Obviously, the woman liked company and conversation.

Ms. Van Owen apparently had a soft touch for animals as well as people. No fewer than four bird feeders dangled from hooks on the aluminum roof sheltering her carport, and a pair of plastic Canada geese stood silently on the six-by-nine strip of grass serving as her front lawn.

White ruffled curtains fluttered at the open window — no air conditioning in June? — and the sound of a whirling fan roared through the screen. Peyton knocked on the door, and a moment later heard the sounds of movement.

"Coming!"

The door opened. Mary Grace Van Owen was sixty-five if she was a day, with stark white hair pulled back in an old-fashioned, anti-style style. A softly patterned housedress cloaked her solid figure, while plain white Keds covered her feet.

In the bright light of the summer sun Peyton could see that age had painted dark spots on Mary Grace's square face, especially her cheeks and forehead. But pink lipstick provided a bright note, and her blue

133

eyes gleamed as gently as a happy baby's. "You must be the lady from the paper," she said, her voice a mild croak in the hot afternoon stillness.

Peyton felt a slow smile spread across her face. "I am. King Bernard said you could help me."

The woman's grin widened, showcasing a perfect set of yellowed dentures. "How is ol' King doing? Still got that adorable little boy?"

"The boy's grown now; he's a sophomore at USF. But King's fine and he still thinks a lot of you." Peyton paused to swipe at her bangs, damp with perspiration now that she stood in the sun. "He said you were some kind of genius when it came to dealing with people."

Mary Grace chuckled. "Well, I don't know about that, but you come on in, and we'll talk for a few minutes. My ride comes at 2:20, though, and I can't miss my jail time." One corner of her bright pink mouth turned up. "Gladys — she's the lady who drives me — always gets a kick out of hearing me talk about my jail time."

"I can see why," Peyton murmured, her gaze sweeping past the woman into the trailer.

Mary Grace opened the door wider, and

Peyton stepped in, inhaling the scents of dust, heat, and Lysol. Her first impression was *dark*. No lights burned, but perhaps the shade helped the place feel cooler. As her eyes adjusted to the dimness, she saw a small, spotless kitchen to her left, a living area to her right. The kitchen seemed unremarkable except for an abundance of crochet — a hand-worked orange-and-green cover for a Crockpot, several blue potholders on a wall hook, and a little apron for the bottle of dish soap by the sink. Very grandmotherly, Peyton decided, and even the darkness seemed appropriate. After all, most of Florida's retirees lived on fixed incomes, and electricity cost a bundle.

"Can I get you something to drink?" Mary Grace lifted her voice to be heard over the roar of a box fan in the hall. "It's awful hot today."

"No, thanks." Peyton turned to face the living room, paneled in dark walnut, with darker brown shag carpeting on the floor. A faded floral sofa sat against the wall, most of its surface covered with pillows and — she felt her heart lurch — *babies*. For a moment she thought she'd stumbled onto some sort of mad grandmother kidnapper, then she realized the infants filling the sofa, a chair, and a cradle were dolls.

"Wow," she said, placing a protective hand over her heart. In time, it might settle back to a normal rhythm. "You must be a collector or something."

"Aren't they adorable?" Mary Grace scooped up one black-haired infant, nestled it in the crook of her arm, and pointed to the sofa. "Just pick up a sweetie and make yourself at home. The babies like to be held, and it doesn't do us any harm to hold 'em, either."

Peyton looked for the least crowded space on the couch, then picked up the doll sitting there. She had grabbed it by the arm, but it felt so fragile in her grasp that she reflexively dropped her backpack and caught the doll's body with her free hand. A cold panic started somewhere between her shoulder blades and prickled down her spine. Holding the doll in front of her, its head lolling from one side to another, she cast a look at Mary Grace, who had settled into a padded rocking chair.

"They even feel real," she murmured. *Like an honest-to-goodness Chuckie doll . . .*

"They're weighted," Mary Grace answered, propping her elbow on the chair's armrest. "They use these dolls in all the TV shows like *ER* and *General Hospital*. Whenever there's an infant in the scene, you can almost bet they're using one of these babies."

"How interesting." Though her stomach had clenched tight, Peyton forced a smile and sat down, settling the wide-eyed baby on her lap. She would have dropped the doll to the floor, but something in Mary Grace's solicitous manner warned her that might not be a good idea.

She'd have to ignore the spooky thing. Resting the doll's head against her knees, its bare toes brushing her belly, she leaned forward and pulled her backpack to the sofa. "I need to grab my notebook and a pen . . ." She lowered her head to dig in the depths of her bag.

"You never had children, did you?" Mary Grace's voice was soft, filled with quiet sorrow.

Peyton stopped digging, but didn't look up. "No," she said, struggling to maintain her control. "My husband and I didn't have time to start a family."

From the corner of her eye, Peyton saw Mary Grace nodding in the slow rhythm of the rocking chair. "You were a young widow, then. So was I. Pneumonia took my Donald back in '54. Of course, they have better drugs today."

Peyton found her notebook and pencil,

then let the mouth of her backpack droop over the baby in her lap. The woman was a good observer, but reporters were trained to observe, and she'd undoubtedly noticed that Peyton had no clue how to handle a baby. Mary Grace wasn't a mind reader, after all.

"How do you know my husband died?" Peyton said, keeping her voice light. "We could have divorced."

Mary Grace gave Peyton a bright-eyed glance, full of shrewdness. "Divorced women don't usually wear their wedding bands, not even on their right hand like you're doing."

Peyton reached for the slender gold ring and spun it on her finger. "You didn't know this was a wedding band. It could have been simple costume jewelry."

"Don't think you're much into froufrou." Mary Grace lifted a finger and pointed. "You're wearing a wide leather watch. Sort of a mixed look, don't you think? Sportswoman's watch and engraved gold band? I could be wrong, but I doubt it. There's a story in you."

Peyton froze, her mind reeling in momentary panic. This woman knew everything. She *could* read minds. Peyton would have to leave, escape this stifling heat and these creepy dolls —

She closed her eyes and forced herself to take a deep, slow breath. She would *not* panic. The air was *not* growing thin; her pounding heart was only demanding more oxygen because this trailer was as hot as Hades. Mary Grace Van Owen could not see into Peyton's past. She was a skilled observer, an exceptional reporter. After all, King had recommended her, and only pretty spectacular people earned his recommendation.

She counted to five, then opened her eyes. "Maybe there is a story," she said, forcing herself to focus on the woman. "And I can see how you picked up the details. But you could have been wrong, too, so how am I to know —"

"There's a story in everybody." Mary Grace gave her a soft smile of concern. "You can't spend all your energy looking at the forest, honey. You'll miss the trees if you do."

Not certain how to respond, Peyton stared at her hostess.

Mary Grace's bright blue eyes grew larger and darker, the black pupils training on Peyton like binoculars. "People are like newspapers, sweetheart, and most of them don't want to open up when you first meet 'em. They'll show you their front pages, maybe even let you read some ads on the back page. If you take a little time and ask the right questions, you might be trusted enough to peek at the masthead on page two. But if you really want to read everything, you've got to convince them to open up all the way. Not until then will you be able to read the fine print of the soul."

"The classifieds?" Peyton forced a laugh, her heart sinking with disappointment. She'd hoped for some concrete tips on dealing with grief-stricken people, but this woman had given her nothing but generalities and metaphor. "How, exactly, do you get people to open up?" she asked, shifting on the sofa. The doll slid from her lap, but she caught and repositioned it, resting its head against her clammy legs. "In the next two weeks I'll be interviewing people who lost a father in the crash of Flight 848. I won't have much time, but I want to get to the heart of the matter without evoking a lot of grief."

One of Mary Grace's penciled brows tilted uncertainly. "You want to mine gold without digging and scraping?"

More metaphor. Peyton sighed. "I don't want these interviews to get . . . messy. You talk to prisoners all the time, right? How do you keep the conversations focused? Surely you have a technique for keeping people on track during an interview, a way to avoid emotional jags and pitfalls —"

"Honey, I just let them talk." The expression of good humor faded from the curve of Mary Grace's painted lips as the depths of her eyes shone with a serious light. "The most precious gift you can give a hurting soul is the freedom to express pain and pleasure. Go in to the interview empty-handed; leave your notepad and pencil outside. Ask one question, only if you have to, then sit still and listen. People will talk if you give 'em a chance. It's when you try to direct things that they fall silent. When you're as quiet as a held breath, that's when other people open up."

Peyton looked at the woman, letting the silence stretch. Maybe Mary Grace had a point, because the quiet that wrapped around them now was anything but comfortable. The air seemed to grow thin again, and if the silence continued, she'd have to go outside for some fresh air —

Mary Grace's lined face crinkled in a smile. "I think you're getting the idea, hon. Humans are sociable creatures, so not many of us take naturally to silence. Your interview subjects may cry, they may get hung up in all kinds of what you call pitfalls, but their pages will open. You mark my words, that's when you'll find your story. More than that, you'll likely find a friend, too."

Peyton could have melted in relief when a car honked outside. Mary Grace shifted her weight forward and pushed off the rocker's armrest. "That'll be my ride," she said, standing.

Peyton picked up her backpack and stood, too, feeling a little foolish as she propped up the creepy baby she'd displaced on the sofa. One of the advantages of advanced age, she supposed, was being allowed to bring one's eccentricities out of the closet.

"Thank you, Mary Grace." More than ready to leave, she extended her hand, and felt the soft warmth of the woman's crinkled skin. "I'll try to remember what you said."

She tried to withdraw, but Mary Grace held on, bringing her free hand up to cover Peyton's in a double grip. "I'll be praying for you, hon," she said, her eyes blazing with a light that had nothing to do with the darkened trailer. "I have a feeling our little talk wasn't what you expected, so I've got one bit of practical parting advice. Remember — if you want to really know people, you have to love them. To love them, you have to forgive their faults. If you forgive folks enough, you'll belong to them, and they to you, whether either of you likes it or not. It's a natural law James Hilton once called squatter's rights of the heart."

"James Hilton?" Peyton asked when Mary Grace released her hand. The name didn't ring a bell.

"A novelist, one of the greats. He wrote *Lost Horizon*, *Random Harvest*, and *Goodbye, Mr. Chips*." Her voice softened. "He was one of my college professors, and I admired him greatly."

Peyton looked away as heat stole into her face. Faced with Mary Grace's plain appearance, quirky collection, and Southern speech, Peyton had forgotten to consider the woman's education and background. Clearly, if she intended to conduct successful interviews in the coming weeks, she'd have to do thorough preliminary research and pay more attention to her subjects.

She moved to the door and opened it, then inhaled deeply of the fresh air. Compared to the stifling heat of the trailer, the shady carport seemed cool and invigorating. She moved down to the first concrete step, then turned. "Thank you, Ms. Van Owen. I hope you'll read my column for the next few days. The story I'm following could be interesting."

Mary Grace took a moment to lean out the door and wave at a woman in an older-model white Lincoln on the road, then she gave Peyton a pink-rimmed smile. "I'll look forward to it, hon. You take care now, and God bless."

As Peyton began the walk back to her Jetta, she heard Mary Grace yell, "Just a minute, Gladys. Let me grab my pocket-book."

Peyton sighed as she slid into her own car, turned the key, then lowered her perspiring face into the AC's frigid blast. She wasn't certain she'd be able to use anything Mary Grace had told her, but a savvy reporter tucked everything away in a mental trivia file. One never knew when a contact would come in handy.

She shivered as she put the car in gear and turned to check the road. If she ever had to do a column on baby dolls, she knew exactly where to go.

Comment by Mary Grace Van Owen, 67 Retired Feature Writer for the St. Petersburg Post

What did I think of Peyton MacGruder? Oh, honey, you don't want to get me started. I could tell you plenty about that one, but I doubt she'd like me making presumptions about her. Seemed pretty evident there's plenty she doesn't want anyone to know . . . and maybe she doesn't want to know herself.

I'm no professional interpreter of body language, but any observant person knows that when a woman sits with her arms crossed over her chest, she's either being defensive or she's got a stain on her blouse. And no ordinary woman picks up a baby with one hand, even if it *is* a doll. Most telling was the way she covered the baby's face with that canvas thing she carried instead of a purse — what do they call them these days? Bookbags? Backsacks? Whatever.

Yes, I'd bet my old manual typewriter there *is* a story behind the wedding ring, the leather watchband, and the wide-eyed look she gave my babies. But Peyton MacGruder changed the subject real quick when I attempted to draw her out. So whatever her story, it's locked deep inside, probably behind a wall as thick as Gibraltar.

There was something else, too. I'm not sure, of course, and wouldn't gossip for all the world, but at one point Peyton went all pale and fluttery, like she'd discovered a hunk of slime at the bottom of her soft drink glass. I was about to point the way to the bathroom, but then she seemed to get control of herself.

She changed the subject, anyway, and that seemed to keep her from bolting from the sofa.

Maybe I'm wrong . . . maybe she was feelin' poorly on account of the heat. Florida summers can sometimes affect people that way, especially if they're not used to it. The heat can make a person feel downright lightheaded.

It's like we always say here at Lakeview: "If you can't stand the sun, go back up north."

Seven

Monday, June 25
In her glass-walled office on the twenty-first floor of the World Trade Center, reporter Julie St. Claire clicked her mouse and moodily stared at her computer monitor. The crash of Flight 848 was old news now, but no one could deny that it had been good for WNN and the network's star reporter. The fledgling network, which had been struggling to compete with CNN ever since its debut, had soared last week to the top of the ratings heap, largely because of Julie's extensive on-scene coverage. Fortunately, Walt Rosenberg, head of the news division, was smart enough to realize who had attracted so many new viewers.

Just this morning she'd typed *Julie St. Claire* into the Google Internet search engine and pulled up three newspaper articles specifically commending her work. "Not since the Gulf War produced Arthur Kent, the 'Scud Stud,' has reporting been so intrinsically linked to personality," wrote a reporter for the *Dallas Morning News.* "Now Julie St. Claire, the 'Babe from the Bay,' has charmed her way into our hearts with her concise, comforting, and often confrontational coverage of the PanWorld crash."

Crossing her legs, Julie smiled at the computer screen. Her producer had thrown a fit the day she told the cameras to roll and then stopped a navy diver to press for details about recovered bodies, but she knew the confrontation would look good on tape. The diver, exhausted and mentally drained, had no patience left. His crude remark, edited so it was visible but not audible, won Julie boatloads of sympathy and increased her ratings by ten percentage points. In the end, her producer had admitted the encounter made sense, and Julie enjoyed the affirmation of one of her core beliefs: people watched television news for entertainment first, information second.

Let Dan Rather and Tom Brokaw read the news in their conservative dress shirts and ties. They might as well be on radio for all they seemed to care. Julie, on the other hand, had come to value the unblinking eye of the camera. It could be harsh, but it could caress a reporter who knew how to handle it.

Yes, the tragedy of Flight 848 had been

good for her. She almost hated to see the coverage fade. There would be at least one more report once the FAA published its findings about the cause of the crash, but their investigation could take months.

Out of habit, she logged on to Nexis, the information database, then clicked her way to the search screen that would limit her search to data entered in the last twenty-four hours. Once again she typed in *Flight 848*, then snapped the enter key. She doubted she'd find any new information, but as long as the FAA investigation remained active, the tight ship of bureaucracy could always spring a leak.

Only two stories appeared in the results list. The first was an updated report on PanWorld's plummeting stock. The second caught her attention:

Treasures from the Deep, by Peyton MacGruder.
"The Heart Healer" is a regular feature of the Tampa Times.
Dear Readers: I met a woman last week — a woman a few years younger than I, with blue eyes as —

The rest of the story had been truncated, so Julie clicked on the link. The link took her to TampaTimes.com and a frame containing a feature column.

She skimmed down the page, her pulse quickening as she read:

The treasure, which came to me wrapped in a square of fine linen, is not jewelry or currency, but a simple note. From inside its protective plastic sleeve, its words speak of a love as wide as the sea and as unfathomable as the ocean. The note was, I suspect, another scrap from Flight 848, but no single piece of luggage or debris carries the emotional weight of this fragile slip of paper. It is addressed to a particular person, and it is signed simply Dad.

Julie tightened her hand around the mouse as an anticipatory shiver of excitement rippled through her limbs. A note? Whoever heard of such a fragile thing surviving a major crash? Never had anyone found a note in the debris from an airline disaster, not from EgyptAir Flight 990, or TWA 800, or the ValuJet DC-9 that slid into the Everglades in '96 . . .

She sat back, her mind vibrating with a thousand thoughts and pictures. *A note.* From a father to a child. Why, the human interest in such a story would send her ratings through the roof! WNN was holding its own now, having picked up millions of viewers and advertising dollars during the crash coverage, but a story like this would *keep* them at the top of the charts. And if she reported it, her Q-rating would soar. Every man and woman in America would know her face and name.

She skimmed the rest of the story, then clicked on a link to the paper's home page. The *Tampa Times* was owned by Howard Media & Entertainment, WNN's parent company, and the columnist was someone called Peyton MacGruder — she scrolled down to the bottom of the frame — who could be reached at pmacgruder@tampa times.com.

Without hesitation, she clicked on the reporter's e-mail address, then paused when her computer shot up a blank message template. How did one reporter tactfully ask another to share a story? Unless this Peyton MacGruder was a complete fool, she had to know she'd been handed the story of the month, perhaps even of the year. E-mail was too impersonal.

Shoving her rolling chair away from the computer, Julie swiveled and picked up the telephone.

★ ★ ★

Back in the newsroom, Peyton pulled her rolling chair closer to the desk and forced herself to concentrate on the passenger list in her hands. Since returning from Clearwater, every time she closed her eyes she saw Mary Grace Van Owen's gloomy living room, complete with smiling, wide-eyed infants all in a row. The effect was spookier than reading Stephen King in a thunderstorm, and the last thing she needed now was to be distracted.

Staring at the passenger list, she ran her finger over the names, checking to be sure she'd highlighted all those who had been Tampa residents. Those obits were waiting in a stack next to her computer, culled from the pages of her own paper. At the little typing table that today served as Mandi's desk, the intern was engaged in the same task, double-checking Peyton's findings. The girl had seemed a little exasperated when Peyton told her they'd be working together for the next two weeks, but all signs of annoyance vanished when Peyton explained what they'd be doing.

"Oh, man, how major!" Mandi had slapped her hand on her chest as though she'd felt the first pang of a coronary. "What a story! I'd love to go undercover with you!"

Peyton refrained from rolling her eyes. "We're not cops, Mandi, and this won't be much fun. It'll be a lot of reading, probably quite a few phone calls, and I'll expect a certain level of discretion. I don't want anyone else to know all the details until we discover the right recipient." She frowned. "Assuming there *is* a right recipient. If this is a hoax, we've got to leave ourselves a way out."

"I hear you, boss," Mandi had answered, just before striking out on a search for a desk to call her own. And though both the title and the gung-ho attitude had made Peyton grimace, it *would* be nice to have an extra pair of eyes for research and someone to cover the phone while she was out.

She pinched the bridge of her nose and closed her eyes, refocusing her thoughts. At least she'd learned that finding prospects to receive the note might not be as difficult as she had first feared. At the beginning, she struck all the women and children under twenty-one from the master passenger list, thinking the note's author had to be a man of a certain maturity. Out of the 147 names remaining, 82 had lived in the Tampa area, so she had those obits within reach. If all went well, she would know by dinnertime if any of them had children with *T* names.

She'd need one — her Wednesday column was due by 11:30 Tuesday morning, and without a name she had nothing to write about.

Peyton opened her eyes and returned to skimming through the Tampa passenger obituaries, then frowned when her phone rang.

From her little table, Mandi looked up. "You want me to get it?"

"No. You keep reading. As soon as you get through the list, start calling the out-of-state papers — use the phone at Karen's desk; she'll be out for the day. Have them fax the passenger obits to us at the features fax line and tell them we're on deadline. Be nice. We'll get results quicker."

Annoyed by the persistent ringing phone — didn't everyone use e-mail these days? — Peyton snatched up the receiver. "Mac-Gruder," she said, scratching through a female name they'd forgotten to strike.

"Peyton MacGruder? This is Julie St. Claire of WNN."

For a moment the name didn't register, then the association clicked. Peyton took a quick, sharp breath, then grinned. "Julie St. Claire — I watched you during the crash coverage. I thought you did a good job of handling a difficult situation."

"Thanks." The woman's voice sounded flat and listless. "Listen, I read your column today. Wonderful writing. And how incredible that you found a note."

"I didn't find it." Peyton stared at a photo of her cats taped to the border of her computer monitor. "As I wrote in the column, the note was given to me."

"Listen." St. Claire's voice took on an edge. "While I was reading, a great idea came to me. If you want to wrap up the mystery as quickly as possible, why not take your search national? I could come down there and do a story on you and your little quest. We'll get some videotape of you with the note and maybe some still shots of the actual page. With the additional coverage provided by our network, you could find your missing person in no time."

Peyton stiffened, slapped by a wave of shock. "You want me to go on network television?"

Like a bright-eyed jack-in-the-box, Mandi's head popped up into Peyton's field of vision.

"I think it'd be a great feature," Julie continued. "Maybe we could do an entire hour on the note, even an extended special feature. We'll do the background research together, then my crew and I will go with you as you search for this person. After all" — a smile found its way into her voice — "we *are* owned by the same corporation. Working together seems only natural."

Peyton rubbed her temple. Howard Media & Entertainment, which owned a host of newspapers, magazines, film companies, and the World News Network, had always allowed its subsidiaries complete autonomy. She'd never heard of a project shared between a newspaper columnist and a television reporter — even at the *Times*, except in a time of crisis or when projects were conceived as joint efforts. Writers rarely shared stories.

The idea of television — if Mandi's wide eyes were an accurate gauge — was fairly amazing, but TV coverage would do nothing to help Peyton keep her column. And the calm voice of common sense reminded her that anyone with enough chutzpa to make an offer like this without so much as a *how are you, let's get to know one another* might want to run the show entirely.

Peyton had enough bosses in her life.

She strengthened her voice. "Thanks for the offer, but I really want to cover this story my way. You see, I've thought a lot about it and I want to do this as a continuing feature

156

for my readers. I have four columns a week to fill, and two weeks to interview prospects for the note. Television coverage isn't part of my vision for this story."

Silence rolled over the phone line, and for a moment Peyton wondered if the connection had been broken.

"You sure I can't change your mind?" St. Claire's voice now contained a teasing note. "You'd be surprised how a little airtime can boost your ratings."

"I don't doubt it, but yes, I'm sure. Thanks for thinking of me." Peyton smiled into the phone. "I guess I'm a little amazed someone like you even reads the *Tampa Times*. Where are you headquartered? New York?"

"I read it on the Web," Julie answered, then the phone clicked.

Peyton pulled the receiver from her ear, frowned at it for a moment, then dropped it back to her desk.

"Was that really Julie St. Claire?" Mandi whispered, breathless. "I heard you say her name, and then I heard something about TV—"

"Cool your jets, girl, it's not going to happen." Peyton pressed her lips together for a moment, thinking. If she'd been forewarned she might have come up with an alternative to cutting off Julie St. Claire completely. Television coverage might be useful in her search . . . but she'd made a decision to follow this story until she ran out of road and she'd promised her readers she'd give it her best. The distraction of television wouldn't help her accomplish either goal.

She gave Mandi an apologetic smile. "Sorry to disappoint you, kiddo, but this search isn't going to be romantic. Most newspaper work is reading and research, and we need to get back to it. I need at least one *T* name before we leave tonight."

"Okay, boss," Mandi said, heaving a sigh as she lowered her head back to the paperwork. "Whatever you say."

Julie St. Claire glared at the phone and drummed her acrylic nails against the polished desktop. Peyton MacGruder's words kept buzzing in her brain: *Television news coverage isn't part of my vision for this story.* What did a thirty thousand dollar per year newspaper columnist know about vision? The woman was a pencil pusher, and she had no idea what she held in her hands. That little scrap of paper would translate into emotion and ratings, and ratings were the key to everything in this business.

Julie stood, fumbled in a desk drawer for

her cigarettes, then shook one out. She lit it, then drew deeply on the fragrant tobacco and moved to the window. Her reflection stared back at her — large eyes shadowed by dark hair, one arm crossed at the waistband of her leather skirt, the other holding the smoldering cigarette. Adam was constantly on her case about smoking — bad for the public image. But this was her private world, and cigarettes her private indulgence.

Staring at her reflection, she brought the cigarette to her mouth and drew heavily on it, making the tip glow bright, then allowed a thin plume of smoke to drift from her pursed lips. Too bad she wasn't an actress. She could cop an attitude with the best of them, maybe even manage to bring a semblance of sincerity to a role. But actresses, when they hit it big, attracted too much attention. No one cared about the private life of a newscaster; no one was likely to go digging into her past. So Esther Hope Harner would remain hidden forever.

Not that it'd matter much. Anyone who knew that Howard Cosell began life as Howard William Cohen or that Wolfman Jack was really Robert Smith wouldn't bat an eye to realize that Esther Harner had reinvented herself as Julie St. Claire after leaving Mississippi. A nosy reporter might be surprised by the trailer . . . and the skinny man in the white T-shirt who had left his thumbprints above Julie's collarbone on several occasions. A tabloid snoop might even be horrified by the woman who sat in front of the TV in an indentation of the couch that had literally formed around her ample behind. That such a woman, whose grease-caked hair straggled lank around her face, could have given birth to a luminescent star like Julie St. Claire — well, such an idea would be immediately dismissed. No reporter in his right mind would want to report that story, for it would call attention to the unwilling and unmotivated poor — a situation not even the politicians wanted to address.

Julie tasted her cigarette again. She'd started smoking at eleven, when Jimmy Tennant caught her behind the school and taught her how to kiss and smoke, two lessons in one day. She'd learned a lot since then — and from men far more knowledgeable than Jimmy. She'd left the tracks of her stiletto heels on a few backsides, but she'd climbed out of poverty and left Mississippi in the dust. She'd left Esther Harner in the trailer, along with the woman and the man in the sweat-stained T-shirt.

She brought the cigarette to her lips but

didn't inhale, staring instead at her reflection in the wide window. The brute in the trailer wasn't her father, and somehow she'd known that for as long as she could remember. Her mother didn't like to talk about the husband she'd abandoned, but sometimes Julie would dream of a man with kind eyes and a soft voice . . . *a weakling,* her mother would have called him, a weak-livered fool without the gumption to say boo to a goose.

One afternoon, just before passing out, her drunken mother had looked Julie in the eye and cackled like a crazy woman. "He wanted to adopt you," she said, wiping spit from her chin with the back of her hand. "What a fool! You weren't even his brat, but still he wanted to give you his name!"

Drawing deeply on the cigarette, Julie felt the acrid smoke invade her throat and lungs. Her mother had played Mr. Harner, whoever he was, like a violin. She'd married him, taken his name and given it to her daughter, then cleaned out his bank account and left town on a Greyhound bus.

Julie exhaled sharply, sending twin streamers of smoke through her nostrils. Her mother probably wouldn't have hesitated to leave her daughter behind if the man hadn't been weak enough to care. She wouldn't have wanted to leave him with anything worth caring for.

Like her mother, Julie had gathered the courage to run away, but at sixteen she turned her back on that listless life, more than happy to leave the beatings and abuse and ignorance. She lied about her age and took a job at a diner in Tupelo, working hard to change her speech, appearance, and manners. Her hard work paid off when she earned a college scholarship. At school she made new friends and a new life, all but forgetting the past. And now . . .

The ghosts from that trailer couldn't touch her now.

A thin covering of gray fog hung over the Manhattan skyline at this hour; the noise of late afternoon traffic bustled far beneath her. Common sounds could not reach this plush office; no annoyance should be able to slip past security to enter her door . . . but one had. Irritation had invaded Julie's cocoon in the person of Peyton MacGruder, and she could not rest until she set things right again.

She walked back to her desk, took a last drag, then placed the cigarette in an ashtray to smolder. Curling in the leather chair, one leg tucked beneath her, she picked up the phone and pressed a button on the speed dial. As the number rang, she ran her nails through her bangs and drew a slow, deep breath to soften her voice and attitude.

Adam Howard, CEO of Howard Media & Entertainment, did not care for irritation either. He had to be approached in exactly the right way.

"The best thing about the World Trade Center," historian Francis Morrone wrote in his *Architectural Guidebook to Manhattan*, "is that when you're in it, you don't have to look at it." From his office on the one-hundredth floor of the WTC, Adam Howard agreed that the view from thirteen-hundred feet above the city was far superior to what the average man saw from the gray and granite street.

He was not enjoying the spectacular view, however, when his phone chirped. He glanced toward the desk, annoyed that his secretary had put a call through when he'd expressly told her he needed time to consider the Digital Media offer, then he remembered that the chirping phone belonged to his private cell number, known only to fifty or so close associates who owed him money, time, or a personal favor.

He pulled the tiny phone from his coat pocket, flipped open the case — *Why do they make them so small?* — and held it to his ear. "Yes?"

"Hello, Adam. This a good time?"

He recognized the husky voice immediately. "Of course." Actually, it *was* a good time. The entire month had been a continual banquet. His World News Network had finally crested and crashed over CNN, and his magazines, the monthly *Newsworld* and weekly tabloid *Celeb!* had sold out their print runs, largely because of articles featuring victims of the recent plane crash. As luck would have it, an ex-convict had been aboard the ill-fated flight, seated next to a reclusive multimillionaire's mistress. The major newspapers had missed both stories, but his bloodhounds had ferreted out the connections and hit pay dirt two days ago.

"I'd love to see you tonight." He smiled. No mistaking the seduction in the voice now.

Adam pulled his electronic organizer toward him and glanced at his list of appointments. He had a dinner with Mavis and her theater group scheduled for tonight, but he could blow it off. Mavis wouldn't be the only woman present without her husband.

"How's eight o'clock?" he asked, reaching for his stylus. "I'll meet you at the apartment."

"Eight is great," she said, then she hung up.

Adam smiled as he snapped the phone shut. Julie St. Claire possessed many talents, but he especially appreciated her directness.

By five-fifteen, most of the desks in the *Times* newsroom had emptied. The telephones fell silent, and the constant waves of chatter and clatter had faded to the dull roar of a cleaning woman's vacuum. Peyton thought she could actually hear the hum of the overhead fluorescent lights, a sound usually drowned out in the bustle of the newsroom.

Hunched over her desk, she picked up yet another page of local obits and forced herself to read every formulaic word. Halfway down the page, her heart skipped a beat: PanWorld passenger Winston Manning of St. Petersburg was survived by two children: a daughter, Victoria Manning Storm of Brooklyn, and a son, Reverend Timothy Manning of St. Louis.

She whooped. "Bingo!"

From two desks over, Mandi's head lifted from her reading. "Find something?"

Peyton shot her a triumphant smile. "Timothy Manning — a reverend, no less.

The son of passenger Winston Manning of St. Pete." She dropped the page to her lap and reached for her computer keyboard. "Let's see . . . if I fly out of here tomorrow, I can meet with the man on Wednesday and fly home Wednesday night or Thursday morning. I can write Friday's column on the plane if I have to."

"That's a lot of *ifs*." A doubtful look crossed Mandi's face. "What if something goes wrong?"

"I have a backup piece, but I don't want to use it." Peyton stopped typing and looked at the desk where Mandi sat. Obituary print-outs, Diet Coke cans, and pretzel wrappers covered the wooden surface. "Any luck on your end?"

"Not yet."

Peyton lifted a brow. "Well?"

After casting a longing glance at the clock, Mandi took the hint and went back to her reading. Clattering at the keyboard, Peyton accessed her Web connection. She had just located a direct flight to St. Louis from TIA when Mandi shouted, "Got one!"

Peyton's heart dropped. Two *T* names? She'd been half-hoping to hit a home run with her first attempt.

"Who?" she asked, rolling her chair away from the desk.

"Tanner Ford of Gainesville, Florida." Mandi's highlighter moved across the printout in bold strokes. "His father was first-class passenger Trenton Ford of Dallas, Texas."

Crossing her arms, Peyton rocked back in her chair. Both Tampa and LaGuardia seemed odd airport choices for someone who wanted to visit Gainesville from Dallas, but perhaps Trenton Ford had been visiting friends or business associates. Who knew?

"Okay." She scooted forward to pick up her steno pad. "Two *T* names — that's not bad. How many obits left on your list?"

Mandi paused to count down the page. "Fifteen."

Peyton drew a deep breath. She'd love it if no more prospects surfaced. She'd *really* love it if Reverend Timothy Manning could prove the note had been intended for him. Then she wouldn't have to bother Tanner Ford, nor would she have to go to Gainesville . . .

"What about Wednesday's column?" Mandi interrupted her thoughts, glancing up at the clock. "You gonna get started on that?"

"It won't take long. I wrote an outline last night, so it just needs a couple of tweaks." Peyton grabbed a pencil and scratched out a

167

list of things to pack for St. Louis: her digital recorder, notebook, and her laptop. And her credit card, of course.

The *Tampa Times* wasn't wild about reimbursing expenses for columnists on assignment, but this was an extraordinary situation. Curtis DiSalvo had recognized it, and so had King. Even the Dragon Lady knew a story like this came around only once in a blue moon.

"You still here?" The deep, masculine voice startled her. Peyton glanced over her shoulder to see King leaning against the desk behind her. Grinning, he crossed his arms and stretched out his long legs, then gave her chair a playful push with his sneaker.

Peyton felt her cheeks flush hotly in the cool air. What must Mandi be thinking?

"Imagine seeing you here." She swiveled to face him. "Slumming, are you? Come to visit the droids in the desks?"

His dark eyes sparked with mischief. "I thought we had to settle a bet."

Peyton closed her eyes as the memory washed over her. King had promised to buy her dinner whether her time with Mary Grace was useful or not. She'd been so busy reading obituaries she'd completely forgotten.

"Well?" His left brow lifted. "By the way, how's Mary Grace doing these days?"

"Very well, if she's always been eccentric." Peyton hugged her steno pad to her chest. "She's sharp, I'll give her that, but you didn't mention the doll museum or the fact that she doesn't believe in air conditioning. I thought I was going to melt in her living room."

"Did she give you good pointers?"

"She gave me analogies: 'People are like newspapers. If you're nice, they'll open up and let you take a peek.' She was okay, King, and thanks for the offer, but I really can't do dinner tonight." She gestured to the papers on her desk. "I've got to settle a few details tonight or my Wednesday column is shot."

His gaze shifted, and for a moment she thought he might actually be disappointed, but then he grinned and snapped his fingers in Mandi's direction. "Don't let her work you too hard, young lady," he said, moving away through the newsroom maze. "And tell her she missed a great night out with the guys."

Peyton watched him go, then shook her head. Some dinner proposition — he would probably have taken her to his favorite sports bar and sat at the counter, downing a

169

greasy burger and fries while he yelled at whatever game played on the TV screens overhead.

Sure she'd dodged a bullet, she went back to work.

By the time eight o'clock arrived, Julie St. Claire had lit scented candles, set Secret Garden to spinning on the CD player, and donned her most provocative little black dress. The scent of vanilla hung heavy in the air, her hair gleamed in the candlelight, and her reflection in the foyer mirror revealed eyes bright with the thrill of the chase. The dress had cost twelve hundred dollars, about six hundred dollars a yard, but she considered the expense an investment in her career. The silky fabric accented her curving figure, and the color brought out the milky paleness of her skin.

She glanced at her watch. Adam was late, as important men usually were, so she reminded herself to be patient. This little drama had a purpose, and she couldn't let herself be distracted. She was going to give Adam Howard a night to remember, and in return he'd do whatever it took to get her the note. A simple exchange of favors.

At eight-fifteen, the key turned in the lock. She stood motionless at the edge of the foyer, beneath a single overhead light, and waited. Adam let himself in, then stood beside the door, his eyes shining as she tipped her head back and slowly slid her hands from her throat to the not-so-distant hem of the little black dress.

"Hello, Adam." She issued the greeting in a throaty whisper. In a heartbeat he stood at her side, dropping his briefcase to the marble floor before he lifted her into his arms.

By 10:00 p.m., the black dress had found its way to the floor. Because someone had once told her there was nothing sexier than a woman in a man's dress shirt, Julie now wore one of Adam's, a blue oxford she'd pulled from the closet, then buttoned. With one button.

The CEO of Howard Media & Entertainment lay facedown on the rumpled king-size bed, his eyes closed.

Knowing the time had come to act, she crawled over the bed toward him, then planted a kiss on his cheek. "Hey, sleepyhead," she whispered, using the shirttail to wipe a lipstick smudge from his throat, "it's time for you to make yourself presentable."

His eyes flew open, then closed again, but sleep, apparently, was the last thing on his mind. His powerful hands reached out and

171

grabbed her, circling her waist in a grip at once possessive and powerful.

"Adam," she warned, covering his hands with her own, "you've got to go soon."

His head lifted, his eyes open and fixed on her as he sighed heavily. "You're right," he said, releasing her. He rolled onto his side and propped his head on one elbow, then reached out and caught her chin. "But you're hard to leave when you're this adorable."

After pulling her toward him for one last kiss, Adam sat up and began to dress.

Julie quietly launched her attack. "Adam" — she kept her voice low and controlled — "this morning I found a story on the Web about PanWorld Flight 848. Apparently someone recovered a note from the crash; can you believe it? A columnist for the *Tampa Times* has instigated some sort of private crusade to try and discover the author. She'll be making reports over the next few days, documenting her progress."

Adam grunted as he buckled his belt. "Interesting."

"Truth is, I think it's a great idea. I'd like to follow that story as well."

Adam plucked an invisible bit of lint from his shirt, then gave her a knowing look. "I'm sure you would, but if the columnist has already gone public, every reporter in the country will be following that trail."

Tilting her head, Julie turned up the wattage of her smile. "But not every reporter has an inside connection. The *Tampa Times* is one of your papers." She lowered her gaze and idly traced one of the shirt's buttonholes with a manicured fingernail. "So we have an edge CNN doesn't."

Adam picked up his suit coat, then paused. "What aren't you telling me?"

Julie dropped the coy routine and gave him a straight answer. "There are missing pieces: the note itself, and clues it contains as to the identity of the writer. The reporter won't divulge details."

"And you want her to share her secrets with you?" He laughed, his chuckle a dry and cynical sound. "Sweetie, I hate to tell you, but freedom of the press has been twisted a million ways to Sunday. It covers *everything* these days. If that columnist doesn't want to share her cookies, I doubt even I can force her hand."

"There are certain inducements you could offer," Julie said, reclining on the satin sheets. "You have power, Adam. And you've never been afraid to use it."

"You don't know newspaper people like I do."

His voice had gone flat and dry, which meant she had to act quickly or be dismissed.

"If she won't give us details, we can at least convince her to let us work alongside her." Rolling onto her side, Julie propped her head on her hand and met his gaze. "That will still keep us ahead of CNN and the other networks. They'll be at least a day behind because they'll be depending on news dribbling out of her column. If she'll let us know what she knows, when she knows it, we'll win. We could do a special — prime time, of course — and blow the competition away. It'll be bigger than anything, but we need to work fast, before the public's had a chance to forget about Flight 848." She needed to be in front of the cameras with a major story before the public forgot her, too, but she bit her lip, suppressing that thought.

Adam did not speak for a moment. He adjusted his coat, straightened his tie, then stepped into the bathroom. Leaning sideways to peer through the open door, Julie could see him in the bathroom mirror, swiping his hands through his silver hair, giving himself that *end-of-a-long-day* look.

When he came back into the bedroom, he wore an almost gloating expression. He bent to kiss her, then pulled slightly back and held her face in his hands. "Beautiful *and* smart, aren't you? I knew there had to be a reason I can't stay away."

A thrill shivered through Julie's senses. "Then you'll contact her paper?"

"Why not? It's mine."

She pulled him closer, thanking him amid an eager flood of kisses. He laughed with the mirth of a master who enjoys bringing occasional joy to the hired help, then stood and gave her cheek a playful — though painful — pinch.

"We'll need to contact the *Tampa Times* tomorrow." Julie spoke quickly, before he could walk away and forget the entire matter. "The columnist, Peyton somebody-or-other, blew me off today."

A warning cloud settled on Adam's features. "Not a team player, eh? Well — I'll make a call in the morning. We'll do what we must to make this thing work."

"Adam." Julie clasped her hands together, then rose on her knees to adjust his tie. "Have I told you today how much I adore you?" She gripped the lapels of his coat, tugging on the fabric until he bent toward her, then she tipped her head back to meet his kiss.

Eight

Tuesday, June 26
Sitting in a Delta lounge at Tampa International Airport, Peyton balanced her laptop on her knees and typed a few more details into the column about her first prospect.

This column, which King would probably describe as much ado about *note-ing,* would set the stage for her first presentation of the note. She didn't want to divulge the prospect's name or details about his background prior to the interview, so she had been forced to wax philosophical and sentimental to fill her column space. Both approaches lay decidedly outside her comfort zone, but Emma Duncan's readers would probably adore the final result.

Peyton pressed her fingertip to her lip and scanned the words on the screen, her foot jiggling in a hyperactive rhythm. This approach, this *story,* was different from anything she'd ever written before, and necessity was forcing her to open mental closets she would far rather leave closed.

176

She'd never been one for overt sentimentality, but she supposed she could pluck the right strings with her readers. After all, she knew what loving parents were supposed to do — enthusiastically attend their children's football games, piano recitals, and chorus concerts. Just because Peyton had never experienced that kind of attention didn't mean other adult children wouldn't identify with the picture she was attempting to paint.

Children spell love T-I-M-E, she wrote.

Sure they did. After all, she'd read that sentiment a trillion times in feature writer Nancy Kilgore's parenting articles. Peyton's mother might have spelled love that way if she'd lived long enough. And who knew? If her mother hadn't died, her father might not have gone to medical school, might not have sent her off to Grandma's and then to boarding school. They might have been quite a cozy threesome, nesting in a tiny house in Jacksonville, living on love and baked beans . . .

She typed in some more blather borrowed from Kilgore's philosophy, then plugged in the final details. *I'll be in [ ]* became *I'll be in St. Louis, Missouri,* then she clicked on the icon for the spellchecker. There. She'd created a column that would cause young mothers across the county to clutch their children and weep over their breakfasts.

She powered down the laptop, then checked her watch. Eight-forty. Her plane would be airborne by nine, and once they'd passed ten thousand feet she'd send the story in by modem, beating her Tuesday morning deadline with time to spare.

Nora Chilton would love this piece . . . though she'd probably tell anyone within earshot that Peyton was wasting over three hundred bucks of the *Times'* money on a wild-goose chase.

Coffee cup in hand, Julie St. Claire paced in her office and silently cursed Adam's slowness. Ten a.m. already. If they were going to proceed with the story on the note of Flight 848, she'd have to get busy. She'd already sold her producers on the idea of a prime-time special, but she desperately needed facts, names, and footage. *Lots* of footage. She'd get nothing as long as she remained in this glass and steel cage. Who knew, that MacGruder woman could be on to something right now —

The phone rang, startling her into splashing coffee on the carpet. In two steps she had lifted the receiver to her ear. "Yes?"

"Ms. St. Claire, this is Edith Kremkau, Mr. Howard's secretary."

"Yes?" Julie struggled to keep the irritation out of her voice. She knew the name, so why bother with useless pleasantries?

"Mr. Howard's been in touch with some people at the *Tampa Times*, apparently on your behalf. I have information for you from a Ms. Nora Chilton, lifestyles editor . . . or is that features? I'm not quite sure what the difference is —"

"Just give me the information."

"All right." The woman's voice took on a chilly tone. "After quite some runaround, I reached this Ms. Chilton, who said Peyton MacGruder is out of the office this morning. You can leave a voice mail if you want to reach her."

"No contact number? Nothing?"

"Nothing else," the secretary said, each word a splinter of ice. "If you want to know more, I suggest you call the *Times* yourself."

Julie lifted a brow, half-amused by the woman's nerve. Pretty confident for an overpaid secretary.

"Thank you, Edith." Julie smiled into the phone. "I will call the *Times*."

She hung up, then sat on the edge of her desk and considered her options. Ms. MacGruder was on to something, no doubt, but if the *Times* newsroom was anything like the television newsrooms she'd experienced, someone was bound to have a willing tongue . . .

She checked her notes, found the number for Peyton MacGruder, then dialed it. She'd probably get a voice mail recording, but if she did she'd dial again and go through the switchboard. Someone at that office had to know where Peyton MacGruder had gone.

The phone rang twice. Julie was just about to hang up when someone answered. A breathy voice said, "Hello?"

Julie felt her lip curl in a wry smile. Not very professional, this one. "Hello?" she asked, crossing her legs. "This is Julie St. Claire of WNN. I'm trying to locate Peyton MacGruder."

"Julie St. Claire?" The voice rose an octave at the final syllable. "From TV?"

"The same." Julie turned toward the window and regarded her reflection. "And who is this?"

"Mandi Sorenson."

Good grief, the woman sounded like a ten-year-old. "Mandi, it's quite important that I speak to Peyton. She and I are working together on the story of the note, and I need to ask her about her trip."

"Oh, she's left already." A note of disappointment lined Mandi's voice. "Her plane left at nine this morning."

"Perhaps I can catch her at the other end. When does she land?"

"Um" — the sound of rustling papers crackled over the line — "her plane lands in St. Louis at ten-thirty, I think. Yeah, here it is, ten-thirty-two."

"Great." Julie scratched *St. Louis, MO* on a tablet. "And her appointment — was it scheduled for later today? I was supposed to meet her, but I seem to have misplaced the address."

"Really?" Amazement echoed in the girl's voice. "She didn't say anything to me about you meeting her."

Julie lowered her voice to a conspiratorial tone. "We're keeping it quiet. She didn't want anyone else in the office to know."

"Oh."

"But I'm sure she wouldn't mind if I told you. Do you work with her?"

"I'm only a college intern," Mandi said, sounding defeated. "But yeah, I'm helping her with this note story."

"Then I'll tell her we talked. There's no sense in us keeping anything from you, is there?"

"Not at all." The girl laughed. "She's got me doing all the grunt work."

Julie forced a sympathetic sigh. "Well, I've done my share of gopher work, so don't despair. Okay — so Peyton's appointment is scheduled for this afternoon?"

"She wanted to see him today," Mandi said, rustling pages again, "but when she called the pastor's office they said he couldn't see her until tomorrow. So she's scheduled for eleven tomorrow morning. She's coming home right after."

"Eleven, good, that'll give me time to get my crew together. And that was Pastor Hargrave, right?"

"No, Manning, Timothy Manning. Do you need the address?"

"No thanks, hon, I've got it right here." Julie jotted the name on her tablet. "All right, I suppose we're all set. Keep up the good work, Mandi, and remember — mum's the word about me. Peyton won't want anyone in the newsroom to know until we're a little further along."

"No one?"

Was that suspicion in the girl's voice? "Well," Julie searched her memory and came up with the name. "Nora knows, of course. But she wouldn't want you to say anything, either."

"Got it." Mandi giggled. "I *told* Peyton this would be like going undercover!"

"Hmm." Julie dropped her pencil and picked up a cigarette. "Thanks, Mandi. You've been very helpful."

Nine

Wednesday, June 27

Traveling on the Wings of Hope
By Peyton MacGruder
"The Heart Healer" is a regular feature
of the *Tampa Times*

Dear Reader:
　By the time most of you read this I'll
be in St. Louis, Missouri. There I will
call on a man I've never met and give
him news he is certainly not expecting.
I'll be bearing a message from beyond
the grave in the hope he's meant to receive it.
　We're still searching, but so far we
have found two people who fit certain
criteria the note seems to require. I will
have no way of knowing for whom the
note was written until after I've talked to
each prospect, of course. I'm hoping for
some sign or intuition or understanding
so we will all know, without a shadow of a

doubt, whether or not a prospect is the note's intended recipient.

The people I will visit within coming days won't be able to discern much from the appearance of the note itself. The paper is plain white, without ornamentation or embossing, and the ink seems to have come from an ordinary ballpoint pen. But I'm hoping for some second sight into the matter. I'm hopeful that one of these prospects will recognize the slope of a letter or the shape of a word. I'm waiting for the right person to catch the shadows of concern upon this note, and recognize them as a familiar love.

What would you say to a loved one if you had only a few seconds to impart a last message? What language does love speak?

Some of you speak love with wine and roses. For others, "I love you" is best said by breakfast in bed, carefully set-aside sports sections, or nights out at the movies, complete with buttered popcorn.

Children spell love T-I-M-E. So, I think, do older folks.

Teenagers spell it T-R-U-S-T. Sometimes parents spell love N-O.

But no matter what the letters, the

emotion beneath the wording must be tangible, demonstrable, and sincere.

That's what I'm hoping to find on this leg of my journey. Some concrete sign of a love strong enough to impel a man on a doomed plane to send a message to a child no longer within reach.

Wish me well, friends. I'll report back in two days.

From a Days Inn motel room in St. Louis, Peyton called Mandi and learned that the obit search had turned up only one other survivor whose first name began with *T:* T. Crowe, daughter of James Crowe of New Haven, Connecticut.

"That's it?" Peyton asked, pressing her fingers to her temple. "We don't have anything more than a first initial?"

"I followed up by calling the funeral home who handled James Crowe's arrangements," Mandi said, a smile in her voice. "Fortunately, the guy there was talkative. T. Crowe is Taylor Crowe — ever heard of her?"

Peyton searched her memory, then sighed. "No. Somebody we know?"

"You wouldn't know her personally, but you probably hear her music every day. Taylor Crowe is the best-selling songwriter of our generation. She writes for everybody

— Celine Dion, Faith Hill, Anita Baker, the Backstreet Boys —"

Peyton scowled as someone in the next room thumped against the wall. She'd barely slept because a busload of teenagers had pulled into the motel shortly after her arrival. She couldn't prove it, but she strongly suspected they were bouncing each other off the walls in the room next door.

"Name a song."

Mandi didn't hesitate. " 'Yesterday my sorrows came and washed my fears away,' " she sang, warbling over the phone. Then she laughed. "Recognize that?"

"Vaguely — but I think the problem lies in the *singing,* not the song. Yeah, I know that one. Okay, she's famous. That's good. Great for public interest." Peyton raked her hand through her hair as a sudden thought struck. "Oh, brother! James Crowe was from Connecticut? That's quite a hike — bad for Nora's expense account. She wasn't thrilled to hear that I wanted to go to St. Louis. She'll freak when I tell her I need to take another out-of-state trip."

"Well — that trip might be a problem."

"Whaddya mean, a problem? Where does this songwriter live?"

"That's a tough question, and I've been working on it all morning. Her only address

187

is a P.O. box in Los Angeles. There's tons of material available on her, but not much of it is personal. I'm not finding very many clues."

"You're doing great work." Peyton murmured the compliment almost without thinking, then blinked to realize she meant it. Mandi had definitely risen to the occasion.

"Well —" She clicked off the dates on her fingers. Two more interviews meant two more columns, plus the report on Timothy Manning, and an additional wrap-up. Barring any unforeseen difficulties, Peyton's last "Heart Healer" would run on July fourth — Independence Day. How fitting — especially if Nora still wanted her out. Though King seemed certain Peyton had pulled her fat out of the frying pan, she wasn't convinced.

"Are we completely positive there are no more *T* names?" she asked. "We'll need to cover all the bases before we can wrap up this series."

"I've checked and rechecked," Mandi insisted. "I'm as sure as we can be."

"Okay. Next order of business: Did you fax the biographical info on Pastor Manning? I'll need to review it before I get to the church."

"It should be waiting in the motel lobby. I

faxed it ten minutes ago, along with an extra copy for you-know-who."

Peyton frowned into the phone. "You think I have a gremlin in my suitcase or something?"

"Never mind, I know I'm not supposed to know. But I do know, so it's okay. But I won't say anything."

Peyton lifted her gaze to the ceiling. What was the girl babbling about? No telling what sort of rumors were circulating in the newsroom, especially with Carter Cummings spouting off in his misguided attempt at matchmaking. King was probably out of the office today, so the rumor mill had ground out a report that he and Peyton had slipped away together . . .

Just what she needed — sheer tittle-tattle. She cleared her throat. "Listen, kid, I don't have a clue what you're talking about, but I really don't have time to work it out. So just keep quiet about whatever, and we'll talk about it when I get back." She searched her brain for any last-minute items on her task list and found nothing. "I guess that's it, Mandi. You're a lifesaver. Tell the Dragon Lady you deserve a raise."

Mandi giggled. "I'm not here to make money, remember? Interns are supposed to gain experience, not wealth."

"Well, plan on me taking you to lunch in a couple of weeks when this is all over," Peyton said, rising with a sense of relief. Three prospects for the note would be far easier to handle than ten. "Thanks a bunch, kid. See you tomorrow."

After calling to confirm her appointment with Reverend Manning, Peyton walked to the motel lobby to collect her fax, then took it back to her room with a Diet Coke and a bag of Peanut M&M's — not exactly a healthy breakfast, but it would hold her until she could grab lunch at the airport.

She'd learned one thing from her bizarre meeting with Mary Grace Van Owen: it would help to have as much information as possible up front. (If she'd known, for instance, that King's friend collected realistic baby dolls and didn't believe in air conditioning, she probably would have postponed that interview indefinitely.) Even so, one of Mary Grace's admonitions kept replaying in Peyton's mind: *Go to the interview empty-handed. Ask one question, then sit still and listen.*

Peyton had never conducted an interview without a preprinted list of questions, a tape recorder, *and* a notepad and pen. The one and only time she left the notepad at home her tape recorder's batteries had died, so she'd had to frantically pull the quotes for an entire column from her memory. Mary Grace's advice contradicted everything Peyton had been taught, but the woman's insights had been impressive, even a little unnerving. Maybe she knew something.

Still, while Peyton might try going into an interview empty-handed, she refused to go empty-brained. She would internalize all she could from the bio sheet Mandi had faxed, plus she'd memorize a few questions about Reverend Manning's relationship with his father. Only with an hour's worth of material stored in her memory would she even attempt Mary Grace's nonstandard interview technique.

She had already gleaned a few facts from the elder Mr. Manning's obituary. Though he had lived in St. Petersburg at the time of the crash, sixty-four-year-old Winston Manning had been born in Wichita, Kansas. He'd been an insurance salesman before retirement, and was survived by two children and six grandchildren.

Since the obit did not mention a wife, Peyton suspected the late Mr. Manning had raised his family in Kansas, then moved to St. Petersburg alone. With a son in St. Louis and a daughter in Brooklyn, he probably cut his ties to the old community and fled to Florida, where the sun shone nearly every day and residents paid no state income tax.

She popped the top on the can of soda, then ripped open the yellow bag and tossed a few candies into her mouth. Happily munching, she scanned the grainy fax of the son's biographical sketch.

Since 1996 Timothy Manning had served as pastor of the First Fundamental Church of Kirkwood, a suburb outside St. Louis. He married the former Debbie Wyndam in 1989, and the couple had three children, Kelsey, Kenyon, and Karrie. Apparently, she noted with a wry grimace, he and his wife were exceptionally fond of alliteration.

Manning had graduated from the University of the First Bible Fellowship in '88, and had received an honorary doctorate from that same institution in '97. His church had received numerous honors, as had he: Outstanding Young Man of America, '96–2000; Who's Who in American College and Universities, '84–'88; and Church Grower of the Year, 2000. According to the *Fundamentalist Monthly*, his fifteen-thousand-member church was the second-largest Bible-believing Fundamentalist fellowship in the United States.

Peyton blew a stray hair out of her eyes as

she lowered the page. Not much useful information here, and nothing at all to indicate what sort of relationship existed between Timothy and his father. They'd been separated by distance at the end, but few American families weren't.

After brushing her teeth and packing her overnight bag, she took a cab from the Days Inn to Manning's church. The First Fundamental Church of Kirkwood, an octagonal brick structure adorned on the street side with tall white pillars and a set of concrete steps, rose from the corner of North Kirkwood and West Adams like a monument.

" 'At's one big church," the cabdriver said as he peeled a receipt off his pad. He handed it over the seat and sent a crooked smile Peyton's way. " 'At preacher is all *over* the TV on Sunday mornings."

With her overnight bag in one hand and her backpack in the other, Peyton stood uneasily on the sidewalk as the cab pulled away. She hadn't visited a church since Michael from the sports department married Marjorie from the news, and the wedding hadn't taken long — certainly not long enough for Peyton to pick up any church lingo. The pastor hadn't said much outside the typical wedding litany — *We are gathered here in the presence of God and these witnesses* — so she hadn't gleaned a single thing that would help her interview Reverend Timothy Manning of the Kirkwood Fundamentalists.

At least she had an official appointment. She'd called his office early Tuesday morning and assured the secretary she wouldn't take up more than an hour of the pastor's time. The secretary had seemed reluctant at first, stating that Tuesday afternoon was booked solid and Wednesday mornings were the pastor's study time and he preferred to keep those hours uninterrupted. But when Peyton said she was coming all the way from Florida to interview him for a newspaper, the secretary had an abrupt change of heart.

Gripping her suitcase, Peyton ascended the concrete steps and entered the building through a pair of tall white doors. They opened into a thickly carpeted foyer, empty except for two tables, one on each side of the yawning space. An assortment of brochures covered the tables, and Peyton glanced at them. *Ten Reasons Why God Supports Conservative Politics*, *Ten Things God Cannot Do*, and *Order Your Timothy Manning Videotape Collection Today.*

Curious as to what God could not do, she opened the brochure and read:

God cannot lie. God cannot save one soul apart from faith and grace in Jesus Christ. God cannot turn away one soul that comes to Him according to His terms. God cannot bless men apart from faith. God cannot fail to answer prayer when unwavering faith is exercised. God cannot change His eternal plan. God cannot refuse to guide His children. God cannot deny His care for His own. God cannot refuse to forgive a child adopted through faith in Jesus Christ. God cannot break His promises.

"I've wandered into the Church of God Cannot," she murmured, replacing the brochure in its stack. Without any clear direction about where she should go, she opened another door — one of four in a soldierly row — and stepped into the sanctuary.

The cavernous space was dense with quiet and completely unpopulated. Subdued overhead lighting reflected off polished pews. A wide aisle cut through the center of the huge room, and television cameras stood at center, right, and left positions, while another perched on the edge of the right balcony. All were trained, even in repose, upon a monstrous podium at the center of the stage.

She was staring at the wooden pulpit, trying to envision what sort of man would stand behind it, when a voice spoke. "May I help you, ma'am?"

Turning, she saw an older man wearing a blue work shirt and dark pants. He carried a whisk broom and dustpan.

"I'm looking for the pastor's office."

The man's face crinkled into a smile. "That's in the building behind this one. Brother Tim should be in his office now. You follow that aisle" — he pointed toward the wide center pathway — "and go through the next set of doors. You'll see the office building right in front of you."

She smiled her thanks and followed the center aisle toward yet another squadron of doors. How many people actually attended this church? Common sense told her that the fifteen thousand on the membership rolls couldn't actually attend services each week — they'd need a stadium to hold that many. She was no expert on pew size, but this place looked big enough to hold about three thousand people, maybe more if people packed the pews.

After passing through yet another foyer and descending another set of concrete steps, she saw the office building — a squatter, less regal version of the sanctuary.

Fortunately, a series of signs gave directions to church offices, the nursery, and rest rooms. Following directions for the office, within five minutes she found herself in the carpeted sanctuary of Reverend Timothy Manning.

"You must be Peyton MacGruder." A genteel-looking, white-haired woman rose from behind the desk as Peyton stepped through the open doorway.

"I am."

"Pastor is expecting you. Let me tell him you've arrived."

Peyton would have enjoyed a moment to look around and gather impressions, but apparently her call had piqued Reverend Manning's curiosity. Less than ten seconds after the secretary disappeared into an inner office, she returned and gestured to Peyton. "Come right on in, Mrs. MacGruder. Pastor's waiting for you."

"It's Ms."

The secretary lifted a brow. "Whatever you say, ma'am."

Leaving her overnight case in the outer office, Peyton took nervous steps toward her first prospect.

Timothy Manning, as it turned out, looked nothing like the rotund television preacher of Peyton's imagination. The man who stood behind the desk wouldn't come close to six feet even in platform shoes, and his slender frame looked more suited for running than Bible thumping. He wore khaki slacks and a blue dress shirt, with a navy tie hanging loosely from his neck. He did wear his hair in the slicked-back style favored by media evangelists, but the brown eyes that smiled at her from behind a pair of contemporary eyeglasses seemed warm and friendly. And he was young — her age, or even younger.

After shaking his hand and murmuring her thanks for his willingness to see her, Peyton took the seat he offered. Remembering Mary Grace's admonition, she folded her hands in her lap and resisted the urge to fidget.

"First" — she looked at him while her foot began tapping out an insistent rhythm on the carpet — "let me share my condolences for the loss of your father. The crash of Flight 848 was a tragedy felt by millions. I was in Tampa when the plane went down, and the event left us all heartsick. I can only imagine what you must have felt when you learned you had lost your father."

Settling slowly back into his seat, Timothy Manning closed his eyes and nodded slowly. "Yes, it was a terrible thing." His voice came out hoarse, as if forced through a constricted throat. "My wife and children — well, we're still in a state of shock, if you want to know the truth. Pop was on his way back to his retirement place in St. Petersburg when it happened. We hadn't seen him in a while, but he was planning to visit us for my little daughter's birthday. Obviously" — his voice cracked — "he won't make it."

"Your daughter Karrie?" Peyton asked, grateful she'd studied the bio.

Manning nodded, then pulled a handkerchief from his coat pocket and dabbed at his eyes. His complexion had deepened to crimson, and Peyton realized he needed a moment to compose himself.

"I'm sorry." Peyton paused, giving him a chance to steady his voice. "The reason I'm here, Pastor Manning —"

He waved a feeble hand. "Please call me Brother Tim. Everybody here does."

"Thank you. As I was saying, I've come to see you because we have found a note that may have washed up from the wreckage of Flight 848. Before I tell you about it, however — and I really hate to ask this, but you know how things are — I must ask you to sign a confidentiality agreement. Basically, this document states that you won't discuss our conversation with anyone else for at least one week."

Reluctantly, she pulled a file from her backpack, then extracted a copy of the document. She stood and handed it to the pastor, who stared at it intently.

He cleared his throat. "I must say, I'm not used to this sort of thing. My word has always been my bond, good as gold."

"I know." She sat again, then clasped her hands. "But you know lawyers — and this is for your own protection. We want to keep the story under wraps until the issue is settled so you won't be badgered by other members of the media."

The confidentiality agreement had actually been Peyton's idea, a last-minute inspiration prompted by Julie St. Claire's phone call. Thousands of people now knew about the note's existence, and the only thing preventing other reporters from beating Peyton to the punch was the note's content. So long as the message remained hidden, Peyton's lead would be protected.

Pastor Manning's brow furrowed, but he plucked a pen from a cup on his desk and signed, as Peyton knew he would. When he finished, he slid the page back to her, then pressed his fingers to his smooth chin. "What makes you think this note might be for me?"

"Your name begins with *T.*" Peyton pulled a copy of the note from her file. "As you will see, the note is addressed to 'T.' The handwriting is a little shaky, but we're fairly sure the plane had developed problems by the time it was written, and the author must have been frightened. The message is simple, and I wondered — well, I thought it might have been intended for you."

Peyton passed the photocopy over the desk, and watched as the pastor took the paper and read it aloud: "T — I love you. All is forgiven. Dad."

He stared at it for a full moment, then shook his head and dropped the page to his desk. "This isn't from my father," he said, sliding the page toward Peyton. "I'd swear it on a stack of Bibles."

Peyton lifted the page and glanced at it, wondering if she could have missed something obvious. "But how can you be so sure?"

"Several things." He jerked his chin in the direction of the paper. "First of all, my father would never have signed a note *Dad*. He was *Pop* to everyone who knew him, including most of the folks in this church."

Peyton studied the signature. "You never called him *Dad?*"

"Of course I did, but not since my own

kids were born. He's *Pop-Pop* to them, *Pop* to me. Besides, the handwriting's not his. Not at all. He never wrote like that, not even when he broke his right hand and had to write like a lefty for eight weeks."

Peyton lowered the note, only half-aware that the rate of her toe-tapping had increased. "We really don't know what happened aboard Flight 848, Reverend Manning, and this note was scrawled under duress. The turbulence could have distorted his handwriting."

"There's something else." The pastor leaned back in his chair as a small smile lifted the corners of his mouth. "My father would never have written 'all is forgiven.' We were on good terms, he and I, with no outstanding debts. We were close and we stayed in touch. There was no reason for him to speak of forgiveness."

Glancing down, Peyton pressed her lips together. Perhaps Pastor Manning was right and perhaps he was wrong, but evidently he had no room for doubt.

One thing Timothy Manning cannot do: doubt his daddy.

She tried another approach. "Tell me about your father." She gave the pastor a confident smile, ready to sit back and wait for him to open like Mary Grace's hypothetical newspaper. "I'd like to mention him in my next column — without going into detail about the note, of course. I've been doing research on several of the crash victims."

"My father was a saint," Tim said, leaning on an arm of his leather chair. "He raised me and my sister, Victoria, on a shoestring budget and taught us the Bible every night before bed. He loved the Word of God, breathed it in and out. Vicki and I could recite Scripture forward and backward before we started school — I suppose I still can." He paused. " 'Earth and heaven the created God beginning the in.' Genesis 1:1, backward."

Peyton blinked. She wanted to remain silent, but Pastor Manning was waiting, one brow lifted, for a response.

"Oh. Well. I hope you didn't have to learn the entire Bible that way."

Manning laughed. "Of course not. Vicki and I did it as a joke."

"Even so, it must seem a terrible tragedy to lose such a creative father. I understand he was only in his early sixties."

"Ms. MacGruder, a long time ago I learned not to question God. He has His reasons, and all things happen for a purpose. Even when I can't see the rationale, God does. And that's good enough for me."

Silence, thick as cotton, wrapped around them as Peyton waited for another revelation. She was about to give up and ask another question when someone rapped on the door. Without being invited in, the secretary stepped into the room, her eyes wide. "There's a TV crew outside," she said, her hand pinching the ruffle at her throat. "They say they want to talk to you."

Pastor Tim's eyes narrowed slightly, then he looked at Peyton. "Some of your people?"

Peyton shook her head. "I came alone."

The secretary stepped forward, a business card between her fingers. "A woman gave me this — she said she wants to come in and do an on-camera interview."

The pastor scanned the card, then flipped it toward Peyton. "Ever heard of Julie St. Claire?"

Momentarily speechless, Peyton stared at the neat, white rectangle, then found her voice. "As a matter of fact, I have. She's with the World News Network . . . and I believe she's following this story." She blew out a breath. "I apologize, Reverend, for bringing this sort of attention to your neighborhood. I have no idea how they learned I was here —"

Undiluted laughter floated up from

Manning's throat. "Don't you worry about them. The camera guys are probably the regular locals, and I know 'em all." He pushed his chair back and stood, adjusting his tie. "We get a crowd of protestors here about every Sunday, and they draw the news guys like magnets. If it's not the femi-Nazis, it'll be the gay rights brigade or the pro-abortion folks." He chuckled as he walked forward and paused by the edge of his desk. "I've learned that if you stick your neck out, folks are happy to come along and take a whack at you. They want us to stay hidden in our pews, but we're American citizens, too, by heaven. And we have a right to tell folks how we believe Jesus would vote in the elections."

Peyton made a face. "Would Jesus vote? I thought He was a pacifist —"

"Of course He'd vote." Manning came out from behind the desk. "He was a responsible citizen, He paid taxes, and He said we ought to render unto Caesar the things that belong to Caesar. So until I reach the kingdom of heaven, I'm going to do my part to make sure Caesar's people are running things properly on earth."

He laughed again, and something in the sound told Peyton the interview had ended.

"Thank you, Reverend," she said, standing. "I appreciate your time. I'd also appreciate you remembering your promise of confidentiality. The reporter outside will want to know what we talked about, so this might be a good time for a case of selective amnesia."

He smiled, which sent a dimple winking in his cheek as he pulled a navy blazer from a coat rack and slipped it on. "Ms. MacGruder, have you ever known a preacher to lie?"

She laughed. "As a matter of fact —"

"Never mind, then." He took two steps forward, ushering her into the outer office where the secretary fidgeted behind the desk. "Rest easy. My pop didn't write your note, so I'll be praying that you deliver it to the right person. And as far as that crowd outside is concerned, you and I were in here chatting about the state of the world in general and nobody-else's-business in particular."

"Great." Peyton glanced around, hoping to spot some sign of a back door. "Any way I can get out of this place without having to run the gauntlet?"

"Afraid not. But if you come with me, everything will be fine." Manning's smile deepened. "You're not afraid of your own kind, are you?"

"No." The answer sounded more snappish than she'd intended. "I'm not afraid of anyone. But my being here attests to something I'd rather not make public yet."

"If they followed you here, looks like at least part of your secret is already public knowledge."

Realizing the truth in his statement, Peyton grimaced.

Julie St. Claire caught her breath when the door to the church building opened. Slipping from the passenger seat of the news truck, she straightened her skirt and nodded toward the camera operator. She'd already briefed the gawking yokel from KTVI on her plan — he was to pan the scene, then focus on the pastor, being certain to catch Manning's expression when she asked him about the note. What he said didn't matter, she could correct any missteps in a voice-over. The expression on his face, however, might be worth a thousand words.

She'd been lucky to convince the manager at the FOX station to send out a crew — only the thought of shared coverage in what she assured him would be a huge story had won his cooperation. Now a microwave truck with the Channel 2 logo growled in the parking lot, its engine running as the director whispered in her earpiece and a camera-carrying Jim Varney look-alike dogged her footsteps.

She walked toward the office doors with long, sure strides. "Pastor Manning," she called, noticing that two women accompanied the minister. The eldest was the flustered secretary she'd spoken to earlier, so the redhead at his side had to be Peyton MacGruder. The columnist was whispering to the pastor now, probably telling him to keep his mouth shut so she'd have an exclusive.

That frump-in-a-pantsuit didn't stand a chance.

"Pastor Manning!" Using her most charming voice, Julie called for the man's attention, but the pastor didn't look up. Though a pleasant smile remained on his face, he held his hands firmly clasped in front of him while he looked down and listened to Peyton MacGruder.

Julie narrowed her gaze and focused on the Tampa reporter. MacGruder's photo on the Web site hadn't done her justice. She wore a hairstyle and clothing suited to a forty-something career woman, but no wrinkles had yet appeared on her face, not even laugh lines at the corners of her eyes. The gold-red color of her hair hid any tell-tale streaks of gray, and the entire presentation wasn't as frumpish as Julie had first thought. MacGruder would have to lose twenty pounds, though, if she ever planned to do any on-camera work.

Tired of waiting, Julie moved closer, her heels scraping the asphalt parking lot. "Pastor Manning, Julie St. Claire here, from World Network News. We've heard rumors that you may have been made privy to information about Flight 848."

Timothy Manning finally turned, a look of well-mannered dislike crossing his face before he donned a saintly smile. "You've heard *rumors?*" He pronounced the word as if it were unfit for public consumption. "Well, Ms. St. Claire, I didn't know WNN came out to cover mere rumors. I thought you all were in the business of reporting facts."

She shot him a cold look, the lively twinkle in his eye fanning her irritation. "Pastor," she began again, "did Peyton MacGruder show you a note recovered from Flight 848?"

The pastor lifted a brow. "I beg your pardon, ma'am. Did we have an appointment for an interview?"

Julie didn't look, but she had the distinct impression Peyton MacGruder was grinning. "Excuse me, Pastor Manning," she said, struggling to maintain control. "Let me explain. We've reason to believe Ms. MacGruder" — she paused to nod at the columnist, hoping the cameraman would follow her cue — "brought you a note reportedly recovered from PanWorld Flight 848. It's public knowledge that Ms. MacGruder is trying to find a survivor for whom the note might have been intended —"

"I can assure you I have no note." The pastor lifted his palms to the camera, like a child displaying just-washed hands. "And I can also assure you that my father didn't pause to write me a note as his plane went down. My father, God bless him, was probably singing a hymn as the occupants of that plane went to their eternal destinations. He was as sure of heaven as if he'd already been there ten thousand years." He gave the camera a captivating smile. "Ms. Mac-Gruder's reasons for visiting our church are personal, and I'm sure you wouldn't want to pry."

Julie St. Claire couldn't believe her ears. She'd been professionally and courteously dismissed. From behind her, she heard the hayseed cameraman grunt while the director in the news van cursed softly in her ear. She dropped her microphone in resignation.

"All right. Off the record," she said dully, glaring at the man. "You're sure the note wasn't meant for you?" She transferred her gaze to the reporter. "You're sure?"

"The only thing I'm *not* sure of" — Peyton MacGruder's gaze was as frosty as her tone — "is how you learned about my trip. I thought I told you I didn't want the network's involvement in this story."

"The story doesn't belong to you alone." Julie folded her arms. "This is an American drama. It involves all of us."

Timothy Manning stepped forward, protectively placing himself in front of Peyton MacGruder. "Not now, it doesn't. Now, Miss St. Claire, I believe you and this crew are on private property. I'd like you to leave, as not to give passersby the idea something improper is occurring at our church."

Julie glared at him, primed and ready to give him her opinion about churches and ministers and all the improper things taking place in the name of God every week, then she bit her tongue. She could afford to give Peyton MacGruder a little leeway, at least for today. The woman hadn't had time to hear from her superiors, so she probably had no idea what awaited her in Tampa.

"We're leaving now." Julie flashed a smile at the minister, then twiddled her fingers in the reporter's direction. "I'm sure I'll see you again, Ms. MacGruder. Have a nice flight home."

Leaving the pastor and the two women standing atop the church steps like a trio of stooges, Julie climbed into the news van and told the driver to shove off.

"Interesting morning, right, Pastor?"

Tim smiled at his secretary and nodded his agreement. "One for the books, Eunice. Let's see if we can keep things quiet around here for a couple of hours, all right? I really do need to prepare for prayer meeting tonight."

"Not to worry, I'll take care of everything."

Stepping around her desk, Tim went into his office and closed the door, then leaned against it. The morning's encounter had been interesting — it wasn't every day that reporters and TV crews showed up at the church without his having done something extraordinary to draw them. And while Peyton MacGruder seemed nice enough, that other one — St. Claire? — seemed like a regular fireball. Trouble with a capital *T,* for sure.

Shaking his head, he moved toward his

desk. St. Claire was lucky he liked and tolerated people, or he might have been tempted
to tell her to take a long walk off a short pier.
He knew he could never say that — or even
admit that's how he felt. People were always
surprised to discover that a minister's
thought processes mirrored most other people's — just because a person was saved and
called to ministry didn't mean he wasn't
flesh like everyone else. And sometimes the
flesh could get a little cramped under the
mantle of holiness everyone expected him
to wear.

He settled at the desk, pulled out a blank
tablet of paper, and opened his Bible to the
book of Mark. He'd been planning to preach
on hypocrisy, but as his eyes drifted over the
passage, a pair of verses seemed to rise up
before him like an accusing finger:

> *But you say it is all right for people to say
> to their parents, "Sorry, I can't help you.
> For I have vowed to give to God what I
> could have given to you." You let them
> disregard their needy parents.*

He slammed the Bible shut. He had told
Peyton MacGruder the entire truth, plus
he'd managed to keep his cool with the St.
Claire woman, no easy task. Still . . . perhaps

he should have kept a copy of the note on the off chance that his father *did* write it.

He couldn't have. He wouldn't have. Note-writing wasn't Pop's style. And he knew he didn't have to settle anything with Tim; they were on good terms. His father had known for years that Tim loved people and had given his life to the ministry.

Why, Pop sat on the front row when they held the dedication service of their new building! The TV cameras had picked up a great shot of him waving to the television audience the first Sunday they aired a worship service. People wanted to see that a pastor loved his daddy . . . and that his daddy loved him.

Swallowing hard, Tim swiveled his chair to face the window. He had loved his father, truly he had. He couldn't help that he hadn't seen the man in, what, three years? It didn't seem that long, but the last time they were together was right after he finished his sermon series on seed planting and faith reaping. They'd planted a few seeds for Pop in Florida, hoping he'd reap a few new friends down there. St. Louis was too hard on him in the wintertime, and Tim knew Pop missed Mama something terrible. A sunny retirement community was just what he needed.

"Yes sir, just what he needed." Tim folded his hands across his belt and stared out the window at the huge cross in the parking lot. Searchlights lit it at night, beaming the way to the cross to anyone who took the time to look up.

His dad had never seen the cross; they'd erected it last year. But he'd heard about it and he was proud of it, proud of everything Tim had accomplished. And it wasn't as if Tim forgot about his father — his wife made sure cards and letters and the kids' school pictures flowed to Florida like water. Tim knew for a fact that Pop watched his son on TV every Sunday morning.

He'd probably watched the program even at Vicki's house, where he'd been visiting before he boarded Flight 848. That niggling fact was enough to assure Tim that the burning rock of guilt in his gut wasn't going to dissolve. Since Pop had just come from seeing his daughter, maybe he was thinking of his son when the plane went down. And if he had been, did that mean Tim had done something to hurt him?

Surely not. His dad was nothing if not outspoken. He would have said something. He was always closer to Vicki than to Tim, always visiting her, quick to fly up every time she gave him a call. But she was only a housewife; she didn't pastor a fifteen-thousand-member church. She had time for that sort of socializing, which was why she'd gone to Tampa to handle the funeral and all the arrangements. Tim would have gone, but he couldn't get away. And why would he need to? His father was gone, and it was too late to change anything.

Too late. Those had to be the saddest two words in the English language.

Tim turned slowly and looked at the closed Bible on his desk. He hadn't disregarded his parent. He'd treated his father with love and respect.

"And Dad knew I loved him," he whispered. "As God is my witness, he knew."

Leaning forward, he propped his head on his hand and stared at the blank page before him. "Lord, I hope he knew."

Peyton fastened her lap belt, flashed an *excuse-me* smile at the man in the seat next to her, then leaned down to push his carry-on luggage out of her personal space. Honestly, ever since the invention of wheeled luggage, people behaved as though they had inherited an inalienable right to carry every stitch of their personal belongings aboard the plane. Peyton's neighbor, who had conveniently shielded himself behind the latest

Grisham novel, had carried on a camera case, an attaché, and a duffel bag the size of Texas. The duffel bag crowded Peyton's feet even now. The gate attendant must have been asleep at her post to let this guy board with a body bag.

Peyton scanned the aisle, hoping to catch the steward's attention, but the young man apparently had other things on his mind. He walked past her, his lips moving silently, either counting heads or praying for a better job.

For his sake, Peyton hoped it was the latter.

Sighing, she blew her bangs out of her eyes, then bent to pull her backpack from the space beneath the seat in front of her. The black duffel intruded, snagging the corner of her case, and she kicked at it, half-hoping she'd ejected the top of her seatmate's toothpaste. Would serve him right to find Colgate smeared all over his underwear when he reached his final destination.

After pulling out her laptop, she stuffed her backpack beneath the seat again, then slowly exhaled. With a bit of luck, she wouldn't have to move for a couple of hours. She could remain still and gather her thoughts. No sense in powering up the computer until they were airborne. No sense in even lowering a seat tray until then.

While she waited for the attendants to run through their preflight safety routine, she closed her eyes, grateful for a moment of silence. The airport check-in counter had been a zoo. She'd narrowly avoided being shoved in an altercation between two irate passengers, then she'd nearly missed her flight. But here she was, safely buckled in, and soon she'd be airborne and ready to write.

Until then, she needed to consider the implications of Julie St. Claire's appearance at the church. How had St. Claire discovered the pastor's identity? The knowledge could only have come from someone at the *Times*, and King and Mandi were the only two people who knew about Manning.

So — Peyton braced herself as the plane began to roar down the runway — who could have passed Timothy Manning's name to Julie St. Claire?

The corner of her mouth dipped as the plane lifted. Would Nora have tipped WNN about Peyton's visit? Not likely. She didn't even know the television reporter, and Peyton doubted Nora cared much for the World News Network. Born and bred to the presses, Nora was constantly moaning that television news would spell death for the daily newspaper and American literacy unless something changed. Besides, Nora didn't know about Timothy Manning. Peyton had sent her an e-mail about the necessity of a trip to St. Louis, but she felt sure she hadn't mentioned the pastor's name.

Could King . . . ? She shook off the unthinkable. He had too much respect for the journalist's code of ethics — he'd never give away another writer's contacts. He wouldn't reveal his own anonymous sources, not even when pushed.

Peyton sighed as she considered the obvious. Mandi had practically fizzed with excitement when Julie St. Claire telephoned. Perhaps St. Claire had called again, and Mandi had picked up the phone while Peyton was out —

I faxed it ten minutes ago, along with an extra copy for you-know-who . . .

The memory of Mandi's parting comment brought a twisted smile to Peyton's face. The girl had to be the weak link. St. Claire, that charming little snake in the grass, had bewitched the naive intern.

Peyton clutched the armrest as the jet's wheels clunked back into the well. Good grief, why was she so jumpy? She'd flown dozens of times and never been bothered by that particular noise, but that clunk had seemed ten times louder than usual. Was she sitting right above the well? Or had something come loose in the cargo bay?

She turned her head, searching for signs of concern among the flight attendants, but the only stewardess she could see was strapped into her jump seat and idly examining her manicure.

Peyton turned back to face the front of the plane. Her fears were ridiculous. Her nerves were on edge because she was working on a story about a plane crash; her heart pounding only because this plane would probably take the same approach Flight 848 took two weeks ago . . .

She drew a slow breath, alarmed to hear the sound amplified in her own ears. She felt as though she had shrunk somehow, withdrawn to a place deep inside her body, and the mechanism that kept her lungs pumping air had grown irregular and jerky.

The bell chimed; the seatbelt sign blinked off. From the back of the plane Peyton heard the metallic click of the stewardess's lap belt, in a moment she'd be serving drinks and peanuts. Situation normal, time to relax.

Across the aisle, a mother allowed her toddler to kneel in the seat and press her hands to the window. "Oh, clouds!" the little girl squealed. "Wanna go outside."

"No, honey." The mother ran her fingertips through the girl's golden curls. "You can't go outside. Not now."

"Wanna play in dem." The toddler pressed a wet fingertip to the window. "Wanna play! Go outside!"

"You can't play in the clouds." The mother's tolerant smile faded as the girl began to wail in earnest. "Shh, Hillary, not so loud. You'll bother the other people."

Peyton closed her eyes as the child began to scream. The high-pitched sound would have been loud under normal circumstances, but now, with Peyton's strained nerves . . .

Fingers trembling, she reached up and pressed the attendant call button. The waiting seconds stretched into moments woven of eternity, then, when Peyton's breathing seemed little more than sporadic gasps, a slender blonde stewardess appeared at her elbow. "May I help you?"

I-want-off-I-need-to-leave-I-have-to-escape-let-me-out!

By some miracle of will, Peyton's rational brain overpowered the screaming voice of instinct. "Water, please," she whispered in a voice she barely recognized as her own.

"And could you get the kid some pretzels or something?"

A moment later the stewardess returned with a cup of water, which Peyton hastily threw back, then closed her eyes as the stewardess turned to the mother and toddler.

She'd planned to write on the plane, but she couldn't. Not next to a screaming baby.

In an instant of soul-searing reality, she knew she'd be lucky to make it home with her wits intact.

She'd been home — where all seemed blessedly ordinary — for only ten minutes when the doorbell rang. She laughed with relief when she saw King standing on her front porch, a bag of Chinese takeout in his hand.

"Thought you might be hungry," he said, not waiting for an invitation to enter. "The airlines don't want to feed people these days, have you noticed?"

"I have." She closed the door behind him, suddenly grateful for what had become a blessedly low-maintenance friendship. She kicked off her shoes by the door, then followed him into the kitchen, the cats tagging along at her heels.

"How was St. Louis?" he asked, unpacking the bag at the table. The scents of fried rice, chicken, and spices tinged the air.

"Fine." She sniffed appreciatively. "Smells good. Kung Pao chicken?"

"Spicy and crunchy is the only way to go." He poured a smaller bag of accouterments — chopsticks, napkins, and squeeze bags of duck sauce — onto her small table, then took a seat and looked up at her. "So? Was this guy the one you're looking for?"

"Not according to him." Turning, she pulled two plates from her cabinet. "He gave me a list of reasons why his father wouldn't have — *couldn't* have — written the note. It wasn't his handwriting, wasn't his style. Most of all, he kept insisting there was nothing wrong between them — nothing that deserved forgiveness, anyway."

"Did you believe him?"

She paused, a plate in each hand. "At first — yes, I did. He seemed . . . quite confident. The man could sell a prison term as a time share; he's that persuasive."

King's eyes glinted below his dark brows. "But now?"

Shrugging, she set the plates on the table. "I don't know. Can anyone really be certain about other people? I mean, we think we know someone, but every time John Doe is arrested and found guilty of a crime, you can find half a dozen relatives who will swear he could *never* have committed the dirty deed." She opened a drawer, pulled out a spoon, and plunged it into the open container of rice. "I mean — I know you reasonably well, right? When you leave here tonight, I'm fairly sure you're going to go home, get ready for bed, and maybe watch a little ESPN before you fall asleep. But how can I be certain? Maybe you have a secret life I know nothing about."

King's smile deepened into laughter. "Now that you mention it, I am moonlighting at a second job. But I'm out of costume at the moment; my tights and cape need mending."

Peyton lifted a brow. "Let me guess — is there a big *S* on the back of this cape?"

King shook his head. "It's a *K*. For Kingman. I go out every night and search for hungry damsels in distress — damsels who like Chinese, that is."

"Very funny." Peyton pushed Samson off her chair, then sat down and reached for a spoon, wondering what King meant by that crack. He couldn't have known about her irrational attack of nerves on the plane . . . and she wasn't about to tell him.

Silence fell over the kitchen as they piled their plates with rice and chicken. Peyton considered asking whether King had spoken to Julie St. Claire, then realized Mandi had to be the weak link.

She reached for a fork.

"Uh-uh." King picked up a pair of chopsticks and waved them before her eyes. "When eating Chinese, you've got to use these."

"I can't."

"You can. You've probably never tried."

"I've tried, and it's silly, especially when there's a perfectly functional fork at hand."

"If the vast majority of people in the world can eat with these, so can you."

Scowling, she slipped the wooden sticks out of the paper wrapper, then unsnapped them. "Real expensive pair of utensils."

"Disposable," King said, chasing a slippery hunk of chicken around his plate with his chopsticks. "And that reminds me, Curtis DiSalvo came out to mingle with the troops today. He was looking for you."

Peyton swallowed hard. "Really?"

King nodded, then stuffed in another mouthful. She waited while he chewed, but her patience, like her energy, had nearly evaporated. "What on earth did he want with me?"

King lowered his chopsticks. "He said he wanted to congratulate you. Your columns about the note have been a hit. Apparently his office has been fielding calls — some from New York."

Peyton groaned. "I'm afraid I know about New York," she said, her voice dull. "Julie St. Claire and a news crew showed up at the church as I was leaving. They wanted to interview the pastor, but he refused."

King's forehead creased in concern. "That's bad. You've got some real momentum going, not to mention genuine public interest —"

"And if she steals my thunder, I'm sunk." Peyton bit her lip, thinking. "But she doesn't know the names of our other two candidates, and I'm going to talk to Mandi about keeping her mouth shut. I also asked the pastor to sign a confidentiality agreement."

"Did he?"

"Yes. And he says he's a man of his word. I think I can trust him. And if I can't, I can always threaten to sue."

"You'd sue a preacher?"

"Probably not. *Threaten* is the operative word."

King picked up the chopsticks and began to eat again, but a distant expression filled his eyes. After a moment of silence, he looked at her and lifted a dark brow. "You're building something here, MacGruder, and intensity is going to be the key to success. You can't afford to let a television reporter, or *any* reporter for that matter, take the lead. If someone else gets ahead of you, you've lost your edge. Columns run on a fast track, but television news is even faster."

"Tell me something I don't know." Peyton pounded a peanut with her chopstick and felt the satisfying crunch as it broke into three pieces.

Ten

Thursday, June 28

After a good night's sleep, Peyton felt better than she imagined possible. Rather than be distracted by curious coworkers at the office, most of whom had to know she'd begun the first leg of her search, she decided to write the Manning column at home. Samson and Elijah were just as curious as her coworkers, but they were definitely less vocal.

Given Reverend Manning's conviction that his father could not have written the note, she refrained from naming him or his church, identifying her first prospect only as "a successful minister in a Midamerican city." By keeping his identity a secret, she would not only indemnify the paper from a possible lawsuit (she could just see the headlines: *"Manning v. Tampa Times —* Television Ministry Contributions Drop Off When Pastor Denies the Note of Flight 848), but she'd also prevent any other sharp-eyed reporters from discovering the link her prospects shared.

She worked from 8:00 until 11:00 a.m., stopping only for a cup of coffee and a quick peek at the paper, then plugged her laptop into the telephone extension and clicked the send icon.

Done.

Peyton leaned back in her chair, her concentration dissipating in a mist of fatigue. Odd, how this story had drained her. She usually felt like celebrating in the hour when she filed a column; today she felt more like crawling into bed for a catnap.

Leaving her desk, Peyton decided to obey her feline instincts.

Eleven

Friday, June 29

Not My Pop
By Peyton MacGruder
"The Heart Healer" is a regular feature
of the *Tampa Times*

Dear Readers:
    I have just returned from a typical
Midamerican town, complete with neat
houses, white picket fences, and welcome mats before the front doors. The
journey, however, took me not to a
house, but to a church. It's an unusual
church by most standards, with a membership larger than many American
towns. But this institution is home to the
man who was my first prospect to receive
the note: a successful pastor I'll call Jim.
    Jim is an attractive fellow — in his
early forties, slim, and intellectual-
looking. Our interview was pleasant, and
I came away impressed with his abilities

and his honesty. As a minister, I'm sure he often deals with people who are overwhelmed by sorrow, perhaps that's why he seemed to handle his own grief with dignity and reserve.

But after I showed Jim a copy of the note, it took only a moment for him to decide it could not have been written by his father. The handwriting was not familiar, he told me, and he usually referred to his father as "Pop," not "Dad." His most important reason for refusing the note was simple: though separated by many miles, apparently this father and son remained close, so his father didn't need to pen a final farewell. Though I don't want to reveal the note's message until I have found its rightful owner, I can say the writer offered forgiveness — and forgiveness, Jim told me, would have been unnecessary.

Did I believe Jim's assertion? Wholeheartedly, while I listened to him. But now, as I reflect upon the things he told me, I wonder if any of us can be completely certain we know what our loved ones really think of us. If you have not spoken to a parent in days or weeks or months, how can you possibly know what they are thinking and feeling? If you

231

have not called or written, how can they know they are in your thoughts?

Jim admitted he had not seen his father in some time. He assured me, however, that they were close. But how close were they? If the situation were reversed, and Jim had written a note on a faltering flight, would his father have been as quick to deny that Jim could have written it?

Difficult questions, I know. And there are no definite answers.

Even so, Jim has denied the note, and I have no choice but to continue my search. My next journey will take me to see a young woman. Let's hope hers is the heart in search of a healing touch.

It didn't take Peyton long to discover that she'd become a minor celebrity at the doughnut shop. She had no sooner taken her usual seat and ordered her coffee and cruller when two of the regulars moved to the empty stools at her right and left.

"Read your column this morning," one man said, his button brown eyes alert and friendly. "Why'd you think the note mighta belonged to the preacher fellow?"

She shrugged. "There's a clue. It's a little one, but it seemed to point toward the minister."

"So how do you know it wasn't him?" This from a young woman in a booth.

Peyton turned. The woman wore cotton slacks and a printed tunic top, the uniform of those who worked at the nearby doctors' offices. "I don't know for certain," Peyton answered, smiling. "All I know is *he's* sure the note wasn't meant for him. You read his reasons in the paper."

"What are you going to do," a voice boomed from the far side of the counter, "if nobody claims that note?"

Peyton turned slowly. Two men sat at the end of the counter, executives, from the tailored and pressed look of them. As Peyton considered her reply, she realized every eye in the restaurant had turned toward her, including Erma's. The waitress stood with the coffeepot in one hand, her head cocked in Peyton's direction.

She could have heard a frog hiccup in the silence.

"I don't know what I'll do if no one claims it," she finally said, looking around the restaurant. "I suppose I'll feel regret, because a significant gift will have been unclaimed."

When Peyton reached the office, Mandi stood from behind her typing table desk and handed her a stack of mail. "Curtis DiSalvo was asking for you the other day," she said, her eyes bright with interest. "The envelope on top is from him."

"Really?" Peyton dropped her backpack beside her desk and wished, not for the first time, that she had a door she could close and lock — even a cubicle would be nice. Mandi wasn't bold enough to openly eavesdrop, but secrets were nearly impossible to safeguard in the newsroom.

She ripped open the top envelope, addressed only with her name. It contained a single typed request — an order? — for her to appear in DiSalvo's office at 11:00 a.m. on Friday. Today.

"Mandi," she called, dropping the note to her desk, "I need to warn you about something. From now on, don't mention any of our prospects by name, not even on the phone. Let's call them prospects one, two, and three, okay? Delete any files on your computer containing their names, or at least make sure your files are password protected. And don't send any e-mails with their names. Got it?"

Concern and confusion flitted through the girl's wide eyes. "All right — but why?"

Perching on the edge of her desk, Peyton folded her arms. "Yesterday Julie St. Claire showed up at the church as I was leaving. Somehow she learned where I would be, who I would interview, and when I would arrive." Her mouth twisted. "Shoot, she probably had a private jet whisk her into town just in time. She has unfair advantages, so let's not give her any more help, okay?"

Misery darkened Mandi's face. "I — I thought — she told me you were working together."

Peyton leaned closer. "I'm sure she did, but I'd sooner work with Captain Kangaroo. Remember this, Mandi, everyone else, especially TV reporters, is the competition. The *enemy*. We don't want to help them any more than we have to. You got it?"

Mandi nodded, her brows drawing together in an agonized expression.

"Okay." Peyton smiled. "So how are we coming with number two? Any luck on finding out where the woman lives?"

"I have a call in to the publicist at her record company," Mandi whispered, her eyes shifting from left to right as if she suspected spies behind every desk. "I should hear from him this morning. Apparently this woman is a recluse and really hard to reach."

Peyton nodded. "Okay. Just consider this — whenever you're tempted to think somebody is too important or too out of the mainstream to reach, remember that nearly everybody has a telephone. The trick is finding the number. Oh — and try to find her mother. Most people who are famous have a mother who's not, and all mamas love to talk about their kids."

"I'll remember." Mandi's eyes shone with relief. "Um — don't forget your other mail. There was an interesting-looking package with no return address —"

"Not a letter bomb, I hope," Peyton joked, turning. A yellow padded envelope rested at the bottom of the stack on her desk, and it felt heavy when she pulled it out. Though she suspected it was a book from a local author hoping for a plug, she couldn't help feeling a prickle of curiosity as she weighed the package on her palm. No — too light and too large for a book.

Mandi leaned forward, her elbows on her knees and her face alight with curiosity.

"You know, Mandi," Peyton said, ripping the edge of the envelope. "You're not my secretary. I don't expect you to gather my mail every day."

"It's no trouble."

A piece of torn paper fell to the floor. Mandi bent to pick it up while Peyton pulled a picture frame out of the envelope. The plain wooden frame contained an enlarged photograph of her father and Kathy with their youngest daughter, who wore a cap and gown. The other five children were clustered around the happy trio, like overdone decorations on a birthday cake.

She exhaled slowly, then dropped the frame to her desk. The resulting clatter made Mandi lift her head. "What is it? Something bad?"

"Just a picture." Peyton picked up the rest of the mail, shuffling through the inevitable junk mail in search of letters from readers. There were at least a dozen in this batch, not bad when you considered that most people sent e-mails these days.

"What a nice family." Mandi lifted the frame. "Why — this girl looks like you! How funny! Do many of your fans send you look-alike pictures?"

"They're not fans." Peyton tossed the junk mail into the steel trash can behind her desk, then sat down to open her reader letters.

"Then who —"

"The man's my father; the wife and kids are his family."

Mandi's lips parted as if she would say something else, then her gaze shifted and caught Peyton's warning look. She clapped her mouth shut, the words seeming to die in her throat, then placed the picture back on the desk.

Peyton waited until Mandi had busied herself at her typing table, then she shoved the remaining letters aside and stared at the picture. Did she really look like her half sister? The girl had hair of a reddish cast and perhaps the nose was shaped like Peyton's, but the proud graduate definitely had her mother's eyes. Maybe there was a slight resemblance . . . well, obviously there had to be, or Mandi wouldn't have said anything.

Peyton squinted, trying to remember which name belonged to the youngest girl, then smiled as she remembered — *Erin*. She tapped the photograph with a fingernail, then turned back to her work, a half-smile tugging at the corner of her mouth.

Tampa Times publisher and president Curtis DiSalvo's office was located on the top floor of the *Times* building, a hallowed space Peyton rarely visited. Every nerve stood at attention as she stepped out of the elevator, and when she identified herself to the receptionist, the woman pointed toward a hallway and a pair of oak doors. "They're all in there waiting for you," she said, flashing an *I'm-glad-I'm-not-you* smile.

"They?" Peyton smoothed her slacks. "I thought my appointment was with Mr. DiSalvo."

The woman picked up a list. "A planeload of people came in from New York this morning, but the only one I'd worry about is Adam Howard." Leaning forward, she lowered her voice. "I think he owns most of the planet."

Peyton felt a chill pass down her spine. "I've heard that."

She stood still for a moment, resisting the urge to bolt for the elevators, then lifted her chin and walked toward the conference room. Perhaps her fears were groundless. Perhaps this meeting would result in good news. In an hour she might laugh at the memory of her tense nerves.

She opened one of the doors and walked into the cavernous room, simultaneously interrupting several conversations. A few of the men sitting around the elongated oak table stood when she appeared, buttoning coats and smiling as she approached.

Feeling underdressed in her blouse and rayon slacks, she moved forward on legs that felt about as sturdy as spaghetti noodles.

"Peyton MacGruder, I presume." The man at the head of the table stepped out and walked toward her. "I'm Adam Howard, and it's a *real* pleasure to meet the woman who has the entire nation talking."

"The entire nation?" Peyton smiled, feeling her way.

Howard laughed. "Your search is the talk of every news broadcast from here to Hawaii."

"I'm afraid I don't watch much television."

As he took her hand, Peyton tipped her head back and took the man's measure. Adam Howard was a distinguished-looking fellow, far from elderly despite his graying hair, glasses, and the slight spare tire that pushed at the front of his suit. His hand encased hers like a well-worn catcher's mitt.

"I can't believe you didn't know you have the world's attention," Howard said, grinning over his shoulder at the other people around the table.

"I really don't see how that's possible." She forced a smile. "The circulation of our paper is only —"

"The Web site featuring your column is averaging sixty thousand hits an hour," Curtis DiSalvo said, stepping forward. Wide-shouldered and athletic-looking in his dress shirt, the publisher seemed taller than Peyton remembered. His square jaw tensed visibly as he shook her hand, and Peyton suspected he wasn't enjoying Adam Howard's visit as much as he pretended.

"We've been printing extra copies on the days your column runs," he explained, releasing her hand. "Interest is so great, Peyton, that Mr. Howard has come down to see how we can do a better job of broadcasting your search. We want the world to know about the Heart Healer's quest."

Peyton looked around the room. She recognized Nora Chilton and a few faces from the marketing and sales departments, but at least half a dozen people were complete strangers. Television executives, probably, or worker bees from Adam Howard's media hive. Most of the newcomers were grinning at her, while Nora sat silently, her head inclined toward a sheet of paper on the table.

"Please, Ms. MacGruder" — Adam Howard gestured to an empty chair next to Nora — "join us. We're anxious to have your input."

They wanted her "input" on her own series? Instantly on guard, Peyton accepted the proffered seat, crossed her legs, and stared at the faces around the table. Adam Howard settled into his chair, unbuttoned his coat, and pulled his tie — red silk, from the look of it — free from the tailored suit. "I've read every single column in this series," he began, his dark, earnest eyes seeking hers. "And I must say, I admire your work and your insight tremendously. I admire it so much, in fact, that I'm prepared to offer you a contract with my syndicate, Howard Features."

He gestured toward another man at the table, a narrow-faced fellow who peered intently at Peyton from behind wire-rimmed glasses. "Frank Myers is president of Howard Features, and he's got seven hundred papers standing by to shift their layouts to find space for 'The Heart Healer.' That's — what is that, Frank, in terms of revenue for Ms. MacGruder?"

The aforementioned Frank spoke in a voice as narrow as his face: "Nearly ten thousand dollars a week in writer's fees," he said, unsmiling. "Most writers take years to reach that level."

"Peyton, we want to take you to that level now." Adam Howard gave her a bland smile. "We can have your column in seven hundred different papers on Sunday morning. We'll bring the readers up to speed, maybe with a compilation of the past three columns, and let them ride out the rest of the search with you." He dropped his fist to the table with a gentle thump. "How's that sound?"

"It sounds incredible." She squinted in Howard's direction. "How will this syndicate work, exactly?"

"Through technology." Howard spoke with quiet firmness. "You submit your story to your editor as always, but she'll send it to our syndicate electronically. In the click of a button, your column will appear in papers throughout the country, including your own *Tampa Times*."

"But . . . the summation." Peyton struggled to maintain an even tone. "Who's going to put that together?"

"You are." An expression of satisfaction glimmered in his eyes. "I hear you're as dependable as the sunrise. We're not at all worried about you pulling this off."

Peyton's stomach tightened as every eye turned in her direction. Syndication was every columnist's dream — it granted a writer independence and multiplied his earnings exponentially. As a syndicated columnist, she would still work for the *Times*, but she'd expand her audience and her income beyond her wildest imaginings. The larger syndicates also promoted their writers, and promotion built a writer's name recognition, which widened the circle of influence even further.

She had thought the note might be a key to open that door, but this seemed . . . too easy.

"Syndication sounds wonderful," she

began, choosing her words carefully, "but I've got to wonder, Mr. Howard — what's the catch?" She caught Nora's eye. "I know I'm on to a hot story, and my last couple of columns are probably among the best I've ever done, but what will you expect from me after the note story is finished? I really don't think I'm at the level of Ellen Goodman or Dave Barry."

A spark lit Nora's eye — agreement? — then Adam Howard turned to DiSalvo and chuckled. "You've got one forthright gal here, Curt." He laughed again. "One sharp cookie."

Peyton said nothing, but waited until the wave of nervous laughter had subsided.

"Actually, there is something we'd like from you." Howard met her gaze again. "This thing will only go so far via the printed press. Not many people today even read a newspaper, so if we're going to broadcast this incredible story, we're going to have to use companion media. Your people are already using the Net, but even that's limited —"

"You want to put this story on television," Peyton interrupted. She forced a polite smile. "And I'll bet you want it to be a WNN report featuring Julie St. Claire."

She didn't think she had the power to astound Adam Howard, but apparently she did. For an instant his face went blank with shock, then a tide of red flooded his cheeks. Peyton began tapping her toe, a little unnerved by the sudden change in the man. Julie St. Claire's involvement was a given, considering how she'd shown up in St. Louis. So why was Adam Howard blushing?

After a single moment of deafening silence, the CEO of Howard Media & Entertainment coughed a laugh. "I thought you said you never watched TV! But how else would you know Julie St. Claire is one of our best people?"

"I watched her work during the aftermath of the crash." Peyton lifted one shoulder in a shrug. "She was good . . . and she's aggressive."

Howard thumped the table again. "There you have it. Of course we want to put her on the story. We think she'd be great — working alongside you, of course."

"She's already on the story." Peyton shifted her gaze and caught DiSalvo's eye. "I met her in St. Louis — apparently she knew where I was going and who I planned to interview."

Howard spread his hands. "Well, that's proof of her competence, isn't it? What we need to do is share and share alike around here. This story is too big for a single paper; it's too big even for our features syndicate. We'll let Ms. MacGruder keep writing her column, but we need to start making plans for a television special to broadcast the outcome."

He spoke as if the matter rested solely in this ad hoc committee's hands, then he turned to Peyton. "I know you reporters tend to think of stories in proprietary terms. I also know you protect your leads like dogs guarding a chicken bone, but this story's bigger than a simple column, Peyton. Share it with us, and we'll take you to the highest level."

Peyton gripped the armrest on the leather chair as the room began to spin. Howard was right on all counts. Technically, the story was hers and hers alone to follow, but he was offering so much —

"We'll have to set up certain parameters," she said, finding her voice. "First, you may be right about this story being too big for a column, but it began as a column, and I want to be fair with my readers. They are unraveling this mystery with me, so they can't hear about the story's conclusion before they've had an opportunity to read it in 'The Heart Healer.' "

Howard flung up his hands in a *don't*

shoot pose. "No problem. We'll plan to air our special the same day you conclude your series. When will that be?"

"July fourth," she whispered.

Howard picked up a pencil and scribbled the date on a tablet, as did all his lackeys. "That's good. We'll make our employees sign an agreement not to breathe a word before then." He winked at Peyton. "If those people at CBS can keep secrets about who won that survive-on-a-deserted-island show, we can do even better."

"My column goes first," she said, holding him in a direct gaze. "The TV show has to air *after* my series finishes — the next day, I think. Not everyone reads the paper first thing in the morning."

Howard shook his head. "No can do — that's too much lead time, and we'll look foolish covering day-old news. Tell you what, we'll compromise. Our TV special will air during prime time on July fourth. That gives your readers almost an entire day to read the scoop, and we'll capture the evening audience. Sound fair?"

Peyton nodded wordlessly.

Howard scribbled something else on his notepad. "In the meantime, our people will be working in the background and beside you, recording video footage and editing it in New York. And you can trust me — not a single bit of news will leak until after you've made the announcement in your column."

"Nobody works beside me." Her abrupt tone made a dozen heads jerk upright. Glancing around the table, Peyton explained: "These interviews aren't exactly comfortable for me or my subjects. The first one went well, but I don't know what I'm going to encounter from this point on. So no cameras go with me, nobody goes along for the interview. You can follow behind me, but I do the interviews alone."

Adam Howard's jaw jutted forward. For a moment she thought he might object, then he relaxed and lifted a hand. "Okay. We'll send Julie in for follow-ups. I think she'd prefer that anyway." He looked around the table. "Anyone else have any questions for Ms. MacGruder?" When no one spoke, he turned to Peyton. "Anything else you want to know before we settle this?"

Peyton sat silently, examining the situation from various perspectives. Why not accept their offer? Their work shouldn't affect her column. A television special would reach far more people than even a syndicated column, and her readers would probably enjoy reliving the experience in a televised special. She looked at DiSalvo for guidance, but he wore a blank expression. Nora Chilton, on the other hand, looked faintly resentful.

"I'd like to take a little walk to think this through," she said, leaning forward. "Anybody mind if I take five minutes?"

DiSalvo glanced at Howard, who only shrugged.

"You go right ahead, Peyton," DiSalvo said, nodding. "Let us work out the details in the deal. If the *Times* is going to share you with seven hundred other papers, we're going to want to look at this syndication contract."

Peyton breathed easier out in the hall. She walked to the ladies' room — white marble, no less, from the floor to the countertops — then leaned on the counter and stared at her reflection in the huge mirror. Her wide eyes dominated a face that had grown wider with age — and a few extra pounds. Tufts of hair jutted from her head like random solar flares. Her complexion was far too pale for a native Floridian's.

No wonder Julie St. Claire didn't want her on television.

She wasn't cut from the same cloth as these television people, but when else would she walk into a deal like this one? Through a quirk of destiny, she had been handed a story with amazing appeal. Everyone saw the potential, and she wasn't surprised everybody wanted to cash in on it.

Why not accept this offer? She wasn't doing anything unethical or divulging any secrets. If any of the upcoming subjects asked to remain anonymous, she'd promise to keep their identities hidden. The TV people would have to make and keep their own promises, but she'd seen enough blacked-out interviews to know anonymity shouldn't be a problem.

If she joined the team, she wouldn't have to worry about Julie St. Claire rushing ahead of the story. This might be the perfect way to cage that eager beaver until Peyton had finished the series. So why not sign on and deliver the goods?

If she had goods to deliver. She glanced at her watch. Time was slipping away, and she still had to arrange an interview with Taylor Crowe. If she couldn't do that, maybe there was no point in continuing the discussion.

She walked to the receptionist's desk, asked to borrow the phone, then punched in Mandi's extension. "Any luck on finding prospect number two?"

Mandi groaned. "Yes, unfortunately. I did what you said and found her mother, who was thrilled to tell me where her daughter lives. She wouldn't give me the phone number."

"As long as you have an address, that's good."

"Not really. Her mom didn't mind telling me, because you can't exactly drive to number two's house. She might as well be a zillion miles away."

Peyton slumped. "So where does she live? Mars?"

"*The World*," Mandi explained, her voice dropping to a rough whisper. "It's a ship that travels from port to port, all over, um, the world. Mama doesn't know where it is anchored right now. Her daughter likes her privacy and she seems pretty intent upon keeping it."

Peyton stood still, her hopes deflating like a leaky balloon. If Taylor Crowe was truly incommunicado, how could she continue the series? She could always interview the remaining candidate, Tanner Ford, but that would require a trip to Gainesville . . .

The muscles of her throat moved in a convulsive swallow. "Thanks, Mandi." She tried to keep her heart calm and still. "I'll think about what we should do and let you know when I've figured it out."

She hung up, thanked the receptionist, then turned away and crossed her arms, dreading her return to the meeting. Howard's offer might evaporate if she couldn't finish the story, and with Taylor Crowe literally out to sea, it might not be possible to continue.

She began a slow walk back down the hall. But . . . maybe this new team could still save the day. After all, Adam Howard owned nearly the whole planet, and *The World* had to be *somewhere*. A man like Howard would have a private jet, connections, and maybe even enough pull in the entertainment world to get her the interview . . .

She hurried forward and stepped back into the conference room, feeling as if her dazed wits had renewed themselves. "Gentlemen." She smiled around the room, then settled her gaze on Adam Howard. "We have an agreement. But —"

"Great," Howard interrupted. "We'll take you to syndication beginning with Sunday's column, and in return you'll promise to share everything — the note, the leads, and the results of your interviews. We'd also like you to get signed releases from all the principals so Julie can go in and do the follow-ups."

"I'll share everything — when I'm finished." Peyton layered a note of steel into her voice. "You can talk to any prospect after I've had my interview, but not before. My columns will give your people plenty of material to work with, but I have to protect my edge." She sent a tight smile around the table. "I'm sure you understand."

"We do." Howard stood to shake her hand again, and DiSalvo beamed like a proud father.

"We're all agreed on this end," DiSalvo said as she took her seat. "I'm sure you'll want to go over the contract with a lawyer or your agent —"

As if she had one.

"— but everything looks in order. You'll go national with Sunday's column, and the WNN news team will go to work on the Heart Healer's prime-time special."

She forced a smile. "I'm sorry, but there is one other matter. I will agree to your terms, but I'm going to need some help." She shifted her gaze from DiSalvo to Howard. "I've located two other candidates for the note, but one of them is proving almost impossible to reach. I need to interview her tomorrow, and then I'll need a late deadline — as late as you can give me and still make the Sunday paper."

Howard's eyes went bright with the stimulation of challenge. "What's the problem?"

"We know where our next prospect

lives," she answered, not willing to disparage her research abilities, "but our next subject is a celebrity in her own right. She doesn't like publicity and she lives aboard a boat."

DiSalvo's brow shot up. "This is *great.* She lives on a yacht?"

Shaking her head, Peyton said, "It's a ship called *The World*, and it's out to port somewhere."

"Her name." Impatience edged Howard's voice. "We can't help if we don't know the name."

Peyton suppressed a sigh. "Taylor Crowe. She's a songwriter."

Several brows furrowed, but a stocky man opposite Howard snapped his fingers. "No problem, she's one of ours. She's in the stable of writers for our TruBlood division. Best of all" — he flashed a toothy grin around the room — "she's under contract for another five years."

Howard brought his finger to his chin. "Can we get her to do an interview?"

"She'll be thrilled," the stocky man said. "We pay her to be thrilled."

Resting his cheek on his hand, Howard smiled at Peyton. "Problem solved, Ms. MacGruder. Just tell us when you want to go, and we'll arrange everything."

A little breathless, Peyton looked at Nora Chilton. "I should leave as soon as possible. But I'll need to know about the word count and deadline —"

"Five o'clock tomorrow," Nora said, her voice icy.

Peyton felt the corner of her mouth droop as she shifted her gaze to DiSalvo. Nora could do better than five; they often left space open for theater critics who filed much later.

"Ten p.m., but let's not make a habit of this, okay?" DiSalvo looked at Peyton, amusement in his eyes. "And take as many words as you need. You write tight; I'm not worried about you wandering down rabbit trails."

"We'll arrange the transportation." Howard gestured to his stocky associate. "Carl, you set things up for Ms. Mac-Gruder, and see that the writer — what's her name, Crowe? — is ready to talk. Have a camera crew ready to go, too."

"No cameras." Peyton raised her voice, satisfied with the resulting silence. "No cameras at all until after I'm done."

"They're not for Julie; they're for you," Howard said. "People will want to know what you looked like as you went about this search."

"No cameras," Peyton repeated, her voice clipped. "None for me, ever."

Adam Howard cast a questioning look at DiSalvo, then waved in surrender. "We'll play by your rules. No problem."

Peyton thanked him, then stood and murmured that she'd better get to work. The man called Carl promised to phone her with travel arrangements, and the one named Frank promised to messenger a syndication agreement as soon as possible.

As she closed the door and moved back down the silent hallway, Peyton took deep breaths to calm her hammering heart. In a few hours, once she'd signed the contract, her column would belong to Adam Howard . . . and seven hundred newspapers.

She frowned as she pressed the elevator button. It had all happened too fast. She should have been overjoyed, but her stomach churned and tightened into a knot as fear brushed the edge of her mind. She felt strangely like a woman who'd sold her favorite child into slavery.

Twelve

Saturday, June 30
With a copy of the syndication agreement safely in the hands of her newly hired lawyer, Peyton sat aboard WNN's private jet and tried to keep a level head. Though most newspaper reporters prided themselves on being grittier and less pampered than their television counterparts, she had to admit that working the other side of the street had its perks. Howard Features had arranged for a limo to pick her up at 6:00 a.m. and deliver her to a private hangar at TIA. The private jet was taking her to Boston, where Taylor Crowe's floating home, *The World*, would be anchored for the months of June and July. Apparently the ship's residents wanted an opportunity to enjoy summer sailing in the Northeast.

After draining a chilled can of diet soda provided by her own personal flight attendant, Peyton stretched out her legs in the empty cabin, assured the young woman that she didn't want anything else, then patted

257

her briefcase. The leather attaché was a last-minute loan from Mandi, who'd insisted that Peyton could not visit a very important person like Taylor Crowe with a scuffed backpack over her shoulder. In Mandi's soft new briefcase (a gift, the girl confessed, from her father, who was convinced she would become the next Anna Quindlen) Peyton had packed her digital recorder, a copy of the note, her steno pad, and her laptop.

She'd have to write the story on the flight back to Tampa in order to meet her deadline, but she suspected she'd have it in well before ten o'clock — maybe even before five. Frank Myers, president of Howard Features Syndicate, had assured her his top papers would reserve prime space for her debut column.

"Lord, help me make it a good one," she whispered, then chuckled because her exclamation sounded suspiciously like a prayer. She couldn't remember the last time she'd attempted to pray — unless she counted the time she got a flat tire at 2:00 a.m. in one of the most crime-ridden areas of Tampa. Her cell phone wouldn't work, she had no idea how to change a tire, and she'd never quite figured out how to rouse friends from bed in the middle of the night via mental telepathy.

She'd prayed that night, tentatively but sincerely, and a little later a couple of pierced and tattooed teenage boys emerged from the shadows and offered to change her tire for five bucks — each. Nodding like a wary squirrel, she agreed, then nearly fainted when they changed the tire, took the money, and disappeared into the night.

But this situation was nothing like that one. Her experience today would be safe and swift and maybe only a little painful — probably far more painful for Ms. Crowe than for Peyton.

Bracing herself for the task ahead, she opened the briefcase and pulled out a folder of biographical information she'd downloaded from the Internet. Taylor Crowe's father, James, had been fifty-three at the time of his death. An Internet search turned up nothing on his life, and the obit from the *New Haven Register* offered only the bare facts: James Crowe, of New Haven, Connecticut, died June 13 in Tampa, Florida, a passenger on PanWorld Flight 848. He was a construction superintendent and a German Lutheran. He was survived by his wife, Maria, a daughter, T. Crowe, and buried in Evergreen Cemetery, New Haven.

Peyton shook her head as she mentally

filed the information away. James Crowe had probably led a full life. How sad that it had been reduced to a few threadbare lines in a crowded column.

Information about his daughter, Taylor, was far more plentiful. Though neither Taylor Crowe's name nor her face were readily recognized by the general public, music moguls regularly shouted her praises and recording artists showered her with gifts. She was, according to one magazine profile, an incredible one-woman song-writing machine.

She began writing songs at eighteen, and by the time she reached twenty-one she was ripping out four charts a day, writing as she listened to the radio. One of her songs, "If You Looked My Way," had been recorded by both Whitney Houston and Faith Hill, then rode the top of the pop and country charts for more than a year. She'd won a Grammy, an Oscar, and a Golden Globe. Four times the American Society of Composers, Authors, and Publishers had named her Songwriter of the Year. Sales of her recorded songs regularly resulted in six-figure royalty checks.

Crowe's floating home, Peyton learned, was owned by a company known as ResidenSea, builders of a ship billed as history's first residential ocean liner. *The World* boasted 110 spacious, fully furnished apartments offering the comfort and convenience of home along with the services and amenities of a luxury resort. According to the sales brochure Peyton pulled from the Web, *The World* planned to continuously circumnavigate the globe with an itinerary of extended stays for special international events. The small black-and-white photograph pictured a massive boat rising from the water, with six decks visible above the bowline.

Peyton whistled softly. Since apartments aboard *The World* sold for between two and six million dollars, Taylor Crowe had to be a multimillionaire. Still, a ship seemed a terribly unstable place to call home. Had the builders of *The World* never heard of the *Titanic*?

After the plane landed in Boston, the young flight attendant pointed Peyton toward a black limo, which whisked her away from the airport. Once the car arrived at the harbor, the driver radioed information that magically opened an electronic gate, then they drove to a pier bustling with boats and yachts and handsome men in white uniforms.

"The *Misty Sea* has been chartered to transport guests to and from *The World*," the driver said, turning sideways in his seat. "That's your ferry — the big white boat at the second berth."

Peyton checked her watch. She still had plenty of time, but if she got held up here at the dock —

"When does he make his next run out to the ship?" she asked, squinting out the windshield. She could see no signs of life aboard the boat.

The driver eased into a smile. "He's waiting for you. When you're ready, he's ready."

Peyton gulped. *This* she could get used to . . .

"Thanks." She opened her door. "Um — should I call you when I'm ready to leave?"

"I've been instructed to wait here for you." The driver pointed to the briefcase in her hand. "If you wait one moment, I'll get that for you."

"I can carry it," Peyton said, her voice flat. No way was she going to play the pampered socialite, not as long as she carried a press pass.

She got out of the car and lowered her head into the wind, moving quickly toward the *Misty Sea*. As she approached, a pair of men in white uniforms came down the

262

gangplank, then one held her elbow as she crossed.

Five minutes later, she sat in an air-conditioned cabin while the boat churned its way across the harbor. The comfortable cabin had been furnished with cushioned seats and a selection of various magazines on a center table, but the real view lay outside the window. Bracing herself against the boat's motion, Peyton stood and looked at the huge white ship juxtaposed against a royal blue sea.

Incredible. What must it be like to live aboard a luxury ocean liner?

Within ten minutes, the *Misty Sea* had pulled up next to *The World* and a painted steel structure that reminded Peyton of a fire escape, then the polite young men in white assisted her in boarding. More uniformed men loitered on deck, and one came forward to meet her. Holding her briefcase close to her side, she smiled her thanks to the crew of the *Misty Sea*, then shouted an introduction to the officer who stood before her at attention.

"I'm Peyton MacGruder," she yelled, straining to make herself heard over the noise of the departing boat. "I have an appointment with Taylor Crowe."

The attendant nodded wordlessly, then

checked the clipboard in his hand. After running his finger down a computerized printout, he moved toward a telephone on the wall.

"We'll be right with you," he told Peyton, pointing to a narrow flight of stairs. "Wait right there, and someone will escort you to Miss Crowe's apartment."

After a uniformed security guard led her through an elaborate maze of tunnels, decks, and elevators, Peyton found herself standing outside a pair of elaborately carved double doors. Only after the door opened did the security officer retreat.

The woman who opened the door wore a cotton T-shirt, torn at the neckline and sleeves and ending a good three inches above the waistband of her black leather pants. Long black hair splashed over her shoulders and accented a milky complexion. The face was thin and bony; the dark eyes seemed shadowed.

Peyton felt the wings of foreboding brush her spirit.

"Taylor Crowe?" She extended her hand. "I'm Peyton MacGruder, from the *Tampa Times*. I hope you were expecting me."

"Yes." The woman's tone was as expressionless as a robot's, but she accepted Peyton's handshake, then opened the door wider. "Come in. I suppose we should get this over with."

Peyton took two steps, then gaped at the apartment. Black marble lined the foyer, but the living room beyond seemed to shimmer in white — snowy carpet, bleached furniture, milky walls. The wide, uncurtained windows were ornamented only with a series of crystal *objets d'art* that filled the window sill and glimmered with the colors of the steel-blue sea and sky.

Peyton felt as though she were moving into a painting. "I'm not sure what you were told about my visit," she began, following her unenthusiastic hostess into the pristine room.

Taylor Crowe whirled on one bare foot, her face pursing in a moue of distaste. "I was told I had to see you, so here you are. If this wasn't something I had to do, you wouldn't be here."

Score one for honesty, subtract one for tact.

Peyton forced a smile. "Well, then, I'll try to make this as painless as possible."

Taylor only shrugged, then fell languidly onto the sofa. "So sit and tell me what this is all about."

Peyton sank into a chair so white it hurt her eyes to look at it. "First, let me say how sorry I am that you lost your father in the crash of Flight 848. I was in Tampa at the time, and we all felt the loss of so many people."

Taylor positioned her elbow on the back of the sofa, then propped her head on her hand. Worming her bare foot through the plush carpet, she lowered her gaze. "My father and I weren't close. I haven't spoken to him in years, so —" She shrugged again; the gesture seemed habitual. "I said good-bye to him a long time ago."

A black-and-white cat wandered into the room, then leaped into Taylor's lap. The woman welcomed it, stroking the animal with her free hand. After a moment, Taylor lifted her head and looked at Peyton with challenge in her eyes.

Shifting her position, Peyton pulled the briefcase onto her lap. "I hate to begin with formalities, but I'm going to have to ask you to sign a confidentiality agreement. Basically, it says you promise not to share details of this visit with anyone outside Howard Media & Entertainment until after July fourth." She paused, the document in her hand. "I'm going to show you something that might have belonged to your father. If I were in your shoes, I think I'd appreciate a little privacy."

Taylor's dark eyes gleamed. "Something

sort of like not releasing names until the family members have been notified?"

"The same principle, yes." Peyton slid the paper and a pen across a gleaming ivory coffee table. "If you'll sign, I have a few questions for you."

With a careless shrug, Taylor scrawled her signature across the bottom of the page, then dropped the pen. "I probably should have read it," she said, curling up on the sofa. "But if the company people sent you, I know I'd end up signing it anyway. Might as well cut to the chase."

Peyton picked up the page. The woman had a point.

After returning paper and pen to the briefcase, Peyton assumed a relaxed posture, propping her elbows on the chair and folding her hands. How would Mary Grace begin? With an open question — and then she'd sit back, look, and listen.

"Can you tell me something about your father? Do you know what he was planning to do in Tampa?"

Another shrug from the songwriter. "I don't have a clue. I can't imagine why anyone would want to go to Florida in June. Maybe he wanted a vacation. Maybe he had a yen to visit purgatory. I don't know."

Peyton waited. The resulting silence was

deep enough for her to hear the cry of gulls outside the boat, but apparently Taylor Crowe had grown accustomed to quiet. She didn't offer anything else.

Mary Grace would have struck out with this one. Reaching down to the briefcase, Peyton pulled out a copy of the note.

"Taylor, what I'm about to show you might be upsetting, but I think you should see it. A few days after the crash, a woman on the beach found a note protected by a plastic bag. We have reason to believe your father might have written it. If he did, this was written for you."

Something flickered in those dark eyes — but Peyton couldn't tell whether it was interest or a reflection from the window. Taylor leaned forward, dislodging the cat, and took the note, slowly moving her lips as she read the words. For a moment she simply sat there, the note in her hand, then she looked up and caught Peyton's gaze.

"Why did you bring this?"

Peyton clasped her hands. "If it's yours, I thought you should have it."

Taylor studied the note again, tracing her fingertip over the scrawled writing.

Hope stirred in Peyton's breast. "Do you think your father could have written that note?"

"Yeah," Taylor whispered, still tracing the words. "Why not? He could have. Maybe. The writing is pretty clear, isn't it?"

"For someone aboard a crashing plane, yes." Peyton leaned forward, eager to observe the younger woman's thought processes. "If this was written while the plane was going down, I would imagine the other passengers were panicked. Perhaps the plane itself was shuddering, we don't really know."

"My dad had lovely handwriting." Taylor lifted her head and closed her eyes, her dark hair framing her face. "Everything about him was charming, really. He was quite elegant, a quality you don't expect in a construction worker. I used to love that about him. He seemed like the perfect man, and he loved me . . . until I told him I didn't want to be his daughter anymore."

Peyton pressed her lips together, letting the silence stretch.

Taylor didn't speak. Instead she rose from the sofa and carried the note into the next room, out of Peyton's field of vision. Perplexed, Peyton sat still for a moment, then the tinkling sounds of a piano invited her forward.

The living room led to a music room, which was dominated by a gleaming black grand piano. Notebook paper and sheets of music littered the top of the closed instrument. A pair of pencils lay at Taylor's right hand, a coffee cup squatted on a coaster at her left.

"My office," Taylor said, her voice dreamy as she moved her fingers over the keys. "You're a writer, right?"

Peyton nodded.

"Then you'll understand." Taylor closed her eyes and leaned into the keyboard. "This is my typewriter, and this" — abruptly, she reached down and clicked on a tape recorder resting on a small table at the end of the piano bench — "is my computer."

Folding her arms, Peyton leaned against the wall, at once entertained and bemused by the young woman before her. While she watched, Taylor Crowe fiercely played a series of chords, squinting in concentration, then seemed to settle into a pattern. Her left hand picked up a rhythm and moved over the bass keys, providing a running accompaniment while her right plucked out a haunting melody, each note seeming to have been pulled from pain and the most unbearable loneliness . . .

Peyton understood the poverty of loneliness. She could close her eyes and summon memories of playing alone in the dirt behind her grandmother's house, suffering torments when she had no mother to attend her elementary school's mother-daughter tea, and later enduring terminal embarrassment because she had no one to help her fix her hair or teach her how to deal with hormonal males. Even now, as a functional adult, she often found herself sitting against the wall in a movie theater, munching quietly on popcorn and praying for the lights to dim so no one would see the Woman Alone in the Dark . . .

As ghost spiders crawled along the back of Peyton's neck, Taylor began to sing:

"I said good-bye beneath a sky of blue and mingled rainbows,

I said farewell to a love as strong as the sea,

I moved away from an all-protective embrace,

And I hoped you'd forever live in me."

She sang with a surprisingly pleasant voice, and Peyton wondered why Crowe hadn't aimed for a career in performance. A lot of recording artists wrote their own songs, so with her track record and strong voice, she could be right up there with Whitney Houston.

Taylor tinkled the keys a moment more, then moved into a second verse:

"I moved away, into my self-sustaining world,
I walked alone, in search of love and life,
I yearned for you in every face and flower,
But all I had of you was emptiness inside."

A change of mood, an increase in tempo, and she sang again:

"Why'd I go? How could I know . . . your love formed and made me?
Not to say . . . I want to stay . . . for your love will enslave me."

Back to the beginning, a calmer mood now:

"I said good-bye, now I can't cry, for I must live with my choice,
But as I go, you should know, I'll always hear your sweet voice."

Taylor played a final chord, let it fade, then dropped her head. Peyton pulled herself away from the wall, not certain if she should applaud, smile, or weep. She felt like doing all three.

"That was lovely," she finally said, moving closer to the piano. "One of your published songs?"

Taylor reached down and snapped off the recorder. "A new creation. It's a little rough, but I can work with it. And when I sell it, everyone will think it's about the love between a man and a woman." She looked up and caught Peyton's gaze for the first time since sitting at the piano. "Only you and I will know it's about me and my father."

Sensing a rock of truth in the surrounding sea of confusion, Peyton struggled to grasp it. "Taylor" — she moved closer, daring to touch the shiny ebony — "if you're thinking your father died not caring about you, that's clearly not the case. If your father *did* write this note, he wrote it from a heart of love. He forgave you for whatever you said to him all those years ago. The note makes it very clear."

Taylor shook her head. "That note wasn't meant for me."

"But —" Peyton lifted her hand, suddenly choked with frustration. An almost-tangible cloak of melancholy and regret lay upon this woman, so why couldn't she see that forgiveness lay within reach? Whether James Crowe had written this note or not, Taylor did not have to mourn their lost relationship. The key to closure lay within the note . . . if she would only accept it.

"Taylor," she began, injecting a firm note into her voice, "there's no reason for us to doubt this note was written for you. So for you to turn your back on it, to deny it — well, it makes no sense."

Crowe reached up, flicked a hank of dark

hair off her shoulder, and placed her hands on the piano keys. "Life doesn't make sense, does it?" She played a progression of chords, each more dissonant than the last. "It doesn't have to."

Peyton gripped the edge of the piano. "Listen — I've been around the block more than a few times and I've seen things I hope you never see. And let me tell you — carrying sad memories will wear you out. You've got to put them down and walk away. Do whatever you must to put emotional space between yourself and your past. That's the only way you're going to make it through."

Taylor didn't answer, but continued to play, the notes combining into phrases that grated against Peyton's nerves until her heart thumped against her rib cage. A shiver passed down her spine and an odd coldness settled upon her, a darkly textured sensation that sent gloomy thoughts speeding through her brain like bullets. She trembled, seeing her spare school dormitory, her empty house the night Garrett died, and the hospital —

Without warning, the light of understanding blazed in Peyton's brain. The young woman before her had made a fortune singing about love and longing, yet she lived like a recluse in this spotless apartment, with only a cat for company. Taylor *chose* to live this way . . . and she'd hate life as a performer. She *wanted* to remain aloof, feeling only what she allowed herself to feel, sorting through emotions, tasting only those that suited her fancy and ambition. Whether consciously or unconsciously, Taylor Crowe cultivated misery and melancholy, weeding out color and human contact so she could harvest best-selling songs.

Peyton almost laughed as another thought struck her. This girl would *despise* Julie St. Claire and her camera crew.

"Taylor." Peyton bent to catch the musician's eye. "I've got to write a column about this interview. If you'd like to remain anonymous, I'd be happy to use a pseudonym instead of your name. I could describe you as a successful young woman who lives alone."

"I'd prefer that." Abruptly stopping the music, Taylor shifted her weight on the piano bench and sat on her hands.

"That's fine with me, but —" Peyton leaned forward, overcome by an inexplicable urge to rattle this indifferent young woman. "The news people from WNN won't want to hide your name. And since they could pressure you enough to invite me

275

here, I'm pretty sure they're going to want you to cooperate with their film crew."

A pained look crossed Taylor's face. "They won't be able to make me say my father wrote that note."

"But you said he might have."

"Doesn't matter." She tossed her head, sending the mane of dark hair flying. "That note's not mine, and nobody is going to make me say it is."

"Fine." Peyton turned to leave, then pointed toward the note on the piano. "You may keep that, if you like. It's a copy."

Without hesitation, Taylor reached out and handed the page to Peyton. "It's not mine." She lifted one shoulder in a shrug. "I don't want it."

Peyton accepted the note with a curt nod, then left Taylor Crowe to her black-and-white existence.

As the door clicked shut, Taylor slumped and felt some of the tension drain out of her shoulders.

Man, she hated reporters. They stirred things up, made her remember things she hadn't thought about in a long time and didn't want to think about at all . . . but at least she got a song out of the interview.

She pressed the rewind button on the tape

recorder, then stopped and pressed play, humming a harmony line.

Yeah, this song would fly. She'd send it in tomorrow, as soon as she wrote out the chart. The company would probably send it to Mariah or Celine . . . or maybe LeAnne Rimes. Rimes would be best — the country singer was young enough to make it work in all sorts of ways. The tune could become her signature song.

Standing, Taylor stretched for a moment, then reached to scoop up Tuxedo Cat. Tucking him under her arm, she walked into the gleaming kitchen and set the animal on the marble counter.

"I moved away, into my self-sustaining world," she sang under her breath as she pulled a glass from the cabinet. No — maybe *independent world* would be better. Fewer syllables, anyway, and easier to sing. Or maybe *crystal-clear* world. That's how it felt when she first left home. Things were bright and shiny and oh so brittle.

She walked to the bar and poured a shot of vodka into the glass, then lifted it in a toast. "Here's to you, Dad," she said, her voice whispery soft. "I thought I was done with you."

She tipped the drink back with one practiced gesture, then dropped the glass onto the counter and sank onto a barstool. Why couldn't the dead stay buried?

She'd sent flowers to the funeral because she knew her mother would expect her to do something, but she didn't go to the service, and her mother understood. Celebrity status could be convenient that way. Her mother probably thought Taylor would be mobbed at the cemetery, but little did she know that hardly anybody outside the business even knew who Taylor Crowe was — or cared. But it was okay. She was making a good living, and people liked what she did. Nothing else mattered.

The cat walked over to her and rubbed his head against hers, trying to evoke a scratch between the ears or a stroke down the spine. Taylor did neither.

The fates, or whoever ordered these things, hadn't dealt her father an easy death. And he was a wonderful man, really, gentle with his family, good to his friends. The only time he ever lost his temper was with Taylor, and, in retrospect, she could understand why.

Her childhood had been typical and happy, she supposed, the usual stuff, but from the time she hit thirteen she and her parents couldn't agree on anything. They didn't like her friends, her music, or her clothes. They complained that she never talked to them — well, who'd want to? They were so hopelessly out of it. Then one day she and her dad had it out in the middle of the living room, and her phlegmatic father actually lost his temper and went red with fury. He told her to obey the house rules; she said she wouldn't. He said she would or she'd get out, and she said, fine, I'm leaving. By then she was seventeen, so there was little her parents could do to stop her.

A year of shacking up with Daniel taught her that love was nothing like the fairy tale in the movies. When he walked out, leaving her with a stack of bills, a trashed apartment, and an empty bank account, she wrote her first serious song: "Sorry Killed the Dream of You." A friend of hers heard it and gave it to her friend, who gave it to somebody in the record business. Before she knew it, she was a songwriter.

More songs followed, mostly tunes she wrote out of memories. She wrote one of her biggest hits, "Empty Heart," after thinking about the time her father took her fishing at Gaillard Lake. She'd hooked this huge fish — a bass or trout or something — and her dad tried to help her reel it in, but she snapped that she'd rather do it herself. Then the stupid fish got away, so all she reeled in was an empty fishhook.

Nobody knew the real story behind the song, of course. Most of her friends — and she used that term loosely — thought she suffered from some profound lost love. The execs loved "Empty Heart" and used it as the theme for a Julia Roberts movie. It won the Oscar for best song, and after that her stock went through the roof.

She leaned on the counter and pressed her hand to her forehead, the misery of the interview still haunting her. Life was such a joke. People grow up believing that life owes them happiness and a fair shake, then they discover nobody's going to automatically give them anything, so why pretend life was happy and fair? Why love anyone, especially when they expect you to behave a certain way in return?

The only good things that had come out of her past were the emotions that inspired her songs.

Lowering her hand, she stretched it toward the cat. He walked beneath it, arching his back and purring.

Sometimes, when the mood was right, she did miss her dad. When they hadn't been fighting, they'd had good times together. And even though she hadn't seen him in years, at least she'd known he was out there if she needed to call. She hadn't needed him, of course — one of the disadvantages of financial independence — but now that he was gone, she felt disconnected somehow.

And knowing she couldn't call was unsettling.

Leaving the cat, she rose and walked to the window, where the ocean stretched toward the horizon in a palette of blues and greens.

She hadn't been sleeping well since the plane crash. She spent a lot of time looking out over the ocean, watching the waves and thinking that they were part of the same water that covered her dad at the end. Sometimes she wondered if his soul was absorbed by the sea. Where did a soul go when the body died? She couldn't believe death spelled *the end*. A soul was such an expansive thing . . . people couldn't merely disappear into the cosmos. They had to go on somehow.

Closing her eyes, she moved back into the music room and slid onto the piano bench. She played a C chord, then an F, followed by a G7, then another C. The most common progression in the world, one, four, five-seven, one . . .

Life goes on, and so does the music.

She'd frustrated that newspaper woman. For a moment, she'd thought Peyton Mac-Gruder was going to lean across the piano, grab her by the shirt, and shake her into confessing, *Yes, that note was meant for me, no doubt about it.*

But she would never admit that. Never, not even if her father *had* written the blasted thing. The breach between them was too wide. No note could bridge that gap, not now, not ever.

It'd be nice to think her father did write it. If she could believe that, maybe she could sleep at night. But she'd hurt him too deeply to earn easy absolution. Her dad would have to be some kind of saint to overlook the hurt she'd caused.

He was a special man . . . but he was gone.

And she'd give anything to find him again.

Peyton stared at the sun-spangled sea, which slapped rhythmically against the escort boat. Thoughts of her interview with Taylor Crowe ricocheted in her head, pinging off vaults she'd locked long ago —

"Ma'am?" A handsome young man in uniform caught her attention and pointed toward the doorway to the cabin. "This sun is awful bright. If you'd rather go into the cabin, it's shady inside —"

"Thanks, but I'm fine." As if to prove her assertion, Peyton gripped the rail and lifted her face to the sun. "I think it feels nice."

The steward — if that's what he was — smiled, but lifted a warning brow. "Be careful. Sometimes we hit a rough wave, and things can get a little unsteady."

"I'm fine." Peyton looked away, a little weary of repeating herself. She *was* fine, totally and completely, even though she had not been able to stem the tide of frustration that had rocked her thoughts ever since leaving Taylor Crowe's apartment.

Mary Grace Van Owen's little trick had worked in a most unexpected way. Instead of talking, Taylor Crowe had opened up in a song, cloaking her feelings in lyrics that could be interpreted in a dozen different ways. Peyton thought she could sense the true emotion behind the words, but no one else would guess the truth, not in a hundred years.

She felt her stomach tighten as the ship labored through a stretch of choppy sea. A whiff of pungent sea air filled her nostrils even as Taylor Crowe's voice filled her memory:

I yearned for you in every face and flower,
But all I had of you was emptiness inside.

Did Taylor think she was the only daughter ever to miss her father's company? Did she honestly believe she had a monopoly on suffering? Peyton could tell her a thing or two, could teach her plenty about emptiness and yearning and absence.

In the hollow of her back, a single drop of sweat traced the course of her spine. Her hands were damp, too; the brass railing slick beneath her palms. Careful, now, mustn't think of the past. Mustn't dwell on what we've put away. Mustn't unlock the doors, even touch the key.

Why in heaven's name did her father insist on sending letters and pictures and cards? Not a week went by without another envelope appearing in her mailbox at home or at work. When she got back to the newsroom, that stupid picture would be on her desk, the smiling photo of him and her and all the young ones. Why did he do it? He had to know she didn't want contact. Like Taylor Crowe, she'd written off that relationship years ago, but still her father insisted on torturing her.

The sounds of male voices poured out of the cabin area, battering her ears. What were those men talking about? Did they see her out here, wonder why she wouldn't come in? King had wondered why she didn't open the letters from her father, like Mandi had to wonder why she didn't act more thrilled with that sappy photograph of the smiling graduate. But they didn't know. They knew zilch about her life; they had never walked through the valley of the shadow with her, they didn't know about the pain she had locked away. And Taylor Crowe, foolish girl, would learn someday. She'd learn that it was silly to brood on melancholy, stupid to write about it. And because that fool had refused the note, Peyton would now have to go to Gainesville and confront Tanner Ford.

She clung to the rail, her stomach churning. Gainesville had to have changed in the years she'd been gone, but she would never be able to drive through the city without remembering things she'd put away. If only Taylor had claimed the note, then all would be settled and she wouldn't even have to think about Gainesville. But now . . .

How could she pull it off? How could she get in her car and drive northward, knowing each mile brought her closer and closer to —

She brought her fingers to her neck as panic like she'd never known welled in her throat. She couldn't do it! She couldn't go to Gainesville; she couldn't even meet tonight's deadline. Because it was happening again, the racing pulse, the quick breathing, the feeling that she was about to have a heart attack. Sheer, black fright was raging through her, and she had nowhere to run, no place to go. She couldn't go into the cabin and she couldn't stay on this boat. What if it sank? What if a rogue wave came from nowhere and capsized them before anyone even knew what had happened? Or the boat could catch fire — some of the men *were* smoking — and if she stayed aboard she'd face a terrible death by drowning *and* burning.

That couldn't happen. It just couldn't.

All sounds — of the engine, the men's conversation, even the waves — subsided, leaving only a ringing silence in her ears. Unable to control the spasmodic trembling within, Peyton moved toward the stern, hand over hand, clinging to the rail, the only stable object in her field of vision. The wide sky and horizon had narrowed; she could see only the brass cylinder beneath her damp palms. If she followed it she would be able to find a way off this boat.

Because they were going to die. She knew it; could feel it as certainly as she'd felt the sun on her face a few moments before.

She had to leave the boat. Now, as soon as possible, as soon as her heavy feet could find the way to freedom. Gulping for air and finding none, she moved sideways, step by step, until the rail bent and she felt only empty air beneath her hands. Grateful to find a way of escape, she took it.

Half an hour later, wet and wrapped in a blanket, Peyton sat in the back of the hired car with her feet on solid asphalt. She gave the captain of the *Misty Sea* another false smile. "It wasn't your fault," she repeated for the twentieth time. "I must have slipped."

"All the same," the captain said, his eyes dark with worry, "if my first mate hadn't heard the splash —"

"He did, and I'm fine." Peyton pulled the edges of the blanket closer so he wouldn't see that she still trembled. "And if you don't mind, I'd really like to get to the airport."

"Wouldn't you like to get some dry clothes?" The question came from the driver, who'd taken in her dripping appearance with no more visible signs of alarm than a slight scratch of his head. "It might get cold on the plane."

"I have a blanket. I want to go home." Peyton shifted her gaze and gave the captain a grim look. "If you'll hand me my briefcase, we can go about our business and pretend this never happened."

Obediently, he handed her the attaché. "But—"

"Don't worry, Captain, I'm not going to sue you. It wasn't your fault."

Turning, she folded her legs into the backseat, then rested her hand on the door. "Good day, gentlemen. Thank you for fishing me out of the sea."

She slammed the door. A moment later the driver got in, fastened his seat belt, then adjusted his rearview mirror, pausing to catch her eye in the reflection.

"The same terminal where I picked you up?" he asked, his voice soft with wariness.

"Yes, please." Peyton gave him a nod, then leaned her head against the seat and closed her eyes.

She hadn't had a panic attack in years . . . and none had ever literally put her in water over her head. Thank goodness the men who came to her rescue assumed she'd slipped and fallen. Thank goodness, too, that they attributed her fright to the act of falling overboard.

How wrong they were.

Still trembling in terror, Peyton curled into a ball and tried to sleep.

Thirteen

Sunday, July 1

The Heart Healer
By Peyton MacGruder
© Howard Features Syndicate

Dear Readers:

For those of you who've just joined "The Heart Healer," a bit of background is probably in order. Eight days ago, a woman approached me at my home paper, the *Tampa Times*, and handed me something that had washed up behind her home on Tampa Bay. At first glance, any passerby would assume the battered bit of plastic was nothing but another piece of litter tossed out by Sunday boaters on Florida's west coast. The small bag, however, contained a simple sheet of paper, a note hastily scrawled, but legible. Though I will not reveal the note's message until after I have safely delivered it to its rightful owner, I can say this: we have many reasons to believe the bag and its contents came from the tragic crash of PanWorld Flight 848. Because the note was signed "Dad," we know it was written by a father to a child. Through another small but important clue, I have been able to locate three people who could be the note's intended recipient.

Last week I visited the first person on my list, a pastor in a Midwestern town. After glancing at the note for a moment, he assured me that it could not have come from his father. His reasons were credible, his logic sound.

A few hours ago I visited the second person on my list — a successful songwriter who values her privacy. She studied the note thoughtfully, and for a moment I thought her eyes filled with tears. But though she admitted her father *could* have written it — she couldn't rule out the possibility — she refused to accept the note's message. Her father, she felt certain, would never have written those particular words. Especially not for her.

Still, she couldn't help being stirred. While I watched, she went to her piano and created a song that put a lump in my throat — a song with lyrics so polished I was certain she'd labored over it for many hours. No, she assured me, it still needed work.

But it would make a great tune, though no one would ever guess at its emotional source.

She handed the note back to me, drained of emotion and possibility, and told me to keep it. I didn't want to. I wanted her to keep the note and its message; I wanted her to be comforted by knowing her father had thought of her before his death. But you can't force someone to receive a gift they're not willing to accept.

I'm on a plane home now, typing in the pressurized silence of a jet cabin. I'm tired from the long day, and more than a little weary of this forced preoccupation with death. It's been a long journey. I wonder if my songwriter friend appreciates how long and difficult. But I am not to judge her — I'm only the reporter.

Today I met a woman who has everything — wealth, beauty, talent, and intellect. Yet, from what I could tell, she shares her gifts with very few people. Her luxurious apartment held no pictures of friends or loved ones. She lives in a palatial apartment with a cat.

I have to wonder — is she happy? I suppose each of us would define the condition differently. But the life I observed today, while grand, would probably not satisfy the average man or woman. I doubt it would satisfy me.

From what I could gather, this young musician and her father had a falling-out years ago. You're probably familiar with the scene — teenager yells at Mom and Dad; Dad gives an ultimatum — obey the house rules or leave the house. The teen walks out, and the chasm between father and child grows deeper with every missed birthday, Father's Day, and Christmas. Unfortunately, as the father's heart softens, the child's heart can grow harder.

But adolescence is a time of hurts — who among us did not do and say things we regret in our maturity? As adolescents, we are so self-centered and focused on our own desires that we are blind to our parents as real people. We see only their authority, their rules, and their expectations. We do not see their dreams, their strengths, and their ordinary weaknesses. Or, if we see, we do not understand.

I found myself trembling with frustration when I left my second prospect. This young woman carries a burden of loneliness, but it's clear she *chooses* to carry it — it has become a shadow she's accustomed to seeing. Unfortunately, I fear it will walk with her for the rest of her life.

By giving her the note, I hoped to give her balance between loss and love. After all, when do shadows disappear? At noontime, when the sun is balanced and directly overhead.

Tomorrow: a preliminary report on our third and final prospect for the note. Until then, here's a heartfelt wish that you will walk in the brightness of noonday.

In her New York apartment, Julie St. Claire ate breakfast, soaked in a scented bath, and read the entire *New York Times*, followed by a quick skimming of the *Post*. Finally, when the clock on her mantel struck eleven, she tightened the belt on her silk robe, stabbed her cigarette into an ashtray, then picked up the phone to call Peyton MacGruder. Even the laziest Sunday morning sleeper ought to be up by eleven.

The columnist answered on the third ring, her voice heavy.

"Peyton, this is Julie St. Claire of WNN."

"No need to remind me. I know who you are."

MacGruder might be tired, but her defenses were up and armed. Julie sank into a wing chair and pressed forward. "I read your column this morning in the *New York Post*. Congratulations on hitting the major markets."

"Thanks."

MacGruder didn't sound exactly thrilled, so Julie moved on to the reason for her call. "Since we're going to be working together on this note story, I wanted to get an update on your visit yesterday. Tell me about Taylor Crowe."

The phone hissed in her ear for a long moment, then MacGruder said, "There's not much to tell, really, other than what you read in my column. Taylor thought her father might have written the note, but she steadfastly refused to claim it. Apparently they hadn't been on speaking terms for several years."

Julie frowned at the ceiling, irritated both by MacGruder's glib attitude and the interview's outcome. She'd been hoping Crowe would accept the note — what a great story that would make! *Nation's Top Songwriter Receives Last Message from Father!* But now it looked as though her team would be reporting from Florida instead of a floating luxury apartment complex.

Standing, she walked to the fireplace and plucked a cigarette from the case on the mantel. "Let's not give up. Surely we can find something within the message itself that might convince her to reconsider —"

"Afraid not." MacGruder sounded as if she were smiling now. "She was pretty definite. I tried my best to persuade her, but Taylor refused to budge. She has a certain mental image of her father, and nothing I said could alter it."

"You're *sure* she won't do it?"

"I just said I was."

Tucking the cigarette between her fingers, Julie looked around for a light. "What do you think? Could her father have written the note?"

MacGruder snorted. "How do I know? I have no choice but to accept Taylor's word. By the way, I don't think you're going to find her very cooperative if you show up at her place with cameras."

Spying the lighter on a table, Julie reached for it, then flicked a flame into existence. "We've covered our bases there. Howard Media & Entertainment owns her contract, so she'll have to cooperate."

"What a lucky girl."

Though MacGruder spoke in a cool, even voice, there was no mistaking the hostility in her tone. Julie felt her temper rise as she cradled the phone beneath her chin and held the cigarette to the flame. "Listen, lady, I hear you didn't even put up a fight when Adam offered you the syndication deal. So watch yourself and play along."

"Unwilling cooperation is nothing but coercion." MacGruder's voice was cold and lashing. "And I don't think Taylor Crowe will appreciate a heavy-handed approach any more than I do. For heaven's sake, the woman is *grieving*."

"I thought you said they weren't close." Julie brought the smoldering cigarette to her lips.

"They weren't — but Taylor's still not willing to talk about it much."

Julie laughed to cover her annoyance. "Well, I certainly hope she recovers from her grief soon. And I hope your final candidate pays off. If not, we may have to visit Taylor Crowe and convince her to —"

"My columns aren't about *paying off,* Julie. They're about searching for the truth. I really want to know if the note belongs to one of these people or if it's some kind of hoax. If it is, I won't hesitate to say so."

From what asylum had this woman escaped? Exhaling a stream of smoke, Julie blew her bangs off her forehead, then tried the direct approach. "Listen, Peyton, I know about Tanner Ford. It was simple really, once I had two first names, to figure out that

you were looking for names beginning with
T. So we uncovered Ford, and we know
you'll be headed next to Gainesville."

"Really? I'm surprised you did the research. Last time you just weaseled the information out of an innocent kid."

Julie laughed. "I've never had to beg for
anything. People line up to give me what I
want." She tapped a half-inch of ashes into a
mug on the coffee table, making a mental
note to remove it in case Adam dropped in.
"It all depends on how you ask."

No answer from MacGruder but the quiet
sound of a huff.

Annoyed by the writer's self-righteous attitude, Julie gripped the phone. "You know
we've already begun to tape promos for the
special. We're ready to go, so let's stop
playing cat and mouse and put our cards on
the table, shall we? Why don't you fax me a
copy of the note so I can have a handwriting
expert take a look."

"Forget it. What's an expert going to tell
you? That the person who wrote it was
under *duress?*" MacGruder's laughter had
a sharp edge. "An expert can't identify
handwriting without something to compare
it with, and I can assure you neither Timothy Manning nor Taylor Crowe is going to
give you a sample of their fathers' hand-

writing — even if they have one." Peyton's voice went as chilly as the smoke off dry ice. "I'll give you everything as soon as I'm finished, but not before. I don't want anything to leak out and spoil the series for my readers."

"The World News Network doesn't deal in leaks."

"I stopped believing in fairy tales years ago, Ms. St. Claire. Now, if you'll excuse me, I have a deadline to meet."

"I have a deadline, too."

"But you're television news. Don't you all pride yourselves on being up-to-the-minute?"

The phone line clicked. Julie dropped the cordless phone to her lap, then raked her nails across the chair's velvet upholstery. Peyton MacGruder would be no help at all, and she'd ruin everything if she interviewed Tanner Ford and came up empty. A hoax would spell disaster for WNN, but print journalists, especially columnists, had an unfair advantage. They could take a nothing story, paint themselves totally into a corner, and escape by changing the subject to moonbeams and broken hearts, throwing in the mention of a sad little kid for good measure. They didn't have to come up with the goods and answer the hard questions.

But television reporters did. No broadcast journalist worth her salt could forget Geraldo Rivera's much-hyped and disastrous TV special on the secret vaults of racketeer Al Capone. The ballyhooed special featured live footage of construction crews opening the vaults only to find a few broken bottles and bucketfuls of dust. Rivera found not a single trace of Capone or his gang, but for an hour viewers stared at live footage of Rivera gamely trying to pretend he'd accomplished something significant.

Julie St. Claire would not allow herself to be caught empty-handed. Peyton Mac-Gruder's insistence that the network not air the special until she had completed her series was actually a blessing in disguise. If the columnist came up empty-handed, Julie could always proceed with a creative Plan B.

But what plan? The preacher in St. Louis was dull, a story footnote at best. Tanner Ford, according to her preliminary research, was a small-time weatherman, no big deal. But the story of wealthy, reclusive Taylor Crowe and her estranged father's tragic death would tantalize the American public.

Moving to the carved wooden desk beneath the window, Julie pulled her notebook from a drawer and wrote TAYLOR CROWE in block letters.

She could pay Crowe a visit. Even if they couldn't convince *her* that her father had written the note, they might be able to convince a few million viewers. People would believe almost anything if they saw it on television. And live footage of real people was solid gold — the success of reality TV shows had proved it.

Julie parked her chin in her palm, then drew a box around Taylor's name. She could almost hope MacGruder's third candidate wouldn't qualify . . . but if the columnist was right about the songwriter's resistance, perhaps it'd be better to leave Taylor Crowe alone. Unwilling, recalcitrant subjects did not make good tabloid television.

So . . . this third mystery date, Tanner Ford, needed to claim the note. Simple. And if the fates were kind, she'd be able to find something fascinating in his background.

The phone rang, startling her out of her thoughts. The caller was Jason Philmore, a WNN broadcast technician. "You wanted to record a new sixty-second promo?" he asked, his voice clipped in her ears. "You got a studio. We're ready whenever you can get here."

"Did the producer get the still shots of Taylor Crowe?"

"Dunno. But there's an envelope here with your name on it, hand-delivered from TruBlood Records."

TruBlood . . . Julie smiled as she placed the name: another division of Howard Media & Entertainment. She glanced in the mirror above the mantel and pulled at a stray hank of hair. "Let me dress," she said, turning toward her bedroom. "And tell Hattie to dig up everything she can on —"

"Hattie's not here. It's Sunday."

"Call her then, and tell her if she wants a job tomorrow, she'd better come in today. Have her research Tanner Ford — his family, background, present job, everything. I'll be there in twenty minutes."

Seated at her desk in the spare bedroom she used as a home office, Peyton rubbed her hands together, then pressed them over her face and breathed deeply, trying to focus her thoughts. The call from Julie St. Claire had wrecked her concentration, and she had promised to have tomorrow's column in by two o'clock today. This next-to-last in the series had to be perfect; she wanted to set up her readers for the final interview in the most effective way.

But her brain, still centered upon Julie St. Claire, refused to change gears. The harder she tried to ignore the mental picture of a smiling St. Claire the more it persisted, so she surrendered to an impulse and decided to indulge in a moment of imagination therapy — an old trick she'd learned in her Gainesville days. Closing her eyes, she visualized Julie St. Claire on a white sofa, dressed in a soft linen suit, smiling and nodding — and then spilling a cup of coffee all over herself on live television.

No — not drastic enough. Maybe she'd be sitting with Mel Gibson on that couch, and she'd get flustered and call him Gel Mibson, then spill coffee all over *him*. No — too cute. For all the aggravation she'd caused, St. Claire deserved to fall flat on her face on the runway outside the Oscars — wearing a too-tight, red satin miniskirt — or be voted one of the nation's ten worst dressed celebrities in that annual edition of *People* magazine . . .

Cut it out, MacGruder. She's doing her job; you need to get busy doing yours.

Sighing, Peyton opened her eyes. She should have known St. Claire would already be working her nails to the nub on this story. Like Peyton, she had to stay in front of the pack, because the pack was growing larger

303

and more vicious by the hour. Over two hundred e-mails waited in Peyton's mailbox, and she shuddered to think about listening to her backlogged voice mail at the office. Everyone wanted a piece of the story, and there weren't enough pieces to go around.

The days when one reporter could truly own a story were long gone. Once a feature hit print, every newspaper and television station in the country could pick it up and run with it. At least, Peyton reminded herself, she still carried the ball.

Sports analogies. She was reverting to her past.

Dropping her hands to the computer keyboard, she struggled to pull her thoughts together. She wanted to give her readers a picture of the man she was going to meet, but she didn't want to name Tanner Ford. She'd identify him afterward, but only if he claimed the note. And if he didn't . . . she shoved the thought aside. Some bridges could wait until one absolutely had to cross them.

From the Internet and news archives she'd been able to compile an extensive background report on the late Trenton Ford, Tanner's father. Before boarding the doomed PanWorld jetliner, Trenton Ford had been owner and CEO of FordCo Oil of Dallas, a multimillion-dollar corporation. Apparently everything the late Mr. Ford touched turned to gold, including a string of Ford Club hunting lodges scattered throughout Texas and Arkansas. The Ford mansion had been featured in *Architectural Digest* and *House Beautiful*; the lovely Mrs. Blythe Ford had been a close personal friend of Nancy Reagan's and still spoke often to Barbara Bush.

Though Peyton read pages of material on the oil tycoon and his wife, she couldn't help but notice that not a single article mentioned the Ford children. Ford's curriculum vitae, found on the Web site for FordCo Oil, did mention a son, so apparently Tanner was an only child. He was also the only child listed in Mr. Ford's obituary.

Odd, Peyton thought, that Tanner Ford had not stepped into the family business. She knew less than nothing about the oil industry, but in all of Mr. Ford's varied interests he surely could have found a place for his son . . . unless they had parted company.

Her pulse quickened in the way it always did when she suspected she had stumbled onto something important. What the elder Mr. Ford's history did *not* reveal might be far more significant than the details she'd sprinkled through her notebook.

Eager for an answer, she glanced back over her notes on the son: weathercaster Tanner Ford, employed by ABC-affiliate WJCB in Gainesville, lived at 49578 NW Fifth Avenue. From a WJCB Web site she learned that he'd moved to Florida from Dallas, where he'd spent five years at another (smaller, she assumed) independent television station. The station's Web site listed hunting and horseback riding among his avocations — activities that would definitely appeal to his Florida viewing audience. Alachua County people were big on horses and hunting.

For the briefest moment, a picture of Garrett leaning against a three-rail fence appeared in her mind's eye — faint at first, then sharpening like a Polaroid. He had loved riding, even though they couldn't afford a horse, and she'd often gone with him to the equestrian park to watch other riders. He'd been to an equestrian event on New Year's morning, only hours before the accident —

"Stop it!" she snapped, infuriated that her muscles had begun to quiver with the memory flash. She couldn't do this, not now. She had no time to spare, and no energy left for a panic attack . . .

"You've got to focus." She lowered her gaze, staring at the palms of her upturned hands. She knew how to combat the fear; years ago she had memorized the Ten Commandments of Resisting Panic. But it'd been so long since she'd had to use them, and yesterday on that blasted boat not a single coping mechanism had come to mind . . .

"One — feelings of panic and fear are nothing more than an exaggeration of normal physical reactions to stress," she whispered, hearing the calm, collected voice of her therapist through a veil of memory. His voice had once brought her back from darkness; perhaps it could help her again.

"Two — these feelings are unpleasant and frightening, not dangerous. Nothing worse will happen to you."

Unless you jump overboard. Or go into the bathroom and open the medicine cabinet.

A sludge of nausea roiled in her belly. "Three," she said, strengthening her voice. "Let the feelings come. Take a deep breath and let them go as you breathe out."

Exhaling in a rush, she stared at the keyboard, then reached out to touch it. *Four,* she typed, watching the words fill her computer screen, *stop adding to your panic with thoughts of where it might lead. Take one day, one moment, at a time.*

The plastic felt cool under her fingertips, and the quiet clatter of the keys steadied her nerves. The rising fear seemed to flow out of her, borne away by the steady rattle of persistent typing.

Exhaling again, Peyton turned her attention to her notebook. This feature wouldn't write itself, and the longer she put it off, the less time she'd have to craft the column she wanted to share. She had to begin *now*.

"Five," she murmured, skimming through her notes, "try to distract yourself from what is going on inside you."

Like a swimmer about to dive into cold water, she took another deep breath and began to type.

Fourteen

Monday, July 2

The Heart Healer
By Peyton MacGruder
© Howard Features Syndicate

Dear Readers:

As you read this, I'll be preparing for a meeting with the third and final prospect for the note of Flight 848. This young man lives in Gainesville, Florida, only three hours from me, so I'll have many things to consider on the drive north.

Gainesville is a lovely town — actually more like south Georgia than tropical Florida. Alachua County has more pines than palms, and the land rises and falls in soft swells. The University of Florida occupies a solid chunk of the city's real estate, and many area residents are affiliated with the university. Outside the city, owners of graceful farms breed and train winning racehorses within pristine picket fences.

309

This is an elegant area, a place anyone would delight to call home.

Even elegance, however, has to contend with darkness. Gainesville's reputation suffered terribly in the late summer of 1990. Danny Rolling, a.k.a the "Gainesville Ripper," murdered five students in a single terror-filled weekend. Today, more than eleven years later, a single wall near the university campus is painted with the names of Rolling's victims. The people here will never forget, but they are determined to move on.

The man I'm going to interview next is undoubtedly a part of Gainesville's bright future. My prospect, a young professional adult, is a transplant from Dallas, Texas (nearly everyone in Florida is a transplant from someplace), and he seemed eager to hear my news when I called to set up our appointment.

I'll give complete details in my next column when I hope to settle the matter of the note. Its message — which I'll share Wednesday — is disarmingly simple. I have a feeling millions of people would give anything to receive such a note with their name at the top of the page.

I began this search with a simple goal: find the person for whom the note was intended. But over the past few days, the search has broadened for me.

You see, though I lived in and left Gainesville years before Danny Rolling committed his crimes, the thought of that city will always evoke unhappy memories for me. Something in my spirit shrivels at the thought of returning to those rolling hills. The memories are personal, so there's no reason to explore them here, but this realization has made me wonder . . . what sort of memories are my prospects facing when I bring them a note that awakens recollections they have safely tucked away? Most of my memories have been buried deep in the well of memory, but the specter of Gainesville keeps stirring the waters . . .

Perhaps, as Nelson Mandela once said, "true reconciliation does not consist in merely forgetting the past." I used to think forgetting was enough, but life has a way of dredging up even the most deeply buried memories.

Strange, how the note with its six-word message has the power to probe a conscience. Or maybe the note is like radioactive material — the more you're exposed, the more deeply you're affected.

I'm beginning to feel scorched down to the bone marrow.

As I ready to bring this series to a close, I can't help thinking about second chances. Each of the three prospects who fit the criteria defined by the note's salutation has been given another opportunity to hear from his or her father. Yet the first two people I interviewed did not even seem eager to receive the message of the note. I would have thought they'd be eager for an occasion to bring closure to an abruptly terminated relationship.

After all, we pride ourselves on being a country where a man can declare bankruptcy one year and earn millions in the next. You would think our overriding love for the underdog and lost causes would drive us to grasp every opportunity for a second chance.

I don't pretend to understand the reasons behind the reactions the note has received thus far, but I know the note is powerful and power shouldn't be wasted. So I'm hoping this last prospect will be able to truthfully and sincerely tell me, "Yes. This message is for me."

Today, when I present a copy of the note to the final prospect on my list, I'll be giving a child one last chance to hear a message from a loving father.

Will he accept it? We'll see.

★ ★ ★

Knowing she had no answers for Erma and the regulars at Dunkin' Donuts, on Monday morning Peyton skipped her usual cup of coffee and drove straight to the office. She had an hour to kill before she had to leave for Gainesville, and she needed to go through her e-mail and phone messages.

Mandi jumped up like a jerked marionette as Peyton approached her desk. "Tanner Ford called," the intern said, her eyes narrowing. "He's got company up in Gainesville."

Peyton's mouth went dry. "Who?"

"At least two different news vans and a half-dozen reporters." Mandi's eyes gleamed. "He said he's willing to wait until you get there, but those people are getting mighty impatient."

Peyton scratched her head, her thoughts scampering around. "How'd they get his name? I didn't identify him in the column."

Mandi's brow arched. "You didn't see the promo? I saw it last night, and it's playing probably once an hour on WNN. It's a shot of Julie St. Claire promising to reveal the mystery passenger of Flight 848 in a news special Wednesday night." She leaned closer. "She named all the names, Peyton: Tim Manning, Taylor Crowe, and

313

Tanner Ford. That's how everybody found out."

Peyton groaned as her plans for a leisurely drive to Gainesville vanished. It didn't take much effort to envision the scene outside Tanner Ford's house and Timothy Manning's church. All the local stations would be represented, of course. Taylor Crowe could thank heaven she lived on a boat.

And Julie St. Claire . . . that little guttersnipe was probably en route to Gainesville, if she hadn't arrived already.

But St. Claire could do nothing without the note, and she still had no clue what it said.

"Ignorance," Peyton whispered, meeting Mandi's gaze, "*is* bliss." She'd have to take a flight now, one of those puddle-jumping planes that always made her nervous . . .

No. She couldn't. She would need help to get through this, even to get to Gainesville.

She rapped Mandi's desk with her knuckles, then nodded. "Okay. No reason to fear, we'll just pick up the pace a little. Um — go into my mailbox, will you, and print out all the e-mails? Answer any you can and leave the others for me. And be sure you tell Nora how many there were."

Mandi nodded and rolled her chair toward Peyton's computer. "Where will you be?"

"In the sports department," Peyton answered, moving through the newsroom. "I need to ask a favor."

Peyton watched, supremely gratified, as King's face darkened to a lovely crimson color. "The gall of that woman," he muttered, snapping a pencil as if it were a toothpick. "What is it with television reporters? They seem to live by that maxim about forgiveness being easier to obtain than permission."

"You know they'll come up with a hundred ways to justify the promo spot," Peyton said, glancing at the clock on his wall. "They'll say it's reasonable promotion; they'll point out that I promised them the complete story by July fourth."

"But they've revealed all three of your prospects."

"And they'll suffer for it, if any of the three decide not to cooperate. They'll *really* suffer if this Tanner fellow turns down the note, too. They'll be stuck with a prime-time special about nothing."

King's mouth curled like he wanted to spit. "Julie St. Claire won't let herself get stuck. I've a feeling she'll insist the note's authentic, and then she'll find a way to make it stick to one of the three candidates. She has no choice."

Peyton tilted her head. "Which of the three?"

King shrugged. "Doesn't really matter, does it? From what you've told me, it looks like all three are pretty colorful characters. You've given her a television preacher with a flair for histrionics, a wildly successful song-writer, and a weatherman who, at the very least, is bound to be photogenic."

Peyton managed a choking laugh. "Really made it easy for her, didn't I?"

His eyes softened. "You did good. You didn't give her the ball and you stayed in the game."

Peyton glanced down at her hands, swallowing the lump that had risen in her throat. This next part would be hard.

"King?"

"Still here."

"Do you have plans for today — I mean, unchangeable plans? I need someone to go with me to Gainesville."

When she looked up, he seemed to be examining her face with considerable concentration. "Are you not feeling well?"

"I'm fine — a little tired, maybe, but that's not why I need someone to go with me."

Teasing laughter lit his eyes. "You lose your license or something?"

"No." Lowering her gaze to her hands again, Peyton struggled to find the words. She didn't want to tell him anything specific, but if she gave him a general picture, maybe he'd understand. "It's Gainesville. I used to live there and I went through some pretty rough times. I'm afraid I'll —"

The creak of his chair interrupted her. When she looked up, he was standing behind his desk and reaching for the Devil Rays baseball cap he kept on his filing cabinet. "Where are you going?"

King gave her a relaxed smile. "If we leave now, I figure we have a pretty good chance of keeping the wolves outside Tanner Ford's house at bay."

A rush of gratitude filled Peyton's heart. "I'll get my bag," she said, moving ahead of him toward her desk.

Julie St. Claire stepped out of the cab, tipped the driver handsomely, then stood for a moment in front of the small concrete-block house. Tanner Ford's residence looked like the typical three-bedroom, two-bath tract house that popped up every fifty feet or so in this section of Gainesville, and its very ordinariness assured her. Ford would appreciate the uniqueness of his situation — and what she had to offer.

Tossing her hair over her shoulder, she walked toward the news van from WOGX, the FOX station in Ocala. A crew from Ford's own station, WJCB, waited on the curb, too. Either Ford had called them, or one of their other reporters had gotten wind of the story.

The FOX guys grinned as she walked up to the van. "Hi, fellas," she called, pleased by their open admiration. Apparently these guys from the sticks didn't get much in the way of excitement. "So glad you could come help me out."

"A pleasure to meet you, Miss St. Claire." A tall man in a denim work shirt climbed out of the passenger seat and extended his hand. "I'm Reed Nash, and I'll be operating the truck. Michael Green" — he gestured to a man crouching inside the open door — "is our photojournalist."

"Cameraman'll do fine." Green grinned as he thrust out his hand. "Nice to meet you, Miss St. Claire. I've admired your work for some time."

She peered inside the van as she shook his hand, then smiled. The truck was equipped with video editing equipment, television monitors, telephones, intercom systems, audio mixers, speakers, and what looked like miles of cable.

"Nice to meet you both." Julie took a step back and surveyed the truck's exterior. The vehicle was a microwave unit, not as good as the satellite equipment she was accustomed to, but it would do. A retractable mast with a small rotating dish rode on the roof. When they were ready to broadcast, the mast would extend far enough to beam the signal to a receiver, probably located at the station.

She lowered her gaze and looked at Nash. "You got a clear line of sight from here to the receiver?"

"No problem, ma'am, you're in Florida." Reed gave her an easy, relaxed smile that seemed to have a good deal of confidence behind it. "That signal will fly straight home, so don't you worry."

She shifted her gaze to the camera operator. "Did they tell you my plan?"

Green nodded slowly, a grin slowly overtaking his stubbled features. "They sent along a release form, though. Mr. Ford will have to sign it before I can set up."

"He'll sign it." Julie turned toward the house, then lifted a hand to shield her eyes from the late morning glare. "I'm not worried."

After a quick glance at her watch, she shot

a smile back to the waiting men, then tilted her head toward the house. "Come with me, Mr. Green, and bring the release. I want to be all set up before Peyton MacGruder arrives."

Grinning like a child at Christmas, Michael Green unfolded his long legs and followed her.

Tanner Ford felt his heart skip a beat when he opened the door and discovered Julie St. Claire on his front porch. The woman had become a legend among newscasters in the last three weeks; some said she was destined to take Barbara Walters's place within three years. Though she had sprung from a lowly station much like the one where Tanner currently worked, her success proved that intelligence, good looks, and dogged perseverance could propel talent to the top.

"Good morning, Mr. Ford." St. Claire's voice seemed lower and a great deal huskier than on television. "Thank you for agreeing to see me."

For an instant his tongue seemed paralyzed, then his reflexes kicked in. "It's my pleasure." Tanner opened the door and gestured to the inside of his house, momentarily ashamed of his Spartan living quarters. Julie St. Claire probably lived in a penthouse apartment . . .

But she walked in and smiled, admiring his living room as if it were digs fit for a king. "Nice place," she said, walking slowly. She stopped before his bookshelf, as he'd hoped she might. His home might be humble, but the variety of books on his shelves would tell her he was well-read, even ambitious. If she took a moment to examine the titles she'd find books on meteorology, self-discipline, public speaking, even Feng Shui.

"This" — she tapped the shelf, then turned to look at the blue-jeaned bubba who'd followed her in — "would be the perfect spot for the camera."

The bubba moved toward the shelf, and Julie backed away, her gaze now centering on the guest chair before the window. Tanner knew she was planning the shot, mentally placing him and Peyton Mac-Gruder into position.

"I had a call from Miss MacGruder about an hour ago." He slid his hands into his pockets, giving Julie a conspiratorial smile. "She's on her way. Said she'd arrive about noon."

"Oh?" The fine dark brows lifted. "She say anything else?"

" 'Hands off.' " He deepened his smile.

"That's an exact quote. That's what I'm supposed to tell you if you knock on my door."

Her laughter was warm, deep, and rich, and suddenly her exquisite hand came up to touch his face. "Then I suppose," she said, stepping close enough for him to feel the warmth of her breath on his cheek, "we'd better not tell her about this, should we?"

Traffic clogged Interstate 75, vacationers mingling with semis who rumbled cab-to-cab like the cars of an unrelenting freight train. King drove like a pro, though, slanting from one lane to the next, skirting sluggish sightseers and commercial drivers alike.

Peyton sat in the passenger seat, her legs pressed together, her hands clasped, her blood rushing through all the boulevards of her body. They'd talked about several things since leaving Tampa — the Bucs, the Devil Rays, and Darren, King's son. Not much had changed in that situation, King had said, a note of regret in his voice. Darren still came around when he wanted money or needed a place to study, but most of the time he seemed content to remain at arm's length. Peyton accepted this news silently, thinking of the unopened letters on her kitchen table. Weren't she and her father at the same place?

When they passed the huge green-and-white sign announcing their entrance into Alachua County, Peyton flinched, the view pebbling her skin with goose flesh.

"You know," King said, "I read your column this morning. It was great — far better than anything you've ever done. I think you're beginning to figure this columnist thing out."

Despite her anxiety, Peyton flushed with pleasure. "I hardly remember what I wrote."

"You're learning, kiddo. You're opening up and beginning to go deep. And I appreciate what you're doing, as a reader and as an editor."

Peyton lowered her gaze as her cheeks burned. High praise indeed from the man who'd once routinely threatened her with covering nothing but the Senior Adult Synchronized Swimming Association.

"Thanks," she whispered, glancing at him. "Coming from you, that means a lot."

He grinned at her, then reached out and took her hand. For a moment she was too surprised to react, then her lips parted — he'd read her column today. And in it she had confessed to having bad memories of

Gainesville, so King had agreed to drive her on the barest suggestion because —

He cared.

She felt the truth all at once, like an electric tingle in the tips of her fingers and toes. She savored the thought, enjoying its newness, but that thought brought another in its wake: What was she going to do about it?

She didn't have the faintest idea.

"King —," she began, but he dropped her hand and gripped the wheel, slanting the car toward the right exit lane. "We're here," he said, nodding toward another green sign. "Gainesville."

Hurtling back to earth, she picked up her backpack and rummaged for the folder with Ford's address. She'd worry about King later; right now she had a job to do.

After a couple of wrong turns, Peyton and King found Tanner Ford's house on a street dotted with tall pines. The neighborhood was an older one — probably built in the early days of the university — and looked like a hundred other neighborhoods for married college students.

In fact, it looked just like the area where she and Garrett had lived . . .

A sudden chill climbed the ladder of her spine. The street wasn't the same, nor was the neighborhood, but the concrete-block

324

houses could have been designed by the same harried, unimaginative builder.

King's hand closed around hers again and squeezed. "You okay, kiddo? Looks like we have a mob up ahead."

Peyton shifted her gaze from the houses to the street. Ford's place was easily distinguishable by the vehicles around it. Five TV trucks — from WJCB, WTXP, WOGX, and WXFL — straddled gutters on the road, their masts retracted, their motors idle. With a start, Peyton realized they were waiting for her.

"WTSP?" King read the logo on the side of the nearest van as he parked the car. "That's one of our local stations. They're the CBS affiliate in St. Pete."

"News travels fast," Peyton answered, her voice dry. She took a moment to scan the people loitering around the vans — sure enough, Julie St. Claire stood beside the van from WOGX. She'd probably worked out some sort of arrangement to use their equipment for her follow-up interview.

"I see St. Claire's not wasting any time." Feeling a little stronger, Peyton pulled her backpack closer, then gave King an uncertain smile. "Ready or not, here I go." She opened her door, then jerked back around when she heard King open his door, too. "You going with me?"

"I'm going to stand guard," he answered, turning to climb out of the car. "I was thinking maybe you won't feel so outnumbered if you look out the window and see somebody in your corner."

Though she felt a long way from any real humor, Peyton laughed softly. As she walked toward the house, she saw Julie St. Claire straighten, look her way, and offer a little wave. Had the woman no shame? She glanced over her shoulder, then felt cheered to see King leaning on the car, his arms crossed in a defensive pose.

Peyton knocked on the door, and half a moment later Tanner Ford opened it. Her third and final prospect was tall, helmet-haired, and handsome, as she'd expected him to be. He even had the newscaster's requisite cleft chin.

"Hi, Tanner, I'm Peyton." She offered her hand and a smile. "Thanks for making time for me today. And I'm sorry about the circus outside."

Laughing, he invited her in. "Don't apologize. Those are my people out there — some of them, anyway. I suppose you know I'm the weathercaster at WJCB."

Peyton nodded and moved into a tidy

living room crowded with a sofa on one wall and two chairs before the window. A bookshelf of lumber and bricks lined the third wall, the poor man's way to store books. She and Garrett had constructed a similar bookshelf in a house much like this one.

Slamming the door on the unwelcome memory, she walked toward the sofa and forced herself to focus. "I read about your present position. I also learned you're from Dallas."

"Yes — but don't sit on that uncomfortable sofa, Peyton. It's in terrible shape. Here, take this chair instead." Surprised, she turned to see Tanner pointing toward a plaid chair that leaned toward the right and had obviously seen better days. The chair, in fact, looked in far worse shape than the couch. She was about to make a joke about the listing chair when a movement from the street caught her eye. One of the TV guys was telling a story, whooping and waving his arms —

She pressed her lips together. Maybe Ford wanted her to sit with her back to the window so she wouldn't be distracted by the commotion outside. Fair enough.

"Thanks." She sat in the seat he offered, bracing herself against the pull of gravity, while Tanner sat across from her in the opposite chair.

"First," she began, launching into the speech that now felt as familiar as her own name, "let me say how sorry I am about the loss of your father. Flight 848 was a great tragedy. I've never been so close to anything like it before. I think it's safe to say the tragic loss of so many people dramatically affected everyone in my community."

Tanner lowered his gaze and seemed to study his knees. "Thank you. My father was a great man, beloved in Dallas. The funeral was held there, of course, and the church filled to capacity. It did my heart good to see how much everyone respected him."

"And there's this little detail." Bending, she pulled a confidentiality agreement from the folder, then set it on the little table between the two chairs. "I hate to have to do this, but for this story, I feel it's necessary."

Ford's brows pulled into an affronted frown as he skimmed the language. "Really," he said, lapsing into a wry drawl, "and why would this be important?"

"Take a look out your window." Peyton gave him a moment to consider the circus outside, then folded her hands. "I'm sure you're aware of competition in the media marketplace, Mr. Ford. I'm just trying to cover my bases."

Ford nodded, then stood and patted his pockets. "Call me Tanner. And I'll sign, but I'm afraid I don't —"

"Use mine." Smiling, Peyton pulled a pen from her bag and handed it to him. Without another word he scrawled a barely legible signature across the bottom of the page, then handed it to her.

After returning the confidentiality agreement to the folder, Peyton settled back into the uncomfortable chair, then shifted when something sharp — a piece of straw? — poked her through the fabric. "Now we can get down to details," she said, smiling to put him at ease. "Were you and your father close?"

"Very. I've only been away from Dallas for five years, and we kept in constant touch."

"So you must know why he was on that flight. I first assumed he was coming to visit you, but surely he'd take a more direct flight than Tampa. I also wondered — maybe I'm showing my ignorance here, or I've watched too much TV — but wouldn't a man as important as your father fly in a private jet?"

"He usually took the company jet, but it was being serviced." A tremor passed over Tanner's face, and a sudden spasm of grief knit his brows. "He never flew commercial, but he decided to this time. He had to take care of some business in Tampa, then he was planning to drive up to see me." Tanner lowered his head. "If only he'd come to see me first, flown into Gainesville, or hired another plane . . ." His words trailed away, followed by a swipe at his nose.

"Well, Tanner" — Peyton reached for her backpack again — "I'm sure by now you've heard about my reason for coming. We found a note that could have come from Flight 848, we're searching for the person to whom it belongs, and we've reason to believe that person might be you. I'd like you to look at this copy of the note and tell me if you think your father might have written it."

Tanner's expression cleared as he reached for the paper in her hands. Eagerly he skimmed the page, then dropped the note to his lap and pressed his hand to his face. "Oh . . . my . . ." He spoke slowly, emphasizing each word as if it might be his last. "Dear God in heaven, help me."

Peyton leaned forward. "Do you think —"

"It's his handwriting. Of course it is, I'd know it anywhere. Oh, why did this have to happen?" Ford pressed the back of his hand to his mouth, his eyes filling with water.

"It's your father's handwriting?" Peyton prodded gently. "You're certain?"

Ford nodded wordlessly. Tears gathered in the corners of his eyes and slowly spilled from the ends of his dark lashes.

"I don't mean to pry, but can you tell me what he meant by 'all is forgiven'? Did you two have some sort of falling-out?"

His hand still against his mouth, Tanner nodded again, then wiped the wetness from his cheeks. "We had an argument the day before he got on the plane," he said, more tears springing to replace those he'd wiped away. "It was a silly matter, really. Dad wanted me to move back to Dallas; I told him I wanted to move to New York. I've been at this station for five years, you see, and I'm ready to try for something bigger." His mouth twitched with wry amusement. "I don't know what you know about the Lone Star State, Ms. MacGruder, but Texans tend to think of Dallas as the biggest and best city in the world. But that's just good ol' Texas chauvinism, and that's what I told my dad."

Taking a cue from Mary Grace, Peyton leaned back in the chair and said nothing.

"My dad was the kindest, most supportive, most incredible father," Tanner continued, gulping hard. "He was the absolute best. And this" — he rattled the copy of the note — "proves it. That he would think of me as the plane was falling, well, I —"

He closed his eyes, held up a hand. "Excuse me a moment."

Peyton nodded silently while Tanner rose and left the room. She stared at the bookcase along the wall — Ford owned books on broadcasting, public speaking, and a large collection of tattered paperback copies of Garfield comics. A five-by-seven color photograph at the end of the shelf featured Tanner with his arms around a man and a woman — undoubtedly his parents.

Peyton leaned forward, about to stand and have a closer look, but the sound of approaching footsteps forced her back.

Ford reentered the room, sat down, then clamped his lips together. "I'm sorry, I needed to be alone for a moment."

"I understand."

"And I want to thank you." He looked Peyton full in the face, his smile deepening. "Thank you for undertaking this search and finding me."

Peyton gave him a cautious smile. "You're welcome. Can you give me an idea what you're feeling? I know it's not easy, but my readers will want to know."

"I —" He drew a shuddery breath. "The

note means so much." He lifted his teary gaze to meet hers. "May I — do you have the original?"

"I don't have it with me," she said, reaching for her bag. "I've put it in a safe place. But I could have it sent to you."

His jaws wobbled. "I'd appreciate receiving it . . . as soon as possible. I'll treasure it always."

He pressed his fingertips to the copy on the table between them, then stood and offered his hand. Peyton stood, too, a little annoyed at being dismissed so quickly. She had other questions to ask, and she wanted to get a look at the picture of his father.

"Actually, I was hoping we could spend a little more time together," she said, taking his hand.

His face contracted in a small grimace of pain, as though she had suddenly struck him. "I'm sorry, but I just can't talk right now. I need to be alone."

Peyton glanced out the window, where another TV van had joined the parade of vehicles. Somehow she doubted if solitude ranked very high on Ford's priority list — the man hadn't even closed the drapes.

"All right, then." She forced a smile. "But I'd like to ask a favor. Despite the TV cameras on your front lawn, please do not reveal what happened here until after Wednesday morning. That's when my final column will run. If you reveal the result of my search before then —" She shrugged.

"I understand completely." Tanner's handshake was firm and final. "All right, Ms. MacGruder. I won't breathe a word until Wednesday." He shot a grin out the window. "Guess those folks will have to camp out on my lawn for a couple of nights."

"Thanks, Tanner."

Peyton moved toward the door, but stopped when he called out a question: "The note? When can I expect it?"

She glanced back over her shoulder. "I can mail it tomorrow — that way you'd have it by Thursday."

"Would you mind overnighting it?" His throat bobbed as he swallowed. "I'd like to have it by Wednesday — when I read your final column. I don't think it will seem real to me until then."

Peyton narrowed her gaze. The question itself was an indirect insult, since only a fool would believe his story about wanting the note purely for sentimental reasons. The truth was as obvious as roach droppings in a sugar bowl — he wanted the note for Julie St. Claire. He'd seen the woman outside his house, and he'd undoubtedly seen the promo spots on TV.

He was, after all, a newscaster.

But what did she care? She'd held a contest and found a winner, so he could have the prize.

"No problem," she said, opening the door.

Peyton felt a small thrill of victory as King pulled away from the house and left the TV newscasters filming their exit. She had the story. They didn't. Yet.

Score a big one for the team of Mac-Gruder and Bernard.

King listened without comment as Peyton told him all that had happened in Tanner Ford's living room. "So that's it," she said, adjusting her seat belt so she could turn in the seat as they talked. "Ford says the note is his, so I promised to send it to him. I'll write this up today and get it in before tomorrow's deadline, then I'm done. Ford can tell the television people whatever he wants on Wednesday morning."

King nodded, then reached out and turned off the soft rock playing on the radio. "I don't want to throw a wrench into the works" — he shot her a quick glance — "but there's one thing that bothers me about all this."

"What?"

He narrowed his gaze as he watched the road. "The three fathers — tell me their occupations again."

Peyton lifted her hand and counted on her fingers. "Timothy Manning's father was a retired insurance salesman. Taylor Crowe's father was a construction superintendent. And Tanner Ford's father was an oil tycoon and real estate developer. Apparently he had lots of irons in the fire."

King nodded, then pulled left to pass a slow-moving RV on the interstate. "The note — the woman on Mariner Drive found it in a plastic bag, right? One of those zipper-type things you use to carry sandwiches and snacks?"

Uncertain of where this train of thought would lead, Peyton nodded.

"Okay . . . knowing what you do about those three men, which would you say was the most likely to carry food onto a plane?"

The question crashed into her consciousness like surf smashing against a rocky cliff. Why would any of them need food? The flight from New York to Tampa would take less than three hours and had been scheduled to arrive shortly after six. Though the passengers would fly during the dinner hour, PanWorld had been scheduled to serve a meal.

She stared at King while thoughts whirled in her brain. "Trenton Ford would probably be the *least* likely," she said, a sick feeling assaulting her stomach. "He was a first-class passenger. He would have expected dinner complete with china and silverware. If the coach passengers got steak or chicken, he probably ate lobster and filet mignon."

King cocked an eyebrow at her. "What about the construction super?"

Peyton frowned. "Maybe. He flew in coach class and he was coming from his home, so maybe his wife sent him off with a sack lunch. Maybe he hated airline food."

"What about the insurance salesman?"

Closing her eyes, Peyton remembered how the plainspoken preacher had described his simple father. "Definitely, he could have carried food onto the plane. I wouldn't have been surprised if a man like that carried cookies, lovingly packed by his daughter. He was coming from her house."

King looked at her then, and in his eyes she saw the truth.

"Trenton Ford didn't write the note," she whispered, her heart sinking. "But why —"

"The son is in television," King answered, shifting his gaze back to the road. "Television people hunger for on-air time. They need it to survive. By claiming the note,

Tanner Ford has guaranteed his role as the star of a prime-time special airing in two days."

Peyton leaned against the car door, one hand pressed to her stomach as she considered the possibility that her next column would be filled with lies.

"Don't beat yourself up." King's voice was heavy with compassion. "You did your job, you found the three prospects, and one of them claimed the note. You've done the best writing of your career in the last two weeks, so don't worry. Write the conclusion with a clear conscience and let the chips fall where they may. Who knows?" He shrugged. "Maybe Trenton Ford *did* have a sandwich bag in his pocket. We don't know him and we weren't there. We can't know what really happened."

Peyton closed her eyes, appreciating the comfort, but not certain she could accept the counsel.

Alone in his bathroom, Tanner Ford surveyed his reflection in the mirror, then frowned when he lifted his chin and his forehead caught the light.

Shine — sometimes you couldn't do a thing about it.

Opening his medicine cabinet, he pulled

out a plastic container of loose powder specially formulated to match his skin tones, then brushed the puff over his forehead, nose, and chin. There. He'd be ready for whatever happened next.

Sighing, he closed the cabinet door, rechecked his reflection, and stood for a moment. He really didn't look a thing like his father, thank goodness. He had inherited his mother's chiseled looks, her thick hair, her elegance. His parentage had served him well.

The college drama classes had served him equally as well. The tears he'd displayed for Peyton MacGruder were real, but that part wasn't hard. Truth was, he *did* love his father, but he hadn't spoken to him since walking out of his office and telling him to take a flying leap off an oil derrick. He fulfilled any familial responsibilities by calling his mother once a month, but his father never entered the picture. Why should he?

He hadn't been around much when Tanner was growing up — at least Tanner couldn't remember him being there. So why should he miss the old man now? When he tried to remember his childhood, he came up with a fuzzy mental image of his father as a benevolent Santa who brought him the presents he asked for, put food on the table, and paid his college tuition. He pretty much did whatever Tanner asked as long as the son's requests fit into the father's idea of what a Ford son should be and do. So Tanner had a horse, a car, and ten thousand Texas acres to tramp and enjoy.

But he never got the thing he wanted most — freedom from the family, from the reputation, from the old man.

Truth be told, the old man was an embarrassment. Not because he was stuffy or uncool or strict like some of Tanner's friends' parents, but because he was Trenton Ford, one of the richest oil magnates in Texas. Everybody knew his name, and when gas prices shot up, everybody took his name in vain.

Tanner had always figured people would find it hard to believe an important person like Trenton Ford could take time from running his world to even consider having a son. He knew they'd find it impossible to believe Trenton Ford's offspring turned out to be a normal kid who got into as much trouble as the boy next door.

One of Tanner's teachers had once made a (rather obvious) point of telling the class that all men put on their pants one leg at a time. But in his heart of hearts, Tanner knew people in Dallas didn't believe anything about Trenton Ford was ordinary. Sometimes Tanner wondered if he even put his pants on. The tailored suits he always wore seemed to sort of grow on him.

Tanner lifted his hand and touched his hair, smoothing a few wisps that had blown out of place when he opened the front door. Had to be perfect and camera-ready when the door opened again.

He left the bathroom and walked back to the living room, then slipped his hands in his pockets and looked out the window. He grinned at the encampment on his curb. Finally, he'd done something to merit the attention he deserved! Still smiling, he sat on the sofa, where he could see anyone coming up the sidewalk. He picked up a newspaper and stared at the newsprint, but his mind refused to follow the words.

He doubted his father had even noticed when he left town. His mother said he did — she said he was heartbroken when Tanner walked away from the corporate kingdom he'd prepared, but Tanner didn't want any part of his father's world. His dad's work would swallow him alive, smother him in petitions, paperwork, and people. He would rather do his own thing, be his own man.

His father had never approved of the

newscasting idea — he kept saying he had better things in mind for his only son. He didn't like Tanner wearing pancake makeup, or carrying around his own camera, video deck, tripod, battery belt, and microphone. Tanner had thought his father was going to slip under the table the time they went out to eat at the old man's favorite French restaurant and Tanner used his announcer voice to order from the menu.

He'd never castigated his son in public, but always in private, with quiet little suggestions that his son could do better, be more than a painted pack mule who read the weather. When Tanner realized he couldn't escape all the nudging, he left.

He frowned at the paper in his hands. Had his father written the note? He honestly didn't know. It was hard to imagine he would . . . but he hadn't spoken to his father in so long he had no idea what was going through his mind when that plane went down. He could have been thinking of his son . . . or he could have been worrying about his all-consuming universe.

His mother had inherited everything, of course. She would probably give Tanner anything he asked for, but he had never particularly enjoyed spending the Ford fortune. He'd rather live on his own terms, in a little house and in off-the-rack suits, until he made it on his own.

Which he was about to do. Thanks to the note.

He smiled at the irony. This was a great story, and Peyton MacGruder had been wise to jump at it. She seemed like an okay reporter, and he was glad to do her a favor and give her an ending to her series, especially since the other two people she'd interviewed had turned coward and run from the publicity. The preacher probably didn't want anyone digging into his finances, and the songwriter — well, she didn't need help. Rumor had it that she was already sitting pretty.

But he, Tanner Ford, was ready to move up and out of a hick town populated by Joe and Martha Sixpack clones. The Gainesville television market was small time, ranked 165th in the nation, but with the publicity from this prime-time special he figured he could find a job with a station in the top five . . . maybe the top *three* markets. Chicago was nice, but L.A. would be better. And if Julie St. Claire liked him as much as she'd seemed to, maybe he'd be joining her at the top in New York.

Mindful that someone might be peering through the window with a long-range lens, he turned the newspaper page. "Thanks, Dad," he said, staring at a column of meaningless words. "It may sound callous, but dying is the best thing you've ever done for me."

Fifteen

Tuesday, July 3

Distracted by the incessant ringing of the phone, the near-constant chime of arriving e-mail, and the questions of curious co-workers, Peyton carried her notes and her laptop to an unused conference room on the south side of the *Times* building. After crawling on her hands and knees to find an outlet, she plugged in her laptop and settled down to work, keeping her back to the door and her eyes fixed to the computer screen.

She'd fully intended to write this column last night after returning from Gainesville, but the trip had left her exhausted. She went to bed at eight, thinking she'd nap a couple of hours and then sketch out a rough draft, but she slept deep and long, not awakening until sunlight fringed the bedroom blinds.

She'd mentally written this column a dozen times in her kitchen, in the shower, and on the way to work, but the words that sprang easily onto center stage during rehearsal balked in the unwavering light of her deadline. Leaning her elbows on the conference table, she raked her hands through her hair. Unbelievable, that she should develop a case of writer's block *now.*

It should have been easy — yesterday Tanner Ford did all the right things and evidenced all the right emotions — disbelief, shock, despair, sorrow, and finally, joy at the thought that his father had written the note. But that orderly display of emotions now felt fake, almost as if he'd rehearsed his reactions. And King's assertion that Ford had claimed the note for reasons of publicity left a sour taste in Peyton's mouth.

She glanced at her watch — eight-thirty. With an eleven-thirty deadline, she couldn't procrastinate any longer.

Drawing a deep breath, she began to type:

Yesterday I drove north to meet the young man whose name was third on my list of people for whom the note of Flight 848 might have been written. This final prospect is a young man — mid-thirties, tall, and striking — and his good looks have served him well. He is Tanner Ford, the weathercaster for WJCB TV, an ABC-affiliate in Gainesville.

Ford was waiting for me when I arrived — he and half the news people from at least two counties, or so it seemed. Interest in the note from the doomed PanWorld flight has grown to a level that surprises even me. I suppose it's only natural the nation should fixate on a bright bit of hope that survived our country's worst air disaster.

But as I consider all that has happened over the last few days, I have to ask myself: Are we really concerned about finding a home for the note, or are we — myself included — more concerned about how the attendant publicity can advance us?

I'll confess that my motives in undertaking the search are not completely altruistic. When the note was first presented to me, my initial thoughts were of my column. But as I've taken a copy of the note to three grieving people, its message has worked upon the innermost part of me.

What does the note say? Only six profound words, and I'm happy to reveal them now. The man who wrote the note used his last minutes of life to write: *I love you. All is forgiven.* Only the word *Dad* identifies the writer; only the letter *T* identifies the child.

My assistant and I methodically searched through all the obituaries of passengers and crew from Flight 848, and found only three *T* names. And so I traveled to meet with three children, all adults, who lost fathers aboard that plane. All three fit the basic criteria for the note, but none of the three were eager to accept its message.

The first candidate, the pastor of a large church in Midamerica, claimed his father would never have written the note. Though he assured me the handwriting did not match (a disputable assertion, given the circumstances in which the note was penned), his basic argument against the note's ownership was that he did not need forgiveness. He had enjoyed a happy and productive relationship with his father, they never argued, nor were they estranged. Forgiveness, therefore, was unnecessary.

My second interview took me to the port of Boston, where a wealthy and successful woman conceded that her father *might* have written the note. But, she assured me, the distance between herself and her father was too wide to be crossed, even by a bridge of forgiveness. She had strayed too far, she told me, to deserve reconciliation.

My third candidate, the one closest to home, claimed to recognize both the handwriting and the man behind the message. He and his father had had an argument, he told me, and the note was a loving father's attempt to set things right. Tanner Ford, weathercaster and grieving son, took the message to heart and —

"Hey, boss!"

Peyton flinched as Mandi's voice broke her concentration. She turned to see the younger woman in the doorway, her face a study in chagrin.

"I think you'd better come see this."

Alarmed by the note of panic in Mandi's voice, Peyton rose and followed her to the news desk. A group of reporters huddled beneath the television set hanging from the ceiling, but they parted like the Red Sea as Peyton approached.

"Sorry," Karen Dolen murmured, folding her arms. "Tough break."

A closeup of Julie St. Claire filled the screen, and when the camera cut away, Peyton saw Julie sitting with Tanner Ford . . . on the set of the *Early Show*. Bryant Gumbel was seated in a chair opposite them, his brows lowered in concern. "So how did you feel when you saw the note for the first time?" he asked.

"Well, Bryant," Julie said, crossing her long legs in full view of the camera, "we brought a tape. I had a hunch Tanner might be the one we were searching for, so we —

well, why don't we let the video speak for it-self?"

Peyton stared at the television in hypno-tized horror. Tanner Ford must have left for New York right after his interview with Peyton. The ink on the confidentiality agreement had barely dried before he went out cavorting with the enemy. He was prob-ably sipping wine with St. Claire en route to Manhattan before Peyton even made it home . . .

The cozy setting with Gumbel dis-appeared from the TV screen, replaced by a shot of Tanner in a chair, a small table at his right hand, and a window — his living room window — behind him. Peyton was not on camera — of course not, they didn't get her permission — but she could hear herself saying, "Well, Tanner, I'm sure by now you've heard about my reason for coming. We found a note that could have come from Flight 848, we're searching for the person to whom it belongs, and we've reason to be-lieve that person might be you. I'd like you to look at this copy of the note and tell me if you think your father might have written it."

The camera captured every emotion on Tanner's face — amazement, shock, horror. Then he pressed his hands to his cheeks. "Oh my." The audio was weak, but the words came through. "Dear God in heaven, help me."

Fear and anger knotted in Peyton's gut. She turned away. "Let me by, please," she said, shouldering her way through the crowd. Her pulse pounded thickly in her ears, blurring the voices from the television and the soft sounds of sympathy from her coworkers.

"I think you ought to stay." King appeared next to her, his hand reaching out to grip her upper arm. "Don't run, MacGruder. Let's see what they're up to."

Surrendering to the strength in his voice, she turned around. The camera had returned to Julie St. Claire, stunning in a red suit. The coy reporter was now dashing a tear from her eye. "I was so moved when I saw this tape," she told Gumbel. "And I know your viewers won't want to miss tomorrow night's special. We'll show video footage of this incredible man" — her hand fell over Tanner Ford's — "his late father, and the family. We'll have an interview with Mrs. Ford and those who knew Trenton Ford best, then we'll follow up with the latest FAA findings about the crash."

"Look at the bright side," King said, his voice low in Peyton's ear. "Apparently Trenton Ford is a big enough fish that she'll leave the others alone. Taylor Crowe and the preacher won't have to worry."

Peyton listened, her senses numb. She couldn't see a bright side in this mess, and at the moment she didn't feel terribly protective of either Taylor Crowe or Timothy Manning. Julie St. Claire hadn't slit their throats; she'd cut Peyton's.

A dozen sympathetic eyes turned toward her when the *Early Show* cut to a commercial. Under the concentrated weight of attention, Peyton looked down, faltering in the unexpected silence. "Well," she said, finding her voice, "that wraps up my series rather neatly, doesn't it? All I have to do is write up the obvious — Julie St. Claire stabbed me in the back, and Tanner Ford broke his confidentiality agreement. Maybe I should sue them. That'd make a heck of a surprise ending."

"That wouldn't be wise." The words, chilly and clear, came from Nora Chilton. She turned to Peyton, and her smile actually seemed sympathetic. "St. Claire's allied with us, remember? The relationship may not be close or even friendly, but I still don't think Adam Howard would appreciate your writing anything that would put his star reporter in a bad light."

"But —"

"But nothing." Nora crossed her arms. "What you call unethical, she'd call bold and aggressive. Face it, Mac, you're playing by yesterday's rules. And no court in the country would even hear your case because you can't prove she's hurt you. You can still write your column and you might not lose a single reader. So cut your losses, kiddo, and wrap this thing up according to the party line. Otherwise, you'll be the one who loses."

Peyton moved back to the conference room, her mind reeling. Why even bother to write a final column? What could she say that all of America wouldn't have already heard? By breakfast time tomorrow, every man, woman, and child in America with a television set would know about Julie St. Claire's upcoming interview with the note's rightful owner. "The Heart Healer" column would be nothing more than a print commercial for St. Claire's prime-time presentation.

Peyton closed the conference room door behind her and leaned against it, breathing in the stale scents of cigarettes and coffee. A temptation rose in her mind — to hit the delete key, forget the entire ending, and take a real vacation — but she'd brought her readers too far to desert them now.

Comment by King Bernard

For a few minutes back there, I was afraid that conniving St. Claire witch had broken Peyton's spirit. She went pale as she watched that video, and I knew what she was thinking — why bother to do good work and maintain your integrity when you're surrounded by people who are flashier, faster, and unethical?

When I followed Peyton into the conference room, I found her standing by the table, her fingertips barely touching the keys of her laptop. Without looking up, she said, "You were right about the baggie and the sandwich. I don't know who wrote the note — or if anyone from Flight 848 did — but that's not the important thing."

"What is?" I asked.

She shook her head, and when she looked at me, her eyes shone with tears. "I'm not sure yet. But when I figure it out I'll let you know."

She straightened, swept her laptop off the conference table, then moved past me and out the door. I didn't know where she was going, but I knew why. Sometimes you've got to get away and get alone before things can sort themselves out.

I hope Peyton can make sense of this madness. Because if she continues to be hurt by this, I just might go out of my way to run into Julie St. Claire at a future press conference. If I see her, I think I'll forget all about being an enlightened twenty-first century male and deck the broad.

Might as well make a few waves in the press pool.

Peyton sat on the stone bench by the lake, her backpack by her side. She hadn't been able to talk herself into leaving the property — that would feel as if Julie St. Claire had managed to run her out of her own newsroom, and Peyton wouldn't give her enemy that satisfaction. But she couldn't stay in a building where the walls seemed to be closing in on her.

The sun was perilously close to its zenith, a sure sign that her deadline was fast approaching. But what was she supposed to do? The easiest course of action would be to type up a column supporting everything Julie St. Claire would say in tomorrow evening's special, but something in Peyton recoiled from that idea. She didn't want to do

355

anything to smooth Julie St. Claire's path. And she couldn't write a lie.

So what should she write? She could always go off on another tangent and discuss, for instance, the importance of closure after a tragedy, but her readers had been following her column with one question uppermost in their minds. She'd be cruel and unfair not to answer it. And she'd be a coward to hedge and say no one would ever know for certain who'd written the note.

She could subtly damage St. Claire's presentation by mentioning the plastic sandwich bag . . . and the unlikelihood that a first-class passenger would have one in his possession. While that tactic certainly wouldn't win her any praise from St. Claire or Adam Howard, at least she could say she was being honest.

But her readers wanted closure. The stream of e-mails that had been filling her computer cried out for finality. The search for the note's author had become inextricably linked to the tragedy, and a definitive answer would help the nation put the catastrophe of Flight 848 to rest.

Peyton lifted her gaze. Overhead, a breeze cajoled a live oak, which answered in a soft, swaying whisper. Why had the note been given to *her*? Gabriella Cohen had brought the note to the Heart Healer, but Peyton had never felt less capable of healing hearts in her life. All she'd done for Timothy Manning, Taylor Crowe, and Tanner Ford was stir up pain and awaken old memories.

The same thing she'd done to herself.

Wouldn't it have been more convenient for Pastor Manning if the note had never been found? Taylor Crowe would have had one less tragedy to milk, and Tanner Ford wouldn't be tempted to use his father's death for blatant self-promotion. If the note had sunk to the bottom of the sea, life would go on as it always had, and Peyton wouldn't be feeling so exposed.

She took a deep breath as a dozen different emotions collided. Nora said her writing had deepened, that readers were finally beginning to understand the woman behind the byline. King said she was doing the best writing of her life, but something in the compliment sent a thrill of fear rippling through her veins. Writing shouldn't be so . . . revelatory. In college, she'd been taught to cover the who, what, when, where, why, and, if she had space, how. Professional writers, she'd been told, should never reveal too much of themselves lest they come across as sentimental or sappy.

The wind freshened, ruffling the surface

of the retention pond, and Peyton squinted at a ripple in the water. She'd heard that a six-foot gator lived here, and a few of her co-workers had named him Walter. But Walter, like most gators, tended to be nocturnal, and she hoped he wasn't thinking of a mid-morning stroll on the bank.

"Miss MacGruder?"

The voice came from behind her, and for an instant Peyton considered not turning around. No one who knew her would call her *Miss MacGruder,* and she wasn't in the mood for a stranger's company.

But strangers rarely went away until after they'd had their say. Slowly, she turned her head. A woman was coming toward her, her strides purposeful and quick, her head tilted at an inquisitive angle. She was petite, al-most Peyton's height, with strawberry blonde hair and regular features. A pretty thing — who probably wanted a tip on how to get into television reporting. As she drew nearer, Peyton could see that she was young — probably early twenties, if even that. Not exactly in her column's usual demographic.

The girl waited until she had reached the curb before speaking again. "I'm sorry to disturb you," she said, clutching a maroon backpack to her chest. Her voice was high and uncertain, the voice of youth. "When I told the receptionist I wanted to see you, the security guard said you were out here."

Peyton grimaced. Some security they had around here — why didn't he just draw the woman a map? This girl could be anyone, even a madwoman with a gun, and he wouldn't think twice about sending her straight toward her target.

She forced a smile. "What can I do for you?"

The girl stepped forward, then hesitated as her gaze drifted toward the lake. "I'm not sure where to begin."

"You could begin with your name."

The tip of the girl's nose went pink. "It's Lila. Lila Lugar."

Peyton leaned back, taking in Lila Lugar's appearance. She certainly didn't look like a lunatic. She wore a long floral skirt and a summer sweater, the typical garb of a college student. Her hair hung off her shoulders in a casual style, and she carried nothing but the backpack — but who knew what it contained.

Why not let the girl talk? Perhaps she had a story worth using for "The Heart Healer," and Peyton needed some new material. She hadn't gone through her reader mail in days.

She shifted on the stone bench, leaving

room for the girl. "Why don't you sit and tell me about it?"

Smiling her thanks, Lila came forward and sat on the bench, dropping the backpack to her side like a barrier. She swallowed hard and squared her shoulders, then stared out at the pond. "I live in Clearwater," she said, a small smile hovering at the corners of her mouth. "I've lived there since I was six days old, when my parents adopted me."

Peyton nodded, hoping the story would soon pick up its pace. She had her own worries to consider, and she didn't have time for a day-by-day replay of this girl's life, short as it was. But she could be patient a few moments more. She had never done an adoption story, so perhaps there was a column here.

Lila leaned forward, parking one elbow on her knee and her chin in her palm. "I saw that man on the news this morning," she said, abruptly changing the subject. "I've forgotten his name, but I heard him talking about the note from the crash. Then I heard them talking about you, so I jumped in the car and came straight over."

"Tanner Ford." Peyton exhaled the name in a disgusted breath.

"That's it." The girl's polite smile faded,

and a hint of tears glistened in the wells of her blue eyes. "He was lying. That note was mine, Miss MacGruder. I know it."

Peyton lifted her brows. Maybe the girl was deranged.

She stared at the young woman for a moment as a hundred logical objections rose to the surface of her mind, then she selected the uppermost: "Your name is Lila. The note was addressed to someone whose name begins with a *T*."

The girl smiled, then thumbed a tear from the corner of her eye. "I'm sorry I haven't said anything sooner. I mean, if you've explained all this in your articles —"

"I haven't, not really," Peyton said. "And you don't have to apologize for not reading my column. Just go on."

Lila sniffed. "Well, my mom and dad adopted me after they'd had four boys — biological babies, you know. They wanted a girl, so they adopted me. And when I was little, I was always trying to keep up with my brothers — I think I drove them nuts. Anyway, they called me 'Tagalong,' then 'Tag,' and finally, 'T.' They've called me 'T' for as long as I can remember. And I can prove it."

"How?"

"Well — there's this." The girl fumbled

for a moment in her backpack, then pulled out a leather book. She held it out for Peyton's examination — it was a Bible — then she opened it. On the presentation page an eerily familiar hand had inscribed, *To T, from Dad, on the occasion of your sixteenth birthday.*

Peyton's breath caught in her lungs as she read the date: September 2, 1998.

The handwriting matched the note.

And the date —

Peyton felt her breath being suddenly whipped away. "Oh." She reached out to steady herself, feeling the rough cement of the bench beneath her suddenly slick palms.

"Miss MacGruder?" Lila's voice went tight with alarm. "Are you all right?"

"Just —" Peyton threw up her hand. "Give me a moment, will you?"

She closed her eyes, unwilling and unable to look at the girl, the pond, *anything*. Thick darkness swirled behind her closed eyelids, a cloud that came rolling out of a vault she'd locked years earlier and hoped never to approach again. Who'd given this girl the right to open the door?

Clutching her stomach, she leaned sideways until her head hit Lila's backpack.

"Miss MacGruder?" The girl's voice took on a note of authority, though the pitch vibrated with uncertainty. "If you need help, I'll run into the building and get someone."

"Just . . . wait." Peyton forced the words over the boulder in her throat as a horde of memories came rushing back like unwelcome guests.

New Year's Day, 1982. Nineteen years younger and four sizes smaller, she'd been sitting in the living room on a rainy afternoon with a bowl of popcorn in her lap. On the television, Clemson was whipping on Nebraska in the Orange Bowl. The popcorn was salty and she had the thirst of all the devils, but Garrett had gone out to get some drinks from the convenience mart a few miles away. Two ice-filled glasses sweated on the old trunk that served as their coffee table.

The doorbell rang right as a Nebraska running back sprinted for the end zone. Muttering under her breath, Peyton sprang up to answer it, spilling popcorn over the brown shag carpeting. Some part of her brain thought it odd that Garrett would ring the bell, but maybe his arms were laden with groceries. He had a habit of tossing anything that caught his eye into the shopping cart, and he'd been gone long enough to buy groceries for a month.

Garrett was anything but predictable — she'd realized that the afternoon they met, when she'd been playing Frisbee with some friends on the grass outside UF's O'Connell Center. Garrett MacGruder had come walking by, literally swept Peyton off her feet, and carried her away with no further comment than his confident smile.

You had to hand it to a guy that self-assured. Though he'd put her down when she got serious about protesting, she never got over the feeling that Garrett MacGruder would be able to protect her from anything life threw her way.

But Garrett hadn't rung the doorbell. Two uniformed troopers from the Florida State Highway Patrol stood on the concrete slab outside the peeling front door. After asking her name, one fixed her in a somber stare while the other said, "We regret to inform you that your husband, Garrett MacGruder, was killed this afternoon when his car went off the road and hit a tree." They went on, filling her ears with details that made no sense, then telling her she could ride with them to the hospital.

The next few hours passed in a hushed blur as seemingly disconnected visions passed before her bleary eyes: a brick hospital, a pair of pale green double doors

364

without handles, a narrow bed bearing her husband's body. Garret's skin was pale, his lips blue, but she bent and kissed him, then noticed the odd way his head jutted away from his body. A broken neck, someone said. He'd been killed instantly.

She signed some papers, mutely nodded to several questions, and accepted a ride from the same two patrolmen who'd come to the house. When she got home she discovered that the day had died, too. Darkness cloaked the rental house, though gray beams from the television lit the front window with ghostly light. She stood in the living room without turning on a lamp, then sank to the threadworn sofa and slowly turned her life's most recent revelation over in her mind. Beneath the surface of her life lay nothing — just a patch of lifeless earth. The only person in the world to whom she felt close had disappeared, leaving nothing but hollowed-out worm trails in the mud. Like her mother, Garrett had left her without a farewell or backward glance.

From the television, a sports announcer called the end of the football game as fans spilled onto the field: Clemson 22, Nebraska 15. Happy New Year from the Orange Bowl.

Peyton blinked at the screen, the words

and images barely registering. Odd, how certain significant numbers seemed to appear in a life. She'd loved her mother for three years. And she and Garrett had just celebrated their third anniversary.

Happy New Year.

Tonight she did not want confetti or champagne or noisemakers or fireworks. She did not want friends or family. She was done with new years.

Rising on shaky legs, she went to the bathroom and swept the toiletries from the counter to the floor. Toothbrushes, bottles of Halston and Old Spice, a container of Scope, and a discarded box from the drugstore fell to the tile in a crashing jumble. The heady scents of cologne rose up to assault her nostrils, but Peyton paid them no mind as she opened the medicine chest and began to rummage through a three-year-old collection of pharmaceuticals.

NoDoz, the student's friend — no friend today.

Midol — useless now.

She pulled out an amber prescription bottle and read the label. The white pills had been prescribed the time Garrett pulled a muscle in a pickup football game; after one dose he'd pronounced himself well.

Extra-strength painkillers. Just the ticket.

While the television announcers debated the game in the living room, Peyton poured the contents of the bottle into her palm, then moved to the kitchen for a glass of water.

An hour later she was lying on the bathroom floor, her nostrils filling with the faint smells of toilet and cologne and mildew from the tattered rug. Her stomach cramped as it tried to throw off the poison she'd ingested, but she refused to surrender to its spasms. Her heart was beating heavily; she could feel each irregular thump like a blow to her chest.

It wasn't fair. Death had come instantly for Garrett — why was it taking so long to come for her?

Summoning her strength, she pulled herself to the bathroom vanity. Garrett's old-fashioned safety razor sat on the sink, right where he'd left it. Grasping the razor, she twisted the knob to free the blade, then held it in unsteady fingers as she half-pulled, half-pushed herself toward the tub. Breathing heavily, she extended her left arm and made a swift slice across the blue veins, then convulsed in nausea as her stomach won the battle of wills.

A few moments later, spent and slick with sweat, she leaned her head on her bent right arm and watched her life's blood spurt into the tub. She'd made a mess of things, but no one would care except maybe the landlord. And he could always hire one of those cleaning companies who came in and swept every trace of a person's life into a great gray garbage bag. It didn't matter. In a few hours, she and Garrett would be together again, in the morgue or the funeral home, wherever they took people who died . . .

Her ears filled with a fuzzy sound, almost loud enough to block the shrill ringing of the kitchen phone. She closed her eyes, willing the phone to stop, just as their answering machine kicked on. Her voice blended with Garrett's in their silly little message, then another voice cut through the fuzzy noise with the sharpness of a knife: "Peyton? Dr. Morgan called me with the news. Honey, Kathy and I are here at the hospital, and the attendant told us you'd gone home. Are you all right? Are you home? If you're there, hon, pick up. I really need to know you're all right . . ."

Peyton closed her eyes and let the darkness overtake her, leaving her father to talk to himself.

She'd awakened in the hospital, zoned out and dense with whatever antidepressant drugs were in vogue at the time. Her father stood to one side and whispered with the doctor in charge, while Kathy pressed a crumpled wad of tissue to her nose and fluttered around the foot of the bed.

Peyton let her heavy eyelids fall.

For hours — or was it days? — the scene scarcely changed, but people moved in and out, like characters on a stage. At times she'd open her eyes to find a nurse adjusting the drips or fastening a blood pressure cuff around her arm; on other occasions she'd open her eyes and see an empty room. No flowers. No cards. Nothing and no one.

Then she'd withdraw to the deep place where no pain throbbed and no one intruded. Often when she'd come to the surface her father would be there, and the doctor, and they'd be talking — arguing, really. One day her father saw her open eyes and rushed toward her, clutching the rails at the side of the bed. "Peyton, honey, you've got to meet us halfway," he said, a pleading tone in his voice. "Talk to us, stay with us. You can't keep pulling away." As she retreated to the place between deep and shallow, one muffled phrase floated down to her like a sunbeam: *psychiatric ward*. She dived deeper and the words vanished, swallowed up by the wailing, anguished sounds of a weeping man.

She went down again, deeper than before.

The soft sounds of weeping brought her back to the present. Pressing one hand to her temple, Peyton sat up, blinking the memories away. She glanced to her right. Lila Lugar still sat next to her, but now tears were streaming down the girl's face. She looked away when Peyton sat up, then pulled a tissue from her pocket and blew her nose.

"I'm sorry," Peyton said, wincing. "Sometimes — well, I needed a minute to think. I hope I didn't frighten you."

Lila shook her head, then stopped and gave Peyton an abashed look. "Well, you did, a little. I was ready to run for help because I thought you might be sick. But I'm not crying because I was scared. I'm crying because . . . I just seem to cry a lot these days."

"These last few weeks have been difficult for everyone." Peyton scraped her hands through her hair, then pressed her fingertips to her temples and counted to ten. She could focus and get through this. Later there'd be time to sort things out.

"Lila," she dropped her hands as she turned to the girl, "tell me about your dad."

The girl smiled at her through tear-clogged lashes. "You believe me?"

Peyton nodded. "Your story makes more sense than the others I've heard. I'd like to hear more."

Lila's lower lip quivered. "His name was Jerry Lugar, and he was truly special." She twisted the tissue in her hands. "I wish I had a picture in my wallet, but we could never get him to sit for a professional portrait. He coached basketball at Clearwater High School until a few years ago, then he retired."

"What was he doing on Flight 848?"

"Both my parents were on that flight." Her voice broke with this confession, but she managed to keep her emotions under control. "They were chaperoning those students from Largo Christian School. Since they retired, they've had time to do things like that."

Peyton remained silent as her mental images dramatically shifted. Jerry Lugar had not been a solitary businessman on Flight 848, but a husband traveling with his wife, half of a congenial couple volunteering to watch over a rowdy group of high school students who'd been camping out at the airport and hoping for a flight home.

The plastic baggie fit this picture. Lila's mother had probably baked cookies and snacks for the trip; perhaps she had been doling out the few remaining goodies as the group waited for their flight.

Pieces of the puzzle were colliding in Peyton's head like the bits of glass in a kaleidoscope, but at last they were beginning to form a recognizable image. Only a few unresolved questions remained.

"The note" — she pressed her hands together to keep them from trembling — "said, 'I love you, all is forgiven.' But if there were five children in your family, why'd your dad write the note to you alone? And if he was traveling with your mother, why didn't he say '*we* love you'?"

Lila smiled at the lake, but she had shifted the focus of her gaze to some interior field of vision beyond Peyton's reach. "My brothers and I got along fine with my parents — until I had an argument with my mom. I told her I wanted to search for my real mother." She glanced at Peyton, then smiled ruefully. "I know how that must sound — like I don't appreciate anything my mom did for me. That's what my dad thought, too, so we had a big argument right before they left for New York. I felt bad about it, though, and would have apologized, but I never had the chance." Her voice softened. "I think Dad knew how terrible I'd feel — and he was right. I didn't get the chance to tell either of them how sorry I was."

Peyton took a quick, sharp breath. "Did you mean it? Do you still want to search for your real mother?"

Lila exhaled softly. "Martha Lugar was my real mom. I can't help being a little curious about my biological mother, but I wouldn't want to upset her life."

Peyton looked away, her senses floundering in an unexpected sense of loss. "So it was just an idle threat."

Lila fell silent a moment. "Yes and no. I don't *need* to know my biological mother, because my mom gave me everything I needed. Even though I've lost her, I still have the memories of all we did together. But if I ever did meet my bio mom, I think I'd like her to know how much I appreciate what she did for me."

"What she did?" Peyton looked away, a new anguish searing her heart. "But she didn't do anything. She gave you away."

Lila shot her a quick, denying glance. "I don't see it that way at all. She gave me life. She didn't have to, but she cared enough to be sure I was placed with a wonderful family who loved me. They weren't perfect, but neither am I. But they loved me. And that's worth everything."

As Peyton watched, two tears welled up in Lila's eyes and overflowed, rolling down her cheeks. Her lips parted as if she would say something else, but no words came.

"So that's why your dad wrote the note," Peyton finished for her. "I think I'm beginning to understand."

Lila's face twisted, her eyes clamping tight. She wept aloud, slowly rocking back and forth on the bench, until Peyton awkwardly put her arms around the girl.

"There now," she whispered, her own heart twisting as she held the young woman in her arms. "It'll be all right. You are forgiven and you are loved. That's all that matters."

Mandi's shrill voice greeted Peyton as she threaded her way through the newsroom. "Only half an hour until your deadline," the intern called, her eyes wide with alarm. "Nora's already been snooping around here, hoping for a peek."

"There's nothing to peek at," Peyton said, moving to her desk. "I haven't written the column yet."

Mandi sat down with a solid thump, her eyes widening still farther. "Oh, wow. I'm

374

going to see the famous lightning fingers in action."

"Don't hold your breath." Peyton lowered herself into her chair, then bent to pull the blue folder from the desk drawer where she'd stuffed it with a dozen others. Taking a clue from Sherlock Holmes, she'd hidden the original copy of the note in plain sight, knowing no lockbox would be safe in the newsroom. Just last week, the maintenance guy had to put the sugars and creamers for the coffee station under lock and key.

After flipping through several clippings, Peyton came to the note, still encased in its plastic sleeve. After so recently seeing the same handwriting in Lila's Bible, the message hit her with renewed force.

I love you.
All is forgiven.

She still had no idea why she'd been given the note, but she knew the time had come to pass it on.

Without a word she closed the notebook and stood, leaving Mandi gasping. "But what about your column?"

"It'll keep," Peyton answered, moving toward the elevator.

Downstairs at the reception desk, Lila Lugar's eyes filled again when Peyton pressed the note into the girl's open palm.

"It's yours," she said simply, her hand lingering in Lila's a moment longer than necessary. "You and I both know it."

Lila wept again, but these tears were quiet and subdued, nothing at all like Tanner Ford's animated, shiny weeping. She simply leaned on the reception desk and bowed her head, her heart silently overflowing.

"Do you want me to tell people the true story?" Peyton gently probed. "I could release your name or not, whatever you'd prefer."

"Please don't." Lila's eyes met Peyton's. "I don't need that kind of attention."

Peyton reached out and tentatively, gently wiped a tear from the girl's cheek. "I understand."

And as Lila straightened and walked away, Peyton bit her lip and struggled to constrain the cry that clawed in her throat.

Comment by Lila Lugar, 19
University of Florida Student

I never meant to tell Peyton MacGruder as much as I did. I thought I'd meet her, explain about the note and my family, and calmly settle things. She'd give me the note, and then I could take home a piece of my mom and dad and hold on to it for the rest of my life.

I certainly never meant to break down and bawl like a baby in her arms. I thought I'd cried everything out. But sometimes I see something — my mom's slippers under the bed, a grocery list in my dad's handwriting — and the next thing you know, I'm reaching for tissues.

Last night I sat in my dad's brown plaid recliner and went through his high school yearbook. I didn't know a soul in those funny pictures; couldn't place a name with a single crew-cut face. But Dad knew them. I stayed up until two, just staring at the flattops and poodle skirts and grainy black-and-white photographs.

My parents' friends say it's okay to be fragile, but they don't really know what I'm going through. It's hard to lose both your parents at once, but it's devastating to lose them when you've parted in anger.

Funny, but I thought of myself as all grown up until June 13. On that day, after the crash, I felt like a little girl again. It wasn't until several days afterward that I realized I could go on, because Mom and Dad had prepared me.

My parents, Jerry and Martha Lugar, clothed me in the iron virtues of strength, compassion, understanding, and loyalty. I wanted to explain all this to Peyton MacGruder, but my tears kept getting in the way. She seemed so interested, and I wanted her to know that the parents God gave me are the ones to whom I owe almost everything.

There are two other people — a man and a woman — to whom I owe my existence, and I don't mean to belittle their involvement in my life. I respect them, I'm grateful for the way they put my interests above their own, but I don't want to intrude now.

All I want is to hold this note, to press it to my heart and know that everything's okay. Though I can't know for sure, I have a feeling Mom was holding Dad's arm as he wrote this . . . and sending her love along.

It's hard to describe what the note means — having it is like walking in a garden after a sudden spring shower. The note is special to me . . . and I have a feeling Peyton MacGruder will be special, too. Her hard work has brought me a joy and assurance I would not have found any other way. I'll always be grateful for her.

Always.

"Hey, MacGruder!"

Carter Cummings's voice cut through the newsroom clatter as the news reporters scrambled to file before their four o'clock deadline. Peyton had already asked for an extension. With all that had happened in the last few hours, she didn't know how to end her series.

Now she scowled at Carter, who would doubtless toss another distraction her way. "Go away, Carter," she yelled, bringing a hand up to shield her face. "I'm trying to think."

Carter came closer, a sly grin twisting his features. "Just thought you'd want to know that your nemesis has just landed at TIA. They're taping something for her special tomorrow, so she'll be at the crash site for the next hour or so."

Surprise siphoned the blood from Peyton's head, leaving her dizzy. "Julie St. Claire's here?" She grasped the edge of her desk. "In town?"

Carter grinned. "Heard it from a guy who works for the Buccaneers. Apparently he and some of the team were at the airport when the WNN jet landed. It's a quick trip, but if you want to go toss a pie in her face, here's your chance."

Peyton was on her feet before her conscious brain gave the command to move. "Pie tossing's not exactly what I had in mind, but it'll do."

She grabbed her backpack, nearly hitting Mandi as she slung it over her shoulder.

"Can I come?" Mandi's voice rang through the newsroom as Peyton stalked away.

"Stay here in the sandbox, kiddo," Peyton called, well aware that half the males in the newsroom were hissing, mocking the sounds of a catfight. "I'll be back before deadline."

Peyton pushed the Jetta well past the legal speed limit, then set the brakes to squealing as she stopped at the end of West Cypress Street. Carter's informant proved correct; already two television vans occupied the scrubby stand of beach, one with its microwave antenna already extended.

Leaving her bag in the car, Peyton pocketed the keys and set off at a jog. A uniformed cop tried to stop her as she approached, but he lowered his hand when she flashed her *Tampa Times* ID badge.

"You got business here?" he called.

"Indeed I do." Peyton kept moving. "I'm the Heart Healer."

He let her pass without another word.

Julie St. Claire sat inside the second van, a mirror in her hand as a young man fussed at her hair. "It's the wind," he said, one hand fluttering up and down in what Peyton assumed was frustration. "We can't do the fringe bang in this wind. You'll have to let it —"

With the arrogance of a warrior, Peyton leaned into the open doorway. "Julie St. Claire? I need a word with you."

The startled hairdresser dropped his pick, but St. Claire only lifted a delicately shaped brow. "Peyton MacGruder," she said, a hair of irritation in her voice. "How nice to finally meet you up-close and personal."

"I wish I could say the same." Peyton's breath came in short gasps, her lungs squeezed by tamped-down anger.

Leaning forward, Julie gestured languidly toward the beach. "Did you see our friend Tanner Ford? They're filming on the beach. He's tossing a rose into the waves, probably just around that bend —"

"I didn't come to see Tanner Ford. I came to see you."

The brows rose again, graceful wings of

contempt, then Julie reached up to touch her hair. "Thanks, Jacques. Would you mind leaving us alone a moment?"

Jacques shuddered as if the thought of abandoning an imperfect creation grated upon his ethics, then he gave Peyton a disdainful look and slipped out of the van.

Julie waited a moment, then pressed her hands together, the manicured talons meeting tip-to-tip. "All right, you came to see me. What's on your mind?"

Taking a deep breath, Peyton struggled to master the passion that had her nerves in a knot. "I could talk about how you convinced Tanner Ford to break his confidentiality agreement," she began, her fists clenching, "but now that's pretty much water under the bridge. If you're the sort of person who cares nothing about integrity, then I doubt there's anything I can say to change your mind."

St. Claire showed her perfectly white teeth in an expression that was not a smile. "So what did you come to talk about?"

"The truth, Julie. You're planning to tell the world that Trenton Ford wrote the note, and that's a lie. Today I learned who really wrote it — and I gave the original to the child for whom it was intended."

St. Claire lifted her head slightly, like a cat

scenting the breeze. "And who was this mystery person?"

Peyton crossed her arms. "My contact has asked for anonymity, and I'm going to grant it. I won't publish the name, and neither will you."

For a moment St. Claire merely stared at her with a bland half-smile, then her expression hardened. "So kind of you to come down here and say hello. We'll be finishing up in an hour or so and heading back to New York."

Words bubbled up and spewed out of Peyton's mouth in a flood. "Haven't you heard a word I've said? You're taping a lie, Julie. Tanner Ford is only out for publicity; he wants a ticket out of Gainesville! His story rings about as true as a front-page headline of the *National Enquirer*!"

"I think you're wrong." St. Claire smiled as if dealing with a temperamental child. "The story has been confirmed by Blythe Ford, his mother. The pieces fit together perfectly."

Peyton snorted. "Oh, yeah? How many first-class passengers do you know who load their briefcases with Zippup sandwich bags?"

The wattage of St. Claire's smile dimmed slightly, then brightened again. "People are eccentric, Peyton, and wealthy people are more eccentric than most. You can't be sure Trenton Ford didn't reach out and take the bag from his neighbor."

"How likely is that, Julie?"

"Likely enough for TV — this isn't a court of law. I'm making a logical assumption, and if the situations were reversed, you'd do exactly the same thing."

Peyton drew a breath, about to protest, then stopped. Truthfully, she *might* have done exactly the same thing two weeks ago. But she wouldn't now.

The note had made the difference.

The realization was so unexpected she actually began to laugh.

"I'm glad you find this so amusing," St. Claire drawled. "Now, if you will excuse me, I really must have Jacques do something with my hair."

Peyton pushed her way into the van, moving forward until she bent within two inches of St. Claire's perfectly powdered face. "You are going to broadcast a lie," she said, lowering her voice to the pitch of cold steel. "And you don't care. You'd rather deceive the world and have people believe this note was intended for the idiot out there on the sand."

For the first time, St. Claire's brows creased. "I have to give them something," she hissed. "The show's been booked; the advertisers are on board. What am I supposed to give them, if not Tanner Ford?"

"Give them the truth." Peyton paused to let her words sink in. "Tell them about a father who loved his child enough to concentrate his final thoughts on an offer of reconciliation. Don't single out one person — let the message go out to the world."

A cold, congested expression settled on Julie St. Claire's face. "That won't play to my audience," she said, her voice flat. "I'm a serious journalist, and serious journalists don't deal in generalities. My people want specifics; they want names and faces and details. And that's what I'm going to give them."

Peyton moved back as the bitter gall of frustration burned the back of her throat. No truth here — not even compromise. And that's the way it would remain.

She drew a deep breath, straightened her posture, and turned to look toward the water. After shading her eyes with her hand she could see a cameraman squatting in the foreground, his lens pointed toward Tanner Ford's long form. Ford stood near the waves, his face turned out to sea.

He'd claimed the note . . . but he'd never know its true power.

"All right, then," she whispered, more to herself than anyone else. Cold, clear reality swept over her in a powerful wave, leaving her breathless.

If the truth were to be told, she'd have to tell it.

Back at her desk, Peyton pounded the computer keys, concentrating so fiercely that the sounds of the newsroom retreated into static. She wrote without thinking; words and feelings and truths seeming to pour from her. Finally, she gave the story a quick glance, ran a spellcheck, then clicked the send key.

She was staring at the empty computer screen when King's voice cut into her consciousness. "Solve all the world's problems today?"

Grief welled in her, black and cold, and for a moment she couldn't speak. Then the words came, a confession: "I need help, King. I need to talk to someone."

When she turned, his eyes brimmed with compassion. "You're in luck," he said, extending his hand. "Come on. I happen to know someone who likes to listen."

The Lakeview Trailer Park had not changed since Peyton last visited it, but somehow it looked softer in the diffused light of dusk. King parked his Jeep in front of lot 137, then cut the engine and gave Peyton a questioning look. "I hope you're hungry. When I told Mary Grace we were coming, she promised to make tuna fish sandwiches."

"Sounds great." Peyton pressed her hand to her empty stomach, suddenly aware that she hadn't eaten since breakfast.

As she and King walked up the driveway, Peyton tipped her head back and breathed in the scents of mown grass and gardenias. Someone on the opposite side of the park was grilling — steak, if the smell wafting their way could be trusted.

Strains of classical music drifted through the trailer's open window, and Peyton felt her mouth twist as King knocked on the door. *The Magic Flute*? Mary Grace liked Mozart?

A moment later the door opened. Mary Grace's sturdy form filled the doorway, then reached out to trap King in a bear hug. "King Bernard, it's been too long!"

"Likewise, Mary Grace."

A moment later Peyton found herself on the uppermost concrete step, then the woman's arms reached for her, too. "How are ya, honey?" she whispered, breathing a kiss on Peyton's cheek as she clasped her in a warm embrace. "I've been thinking a lot about you in the last couple of days. Reading your column, too, though I usually take the *Post*."

"I'm fine." Peyton's voice, like her nerves, was ragged, but Mary Grace seemed not to notice.

"Come on in. There's lemonade in the fridge and sandwiches and chips on the counter. I didn't have time to make much and it's too hot to cook, but —"

"It all looks great, Mary Grace." King announced his approval from the sink, then gestured toward the small table in the kitchen. "Come on, ladies, let me seat you. I'm starving."

They laughed, and Peyton felt her spirits lift as she sank into the chair King offered. After a moment of silence, during which Mary Grace murmured, "For all we are about to receive may the Lord make us truly grateful," they began to eat. The tuna fish salad was cold and crunchy, the lemonade tart. As King and Mary Grace munched and made small talk, she swallowed her first bite, then held the cold glass to her cheek, relishing the sting of its icy touch. She should have been hungry, but her appetite seemed to have vanished along with her scoop on the story of the note.

"Don't you like tuna fish, honey?" Mary Grace's voice brought her back to the present.

"Oh, it's good; I like it fine. I'm just not very hungry."

With a look that said she understood completely — understood *what?* — Mary Grace nodded. "We'll finish up here," she said, scraping a fallen bit of tuna off her paper plate with a potato chip. "Then we can talk in the living room or outside."

"The kitchen is fine." Remembering the baby dolls in the living room, Peyton dropped her gaze to the mica tabletop. "Please, don't go to any trouble on our account."

Mary Grace chewed her last bite, then propped her elbows on the table and folded her hands. She glanced at King for a moment, then said: "It's all right, child. I hear you need to talk, and we're ready to listen. Go ahead. Share that burden on your heart."

Peyton waved her hands. "It's nothing. I'm fine. Really."

"If you were fine, you wouldn't look like a wide-eyed kid who's seen something she shouldn't have." Featherlike laugh lines crinkled around Mary Grace's blue eyes as her hand reached out to squeeze Peyton's.

"Tell me all about it, honey. You came to see me because you wanted to know how to deal with grieving people. So tell me what you learned."

Beneath the table, Peyton's knees began to shift back and forth, touching and parting like the knees of a girl about to be kissed for the first time. "I interviewed three people — well, four, really. With each of them I shared the story of the note, and each of them had a different reaction."

"The note from the crash? The one I've been reading about?"

Peyton nodded. "The first man, the minister, didn't accept the note because he and his dad were on good terms. The second prospect, a woman, didn't accept it because she and her father were on terrible terms — isn't that ironic? Completely opposite situations, but neither of them wanted anything to do with what I had to offer. The third man claimed the note, but I don't think he did it sincerely and I know his father didn't write it. He sees the note as a ticket to fame and fortune."

She lowered her gaze, her mind darkening as she thought of Tanner Ford and the upcoming TV special. She could almost hope something bad would happen, something that would prevent him from making it to

New York. But long ago she'd learned that life isn't fair.

King spoke up. "You said there was a fourth person?"

As she nodded, all the emotions that had been lapping at her subconscious suddenly crested and crashed. She'd been holding them at bay for hours, and she wanted to tell someone, she *needed* to spill the entire story.

She looked up, trying to control herself, but her chin wobbled and her eyes filled in spite of her efforts. "The girl I met this afternoon," she said, balling her hands into fists and fighting back the sobs swelling in her chest. "Well, maybe I should begin at the beginning."

A shiver spread over her as she lowered herself into the cold well of memory. "I married Garrett MacGruder between my sophomore and junior years of college. And though my father didn't approve of my dropping out of school, I was very happy with my husband. I'd never felt close to my father, you see, and wanted nothing to do with his new wife and kids. So while Garrett taught at the university, I worked to help put food on the table and we rented a little house in Gainesville. Poor and happy, that was us. But one day — New Year's Day,

1982 — Garrett crashed the car into an oak tree and died.

"It seems odd to think of it now, but at the time I thought I was totally alone in the world. Garrett's parents were deceased. And with my mom dead and my dad a million miles away —"

"Was he really, honey?" Mary Grace spoke in a low, composed voice.

Peyton shrugged. "I thought so. Anyway, after going to the hospital and seeing to Garrett, I went home and took a bunch of pills. But they didn't work, so I decided to help them along. Here — see for yourself."

With an effort, she unbuckled the leather watchband at her wrist, then stretched her arm toward King and Mary Grace. "This is what can happen when you're young and alone."

She'd been afraid King would squint in embarrassment and avert his eyes from her scar, but his eyes only darkened with concern.

Slowly, she lowered her gaze. "My dad, who'd come from Jacksonville as soon as he heard about Garrett, found me at the house. Called the ambulance and saved my life, I guess, though I didn't want to be saved. And then, in the hospital, he discovered the surprise I'd been planning for Garrett. I was pregnant." Her gaze shifted from King to Mary Grace. "For months afterward I was a mental and physical wreck. My father got a judge to appoint him as the baby's guardian."

"Was this okay with you?" Mary Grace asked.

Peyton shook her head. "I was drugged and half out of my mind. I didn't care, I didn't feel, I wasn't interested. My psychiatrist had no qualms about declaring me mentally incompetent. It doesn't matter whether or not it was okay with me; I wasn't there."

King's eyes narrowed with sympathy. "My word, MacGruder, you've never said a thing —"

Peyton lifted her hand, cutting him off. "I don't like to think about it, and sometimes it doesn't even seem real. I scarcely remember those months, and the pregnancy was like a dream. One day I had a big belly and the next day I didn't. If not for the stretch marks on my stomach and the scar on my wrist, I might have a difficult time believing any of it actually happened.

"But the baby was born and delivered to a social worker. I never saw it. Didn't want to, really. They knocked me out for the delivery, but they needn't have bothered — I was in a mental fog anyway. Only after the birth was I able to slowly find my way back to myself." She met King's gaze. "My father made an adoption plan for the kid; placed it with a family."

"Boy or girl?" Mary Grace asked, two deep lines appearing between her eyes.

Peyton took a deep breath. "Girl. I didn't know anything about what happened to her for weeks — months, actually. But gradually, as I grew stronger, my therapist gave me the truth in spoonfuls. Over the course of our sessions he told me I'd had a girl on September 2 and she'd been placed with a family in Florida. He also told me I was lucky to have a father who cared enough to take care of all the details."

"And you?" King asked, his mercurial eyes darkening. "What did you think?"

Peyton lowered her gaze. "For a long time I just felt numb. It's like when your foot goes to sleep and you can't feel it. But then, when the blood begins to flow again, it stings and aches and nearly drives you crazy.

"As my emotions reawakened, I found myself hating my father. My baby, all I had left of Garrett, was gone forever. So I hated the man who took her away. My therapist said it was wrong to feel that way, but I hated Dad for everything, even saving my life. Oh, I never came out and actually said so — after learning the buzzwords of psychobabble, I managed to convince my doctor that I'd put away my resentment. For years I've even managed to play the role of dutiful adult daughter. But if you want to know the truth, I've resented my father for years, though time has boiled that emotion down to an emphatic dislike. I've never wanted to have anything to do with him, because seeing him, even hearing his voice, brings back the past more vividly than I ever want to remember it."

She looked up, torn by conflicting emotions and the smoldering memories that had flamed to life. She felt as though she had disrobed in front of them, revealing her stretch marks, the scar, the hatred and the harshness she'd locked away in her heart. What must these two think of her now?

"Go on, honey." Mary Grace's hand reached out and enclosed Peyton's wrist. "What happened after you left the hospital?"

Peyton shuddered softly. "Three months after the baby's birth, they discharged me from the psychiatric ward, and I moved into a sort of halfway house — my father wanted someone to keep an eye on me. For a year I lived there and took classes at the junior college — that's when I began to study journalism. The world seemed strangely off-kilter, but I learned how to cope by repressing the bad memories and living day to day. And all the while, I kept going to my therapy sessions and seeing Dr. Stewart. He taught me how to fend off the panic attacks that had begun to come out of the blue and cripple me. I taught myself how to put the pain away, to bury it in the sea of forgetfulness."

She gave King a halfhearted smile. "Did you know the Jewish people have a ritual about that? On Rosh Hashanah, they walk down to the nearest stream of running water and empty their pockets, letting the water carry the lint and dust away. They call the ceremony *tashlikh,* and perform the ritual to remind themselves that God casts all their sins into the sea of forgetfulness and forgiveness."

As Peyton fell silent, a car passed on the street, the sound of its tires a quiet *shush* on the road. Peyton studied the exposed flesh of her hands, knowing they waited for her to continue.

"The writing helped," she finally said. "After so many months of interior silence, words poured out of me like someone had turned on a spigot." She lifted one shoulder in a shrug. "I learned that I have a gift for putting things together in a clear, concise package. I transferred to the University of Florida, finished on scholarship, and took a job as a copy kid for the *Gainesville Sun*. Amid answering phones, running copies, and making industrial-strength coffee, I learned how to write under pressure. Dr. Stewart read my work — obits, mostly, written according to the paper's fill-in-the-blanks formula — and praised my progress.

"When he pronounced me well, my father begged me to come to Jacksonville to be near him and his brood. I moved instead to Orlando. I wanted to be away from him and away from Gainesville and its memories. And there, working for the *Orlando Sentinel*, I learned everything else I know about newspaper work. Burying myself in my job, I developed a pretty good reputation as a sportswriter." She looked at King. "After that, I came to Tampa, where you and I started to butt heads."

"I know that part of the story," he said, a small smile playing at the corners of his mouth.

Silence fell over the table, and Peyton rubbed her thumbnail. "I wish that were the end of it," she said, her voice heavy. "But today a fourth prospect for the note found me in the little park in front of the newspaper building. Her name is Lila, but her family has always called her 'T' — for 'Tagalong,' because she used to tag along behind her four big brothers."

King's brows silently slanted the question: *What else?*

"Lila showed me a Bible," Peyton said, the words beginning to come faster. "On the presentation page, her father wrote her name and birthday — and the handwriting matched the writing on the note. Even though you can tell the note was written by someone being jostled by turbulence or whatever, there's enough similarity to erase all doubt."

"So that's why you're upset?" King crossed his arms and leaned on the table. "Because Julie St. Claire is presenting the wrong person in her special?"

"I couldn't care less what Julie St. Claire does." Peyton narrowed her gaze. "She's going to do whatever is best for her ratings, and Tanner Ford looks great on television. No — I'm upset because Lila Lugar's birthday is September 2, 1982." She shifted her gaze from King to Mary Grace, whose compassionate blue eyes seemed to invite a confidence. "I'm certain Lila Lugar is my daughter."

Silence, thick and heavy, wrapped around them like wool, punctuated only by the steady ticktock of Mary Grace's cuckoo clock.

"Why — that's wonderful!" King attempted a smile. "Isn't it?"

Was it? She'd lived nearly twenty years with a heart resigned to eternal separation, so how was she supposed to face the future? She'd shoved her child and her father into a deep and secret place, knowing that she could never even search for her baby without having to explain those dark days in 1982. How could she face her biological daughter and admit she had once tried to take both their lives?

"I don't know." Peyton turned tear-filled eyes upon him. "I asked her if she'd ever want to meet her birth mother, and she said no. But then she said she would like her bio mom to know that she appreciated the gift of life, and that she'd enjoyed a wonderful family with the Lugars."

"That's wonderful, honey." Mary Grace patted Peyton's hand.

Against Peyton's will, a sob rose in her throat. "But she lost everything in the crash — her mother *and* father. So now she has no one but me, so maybe I'm supposed to —"

"She has four brothers," Mary Grace interrupted, her strong fingers caressing the back of Peyton's hand. "And probably grandparents, too. And friends."

King picked up on Mary Grace's thought. "I don't know if you should go rushing into that situation. The girl has gone through major trauma with the plane crash, and now with the note. Think twice before you go running to her with life-changing revelations."

"Then why did she come walking into my life?" The cry rose up from within Peyton like the wail of an injured animal. "I can't help but feel that this means something, that the note was given to me for a reason. I must be supposed to take this girl under my wing —"

"Listen to me, child." Mary Grace's grip strengthened, as did her voice. "Perhaps you are, but not right now, and for several reasons. First, King's right. The girl has gone through too much in too short a time; you can't drop this bombshell on her now. Second, she told you she doesn't want to meet her birth mother."

"Maybe she *needs* to," Peyton said, sniffing. "We don't always know what we need."

Mary Grace shook her head. "Maybe later, child, when you've both had some time to heal. But baby, let me tell you something — looking at the situation from where I sit, you don't need to worry about that girl. She sounds like she's doing fine; she's coping. She's mourning the loss of her parents, but that's only natural. What isn't natural is *you*."

Peyton stared. "What?"

"You, honey." Mary Grace's tone softened. "The relationship that's not right here is the one between you and your daddy. He loves you, child, and you have to be as blind as dirt not to see it. He loves you, he's caring for you, and he's done nothing but care for you all these years."

Peyton lifted her chin. "He doesn't care a whit for me. His other kids take all his time and energy."

Mary Grace laughed. "Honey, love isn't something that can be parceled out, giving a smidgen here and a smidgen there. No. People who love give their whole hearts, and that's what you've been receiving. Your daddy's heart will always belong to you, and sounds to me like you've given him nothing but a false-fronted Valentine." Dropping Peyton's wrist, Mary Grace leaned forward, her hand coming up to support her sagging jaw. "When's the last time you talked to him?"

Looking at King, Peyton saw gentle rebuke in his eyes. Of course, he knew. He'd seen the unopened letters in her kitchen junk basket and in the napkin holder. He knew and he agreed with Mary Grace.

"My father took my baby." Peyton underlined the words with a viciousness she didn't quite feel. "He didn't wait for me to recover; he just took her."

"He took charge of that little girl because he knew you weren't able to," Mary Grace said, her eyes soft and shining. "He placed her in a home where she was loved and pampered. Four boys and one girl? You can't tell me she wasn't treated like a little princess."

Peyton glanced at King, hoping to find an ally, but he only crossed his arms.

She turned back to face Mary Grace. "My father was never there for me. After my mother died, I had to stay with Grandmom until she got sick. Then I went to boarding school while he began his residency, then he got married again . . . and I stayed away."

"Did he never ask you to come home?" Mary Grace asked.

"Sure." Peyton shrugged. "But by then I didn't feel like I even knew him. And I had learned to get along without him." She shivered as the curtain lifted on memories she hadn't revisited in years. "I felt like an orphan at school. I had to learn about menstruation from my health teacher. I stole my first bra from a Kmart because I couldn't bring myself to carry it to the cashier. I can't count the times I nearly died of shame and embarrassment and humiliation, and there was nobody to tell me anything. All the other girls had mothers. I didn't, and I couldn't ask my father about any of that stuff."

"Didn't he ever try to talk to you?"

"I suppose. But when we did speak, he stumbled over embarrassing topics. I finally told him not to worry, I'd learned everything from my girlfriends at school. And at school I told my girlfriends that my dad and I had a great relationship, that he would give me anything I wanted. He did send money when I asked, but what I needed was his love."

"What makes you think you didn't have it?" The question came from King, who looked at her with eyes that seemed to read the secrets imprinted on her heart. "He provided for you, he reached out — honestly, Peyton, what more did you want?"

"I don't know." Her voice broke as she admitted the truth. "I just wanted . . . more."

"What you wanted was relationship." Mary Grace gave Peyton an emphatic nod. "Yet that's what you denied him."

Something flared in Peyton's soul. "I did not!"

"Yes, you did." Mary Grace would not relent. "Didn't you just say he came to see you? He sent money? Didn't he come to Parents' Day and all that sort of thing?"

Peyton frowned. "Good grief, Mary Grace, I covered all this years ago. You sound like my shrink."

"But you still aren't seeing the truth. Your dad was available to you, Peyton, probably about as much as any father is around for his kids. Your dad's a doctor, right? So it's not like he can be available at all hours of the day."

Peyton lowered her gaze, knowing Mary Grace had a point. Her dad had come to many of her school events, sometimes even dragging Kathy and the wee ones along . . . but she'd been too annoyed to acknowledge them. And once he had established his practice, every year he had given her the opportunity to choose between boarding school or a local school, and she'd always chosen to go away.

The older woman reached out again, but this time she caught Peyton's left arm.

With one hand she held the scarred wrist, and with the other she slowly stroked the bright slash left by the razor blade. "What you've always considered a grave offense isn't an offense at all, honey," she whispered. "I think it's time you looked at things again."

Peyton closed her eyes. Last Christmas, goaded more by social obligation than fondness, she'd gone to Jacksonville to attend a Christmas party given by one of her high school classmates. After the party, she stopped by her father's house to drop off a load of perfunctory presents. He answered the front door. "Won't you come in?" he asked, looking at her with great dark eyes that glimmered with hope.

"No." She backed away, moving down the elegant brick staircase while she wished it were proper to drop off presents, ring the doorbell, and run, like a trick-or-treater in reverse. "I have work waiting at home."

"You can't stay?"

She had only waved in answer, then turned and jogged toward her car, struggling to forget the haunted look in his eyes. She couldn't wait to get back home to her computer, where the monitor would stare at her blankly and words would obediently leap or twist or curl on the page, whatever she asked them to do.

She *couldn't* stay back then . . . and shame kept her at arm's length now.

Night had fallen by the time King drove Peyton home. He'd insisted on seeing her to her front door even though her car remained at the *Times* office because, as he teasingly pointed out, she was not exactly in a fit condition to drive.

Now, as she unlocked her front door and caught a glimpse of herself in the foyer mirror, Peyton had to agree that while her skills weren't impaired, she did look a little odd. She'd wept her mascara off at Mary Grace's, and during the time or two she'd swiped at it she'd painted swooping black marks at the corners of her eyes. If a cop had pulled her over, he'd probably think he'd found Elvira, Queen of the Dark, on her way home from a come-as-you-are party.

She turned from the mirror, a little embarrassed at her disheveled condition. "You want to come in a minute?" she asked over her shoulder. "I'm going to do a rewrite of my column and file it ASAP, but I have some time and a few Cokes in the fridge. There might even be an apple pie. I picked one up at the grocery a week or so ago."

"A week?" Grumbling, King wiped his boots on the mat, then followed her into the house. "Honestly, MacGruder, you've got to take better care of yourself. There's probably mold growing on that pie. You'll get sick if you eat it."

She turned, a little amazed that he'd actually followed her in. But he'd seen her at her worst now, emotionally and physically, so if he was still here there might be something more to this than mere friendship . . .

"Would you care?" she asked, overcome by an attack of shyness. "If I got sick?"

"Yeah." Standing before her, he reached out and traced her cheek. "I'd miss sparring with you at the office."

"We don't have to." She felt herself blushing. "Spar, I mean. We might try getting along for a change."

His mouth curved in the slow, drowsy smile she suddenly realized she loved. "What's this? Are you honestly thinking of proving Carter Cummings right? He always said you had a thing for me."

She laughed. "That's funny — on our side of the newsroom he was always saying you carried a torch for *me*."

His hand caught her chin, lifted it, and then he bent and kissed her. For a breathless moment Peyton closed her eyes and felt the jumbled pieces of her world settling into place, then she opened her eyes and saw him smiling.

"Um . . . that's two Cokes, right?" She moved toward the kitchen on legs that felt as insubstantial as air.

"Sure."

He sat at the kitchen table while she pulled glasses from the cabinet, then filled them with ice. She glanced over at him a couple of times, noticing how at home he seemed, and when she brought the foaming glasses to the table she saw that he'd pulled two of her father's letters from the crowded napkin holder.

"Thought you might like to read these," he said, deliberately dropping them to the table. "It's about time, don't you think?"

She stared at the letters as realization bloomed in her chest. She and King had just made peace, and he had seen her at her worst. If they could call a truce, and if he could care for her knowing all he knew about her past . . .

She took a deep breath, then turned away. "I've got a better idea." She moved toward the phone. "You doing anything this weekend?"

"Um — no. What'd you have in mind?"

"You'll see." Picking up the phone, she

slowly punched in the number she hadn't dialed in years, then turned when a male voice answered. "Dad? This is Peyton. Listen — a friend and I were thinking about coming up this coming weekend. So if you could clear out a couple of bedrooms —"

She smiled. "No, Dad, nothing's wrong. I just thought . . . well, I have a story to share. One you're not gonna believe."

Glancing across the room, she saw King give her an enthusiastic thumbs-up. She returned his grin, then looked away, unable to hide her pain as her heart twisted.

Her father was weeping.

Sixteen

Wednesday, July 4

The Heart Healer
By Peyton MacGruder
© Howard Features Syndicate

Dear Readers:

Tonight many of you will watch the World News Network's prime-time special on Flight 848 and its surviving note. I don't want to spoil your enjoyment of a televised spectacle, so in this column I'm simply going to say that I visited and interviewed my third prospect, he claimed the note, and at the time I had no reason to doubt him.

But yesterday I broke my promise to that young man. Instead of sending him the original note, I hand-delivered it to a weeping young woman who persuaded me it had been written for her. She offered some pretty convincing proofs, but I didn't need evidence to realize the note had come full circle. It began in me, you see, many years ago. And soon the circle of forgiveness will be complete.

The young woman's identity shall forever be my secret. I've seen the stress heavy media attention can bring, so I pray you'll forgive me this one secret and allow me to keep it.

This search has done something to my own heart — ripping open old wounds and opening doors I hoped never to walk through again. But through the sometimes painful process, I learned something: a columnist should not merely report a list of facts, nor should she confine herself to writing for her peers in the newsroom. If I want to live up to my name, to be a heart healer, I'm going to have to open my own heart along the way.

Tomorrow, a friend and I are driving up to Jacksonville to visit my father, his wife, and six half-siblings I scarcely know. Why? Because in searching for the author of the note, I came to realize that the heart in need of healing was mine.

I'd like to take this opportunity to say farewell, at least for a while. I've been writing this column for nearly a year, and I've begun to realize that I need some time to step back and ask myself what I want to accomplish through this forum. I don't think print journalism needs another platform for a writer to bewitch and bedazzle with information or pretty prose. I think I'd like to make "The Heart Healer" a place of service and connection. To be honest, I think it's time we returned to the vision Emma Duncan presented in this space years ago.

And so the Heart Healer is taking some time to mend. I've done it once before, after a major heartbreak. After that first crisis, I took time to heal body and mind. This time, I'll be taking time to heal my spirit and emotions.

Through this journey, my friends, I've learned something else: the note, in and of itself, is not important. The *message* is the significant thing, for it contains the power of life and love.

Now I understand why the note was given to me. Not because of what I could do for it, but because of what it could do for me. I've recorded my observations as a message of love and forgiveness has gone out to the world. I've seen that message disbelieved, disowned, doubted, and disparaged. Yet to *this* broken heart, it has not lost its power to restore.

At the memorial service for the victims

of Flight 848, the minister said, "Shared anguish can be a bridge to reconciliation." Throughout my search, I've shared the anguish of hurting people, and I've finally learned to share my own. Truly, the sharing has built bridges . . . and I'm confident they will stand for years to come.

Thank you for accompanying me on the journey.

Flush with an inexplicable feeling of happiness, Peyton stepped through the Dunkin' Donuts doorway, then blinked when the customers broke into applause. Amid a sea of congratulations, she walked to her usual spot at the counter (reserved, she noticed, by an ink-stained napkin on the stool that read SAVE THIS SEAT OR ELSE!). Grinning at Erma, she sat and ordered her coffee and cruller.

She glanced around. Folded copies of the *Times*' lifestyles section appeared in every hand, with her column folded front and center.

"Well, girl, you did it," Erma said, speaking a little more loudly than usual as she poured the coffee. "And we're all dying to know — if the note shouldn't have gone to that Tanner Ford fellow, who was it for?"

"You can tell us, kiddo." This from the

man on the stool next to her, his grin backlit by the garish colors of his Aloha shirt. "We're your friends."

Peyton picked up a sugar packet, ripped off the top, and paused. Looking up, she swept her audience with a smile. "I'm entirely convinced, folks — the note was meant for all of us."

The hum of conversation and the gentle sounds of restaurant service ceased for a moment, then Erma nodded. "You said it, hon. Down in my heart, I know you're right."

Peyton turned as the bells above the door jangled. King walked in, his smile glowing above the dark blue collar of his knitted shirt. "You ready to go, Peyton? The car's gassed up and waiting outside."

"In a minute." She looked around, caught Erma's lifted brow, and grinned. "King, let me introduce you to the morning crowd at Dunkin' — some very important people." She gestured to the waitress. "Erma plays a starring role here."

Erma wiped her hand on her apron, then extended it over the counter. "Mighty nice to meet you. I've seen you in here a few times."

"Your coffee's a lot better than the murk they make in my office." King shook her hand. "And I can see why Peyton enjoys the company."

As he moved away, shaking hands with the regulars, Erma leaned over the counter. "Golly, Peyton, you sure know how to pick 'em. You taking that hunk away for a long weekend?"

"Something like that." Peyton met the waitress's wide-eyed gaze. "I'm taking him to Jacksonville. We're going to spend some time becoming acquainted with my father."

Erma laughed. "I'd think a writer would be more particular with words. Sounds like you're planning to get to know your father yourself."

Peyton lifted her coffee cup and picked up her cruller, then gave the waitress a heartfelt smile. "That's the idea."

Then, after gently pulling King away from a group of admiring women in a booth, Peyton led the way out into a cloudless Florida morning.

Resources

Writing this book would have been much harder, if not impossible, without help from the following:

Susan Richardson, Claudia Coker, Gaynel Wilt, and my special secret pal who "test-read" the manuscript and gave me valuable feedback.

Karen Ball, friend and editor extraordinaire, who knows how to spell words like *extraordinaire* and helps me stay focused.

John King, columnist for the *San Francisco Chronicle*. John not only answered my frantic, questioning e-mails, but he did so with grace and style.

Bob Elmer, novelist and friend who recommended John King.

Judy Hill, columnist for the *Tampa Tribune*. Judy corrected several of my misconceptions and generously gave me part of an afternoon to ask questions.

Elaine Anderson, Ed.D., who provided useful information on panic attacks from her Wings of Faith program. Many other friends also shared their stories. Thank you!

Arya, Bob. *Thirty Seconds to Air: A Field Reporter's Guide to Live Television Reporting*. Ames, Iowa: Iowa State University Press, 1999.

Brelis, Matthew. "A Beautiful Night for Flying Evolved Into Doom." *St. Louis Post-Dispatch*, July 28, 1996, 6A.

Discussion
Questions/Study Guide

1. *The Note* is an allegory, a story in which certain elements represent essentials of another, deeper story. Like the story of the Good Samaritan and the Prodigal Son, it is a spiritual tale that does not directly discuss God. What are some of the obvious (and subtle) relationships between the note and the Gospel?

2. God has written a note to mankind. What is it, and how is it similar to the message contained in the note from Flight 848? How does the message differ?

3. Compare how the three "prospects" reacted to Peyton's offer of the note with how people respond to God's message of forgiveness and reconciliation.

418

4. Consider Timothy Manning, who seems secure in his religion and his role. Was Reverend Manning secure in his father's love? Could he have ever reached a place of true security? How did his personal thoughts differ from the persona he presented to the newspaper reporter?

5. Consider Taylor Crowe, the songwriter. Taylor admitted that her father might have written the note, but she claimed the breach between them was too wide to ever be crossed. Does her situation mirror the way some people feel about God? Do they accept this chasm, or do they try to bridge the gap on their own terms? What are some ways people try to "get to God"? Are these man-made attempts ever successful? Have you ever felt that a chasm exists between you and God? Is it too wide or deep to bridge?

6. Consider Tanner Ford, who apparently wanted to accept the note for ambitious reasons. What did he actually accept, a copy of the note or its message? How does this character relate to some people who accept the "trappings" of

belief without ever actually embracing the belief itself?

7. The book abounds with poor father/ child relationships: Peyton and her father, King and his wounded son, and all three of the candidates to receive the note. In this story, each father was patient, but in real life, estrangement between fathers and children is often the father's fault as well as the child's. Can we ever blame our heavenly Father for walking out on His children?

8. We are given a brief glimpse of Julie St. Claire's relationship with her adoptive father. Julie's mother walked out on this man, and Julie scarcely remembers him. How might her life have been different if her mother had not walked away? What does this say to us about the importance of our roles as parents?

9. What attributes of God were revealed in Peyton's father? Timothy Manning's? Taylor Crowe's? Tanner Ford's?

10. Finally, many people are fond of espousing the "fatherhood of God, brotherhood of man" philosophy. Is God the

Father of all, or the *Creator* of all? If He isn't the Father of all, how do we become His children?

Author's Note

The idea for *The Note* came to me one morning in my husband's Sunday school class. As a friend and I were busy checking in our usual horde of active middle-school students, we were reflecting over our week as the mothers of teenagers. The conversation shifted to the recent tragedy of an Alaska Airlines crash, along with the rumor we'd heard about a woman attempting to share Christ with her fellow passengers as the plane went down. Alas, we decided, the rumor probably wasn't true because the flight attendants would be busy giving emergency instructions.

"I know what I'd do if I were on a crashing plane," I said, reflecting on the past week with my teens. "I'd write, 'Dear Kids — I love you. All is forgiven. Mom.'"

We laughed — and what began as a wry bit of humor suddenly struck me as profound truth. What *would* I write if I had one moment to share my most profound thoughts with my loved ones?

And then it occurred to me — God has written mankind just such a note. Just like the fathers in this story, He loves, He cares, He mourns when His children leave Him out of their lives. He wants us to know He loves us and has forgiven our neglect of this all-important relationship.

There were many times in the writing of this book that I felt as though I'd bitten off more than I could handle. At other times (like today, when I am sitting in an airport and separated from my family by Hurricane Gordon), writing about an air disaster struck a little too close for comfort. But I know God is faithful, and will equip us to perform the tasks He entrusts to us.

One final note: in the discussion questions, we ask how one becomes a child of God. I don't want to leave you without an answer.

The Bible (God's note to mankind) says that though God created and loves everyone, His children are those who come to Him by faith.

How we praise God, the Father of our Lord Jesus Christ, who has blessed us with every spiritual blessing in the heavenly realms because we belong to Christ. Long ago, even before he made the world, God loved us and chose us in Christ to be holy and without fault in his eyes. His unchanging plan has always been to adopt us into his own family by bringing us to himself through Jesus Christ. And this gave him great pleasure.

So we praise God for the wonderful kindness he has poured out on us because we belong to his dearly loved Son. He is so rich in kindness that he purchased our freedom through the blood of his Son, and our sins are forgiven. He has showered his kindness on us, along with all wisdom and understanding. (Ephesians 1:3–8)

I hope you will take the message of *The Note* to heart . . . and spread it as a heart healer in a broken, wounded world.

Angela E. Hunt
Charlottesville Airport
Hurricane Gordon,
September 2000